A LIFE OF DEATH
THE GOLDEN BULLS

Book Two

WESTON KINCADE

Introduction
by
Julie Hutchings

"Character driven and suspenseful, this is a paranormal mystery
novel with heart."
~ Bracken MacLeod, author of Mountain Home and Stranded

.

"A Life of Death is quite simply, absolutely superb. I loved this book, it was an emotional and entertaining journey that had me hooked."
~ David King, An Eclectic Bookshelf

"A very good story."
~ Kathleen Brown, author of The Personal Justice Series

"The title drew me in and the novel itself is an experience that should not be left unread."
~ Bruce Blanchard, author of Demon's Daughter

"Mr. Kincade did a wonderful job telling this story. The characters are well developed and easy to relate to. I cannot tell you how much I enjoyed this book."
~ Christi, Alaskan Book Cafe

Copyright © 2011, 2013, 2017 by Weston Kincade
Published in 2013 in Canada by Books of the Dead Press.
For information about special discounts for bulk purchases, please contact Weston Kincade at wakincade@gmail.com or at http://kincadefiction.blogspot.com.
Book Design and Editing by Weston Kincade and K. Sozaeva
Cover Art copyright © 2017 by Claudia McKinney at PhatPuppyArt
The text for this book is set in Cambria.
Manufactured in the United States of America

Summary: Ritual Sacrifice. Terror. Panic. In a fear-filled town, will ghostly visions be enough to stop a serial killer?

After fifteen years of ritual murder, Homicide Detective Alex Drummond must save this year's sacrificial lamb. But who is it? The serial killer's anointed date is only days away. An anonymous tip forces Alex and a high school friend to Washington DC to prove the suspect's guilt, but nothing is as it seems. Unsolved murders abound like cobwebs under abandoned guest beds. Is Alex in over his head?

Time, beliefs, and supernatural abilities collide in Weston Kincade's thrilling sequel in the A Life of Death trilogy. In the end, the stakes couldn't be higher… or more personal. Do your part. Buy The Golden Bulls today.

ISBN 978-1546651147 (Print)
ISBN 978-0-9834648-5-3 (eBook)

A LIFE OF DEATH
THE GOLDEN BULLS

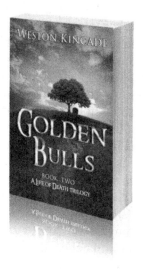

Ritual Sacrifice. Terror. Panic. In a fear-filled town, will ghostly visions be enough to stop a serial killer?

After fifteen years of ritual murder, Homicide Detective Alex Drummond must save this year's sacrificial lamb. But who is it? The serial killer's anointed date is only days away. An anonymous tip forces Alex and a high school friend to Washington DC to prove the suspect's guilt, but nothing is as it seems. Unsolved murders abound like cobwebs under abandoned guest beds. Is Alex in over his head?

Time, beliefs, and supernatural abilities collide in Weston Kincade's thrilling sequel in the A Life of Death trilogy. In the end, the stakes couldn't be higher... or more personal. Do your part. Read The Golden Bulls today.

Acknowledgements

I would like to thank quite a few people who have helped *A Life of Death, Book One* evolve into the trilogy it is today. If only my editor, Katy, could have seen it completed. Firstly, to the late, great Katy Sozaeva who helped make this trilogy what it has finally become. She will be missed, but her efforts will live on within these pages. I could not have flourished as a writer without her painstaking assistance. Also, the support and love of my wife, family, and friends is something I could not live without. A shout out to Tavis Potter, my friend and "brother from another mother," who has always been a personal inspiration and supporter when things looked bleak. Look Tavis, you made it into another of my books! Additionally, thanks go out to Roy Daily and Books of the Dead Press, who published the first two books in the *A Life of Death* trilogy back in 2013. The support and confidence he had in the series will always be remembered. Also, I would like to express my gratitude to fellow writer and peer editor Scott Rhine and the beta readers who made this phenomenal series possible. Last but certainly not least, a huge thanks goes out to Julie Hutchings who believed in the series and my writing enough to provide her own personally written introduction.

Personal Note:

Tranquil Heights, the setting for the *A Life of Death* trilogy, is based on a mountain town I used to teach in, Abingdon, Virginia. Its unique beauty was certainly part of the inspiration for this story and the rest of the series. Walking through the town after reading the novels, I'm sure you will recognize a few features; although, I did take some liberties.

Tempt fate. Destroy destiny. Demand retribution.

If you like delightfully dark diversions from reality, stories strange and wonderful that leave you begging for more, Strange Circumstances is the collection for you. The future is a gamble. Care to place a bet on yours?

Click and sign up to read Strange Circumstances FREE today.

http://strangecircumstances.gr8.com

Table of Contents

Introduction

Julie Hutchings

WE LOVE TO HATE death. It plagues us, it drives us to truly live, it tricks us into living in fear. And so, we read about it, we watch movies and TV about it, we think about it and we write about it. Some of us romanticize it—to make us feel better, take the scary and make it beautiful.

Weston has done something beautiful in *A Life of Death*.

I hate death. I'm terrified of it. I have a grudge against it and I feel like because of that, death has its sights set on me and mine. It's no coincidence that I've loved vampires since death began rearing its head in my personal space whenever it got the chance. I played with the notions of fate being both romantic and gruesome, and with how choice itself is a choice when I wrote *Running Home*. My Ellie, like Alex in *A Life of Death*, suffered parental loss too early in life—as did I. Writing our own story through characters gives us control of the consequences, makes a world where we make the rules. Because in *our* world, there is but one rule, and that is death is coming for you, and you will not get away.

Weston has given our Alex a way to have some power over death, something we all long for. Alex has an ability to uncover some of death's mysteries, and yet it pulls him further and further into an isolation where life in many ways, is passing him by. The gift that takes more than it offers. An irresistible pull that drags him into a sullen and difficult private life, but that helps him heal and partner with death rather than despise it.

Though death is a despicable thing that caused the wound to begin with.

Again, I say Weston created a beautiful thing with *A Life of Death* because he celebrates the inevitability, the trauma of death, and romanticizes it in a way that enthralls me. Romanticism where the ugly face of death becomes an ally of sorts, and yet there's nothing romantic about it. It's a story of an ordinary person, with an extraordinary ability, who conquers the unconquerable in a very human way. It's heroic. A hero in a war that cannot be won, and yet Alex *wins* it.... It gives the death-obsessed like myself the gorgeous false hope against an all-powerful enemy, even as I know that it's fiction. It's a lie. The best, most haunting lie.

If fiction is a lie, and horror is meant only to frighten us, then Weston redefines them. I took *comfort* in Alex's story.

I lost my father at sixteen, and the epitome of all grandmothers weeks later. There have been many other deaths in my family, starting when I was eleven, and they always seem to happen on memorable dates that stick out even more than a birthday, ensuring I'm reminded every year: Christmas. My dog's birthday. Blue Monday. Cinco de Mayo. My anniversary (three times). It's as if death is sticking it to me, then waving it in my face. And like waiting for any tiger in the grass to jump, I'm always on the lookout for it. I expect it when things go too well for too long. Maybe that's why I've always had an affinity for the morbid...it keeps death on the perimeter. My eyes are on it as much as death's eyes are on me. But I think it's quite the opposite—I think my eyes were on death and then death came.

Catholic guilt is a wonderful thing for a writer's mind. Early in life my father made me a reader. We'd spend hours at library book sales and yard sales, poring over old books together. We shared that. It's where my possibly odd taste in books began. I remember reading this picture book about a Pegasus over and over in second grade, far too old for me. It was really dark, with only illustrations, and it made me *think*. I loved *Star Wars,* and the darkest sides of fairy tales and folklore as a child, then comic books, and other stories of strength: for instance, I read the novelization of Rambo about six times in seventh grade. This man who tempted death, lived in its wake, and fought it every minute. I was the only twelve-year-old girl carrying around a copy of *Rambo*, which did nothing but isolate the quiet nerd more, and make me a target. When other girls were swooning over the first boy bands, I was in love with Batman. It was these stories where the good, but dark character prevails that got me through, and part of what made me a good, dark kid to begin with. I had a hard time fitting in, was bullied something horrible, often coming home with a black eye, gum in my hair… but I loved school and learning, despite being misplaced there, and I identified with characters that always had something a little more, a little different, but still wanted so much to be immersed in a world that didn't feel like it belonged to them. Like they were waiting for their real purpose to find them. For me, my strength came from writing when I was very young, and later when my father asked me casually when we walked by a karate school if I wanted to go in. Always afraid, but never willing to show it, I said yes, and that was the day that changed my life, where I felt like I found the place to feel as strong as I was. And as I grew into my strength, I learned to not be embarrassed of my love of dark things that other kids wouldn't understand.

When I was older I loved Dracula, Anne Rice, Stephen King, James Herbert, along with the rich worlds like in *The Mists of Avalon, Outlander, A Wrinkle in Time, 1984*, everything by V.C. Andrews and Terry Pratchett... Combining such morbidity and love and beauty and impossibility and doom in my head gave me a uniquely dark and yet optimistic mindset, where I loved life, embraced challenge, but didn't fear death.

Until it showed up. Forever I'll ask myself if it came because I called it.

It's these obsessions with books and the possibility of life and the randomness of death that beckon me to books like *A Life of Death*. Because Alex can't escape death in such a complicated way, and in another way, he doesn't want to. It's his partner and his enemy, and never quits surprising him, in helpful, horrible ways. *A Life of Death* reaches me in the place that inspired me to write *Running Home*—where I wonder if this purpose that those strong, dark characters overcome difficulty to find is part of a fateful plan where choice is an illusion, or if death is merely a bystander that we try too hard to make sense of. The darkness that hovers over Alex is so complex and rich, uniquely fateful and ironic, that it calls to me, maybe like death always has.

Weston Kincade embraces the morbidity and the beauty. And for readers like us, he lets Alex answer the call.

-**Julie Hutchings**
Author of Running Home

Bio:

Julie Hutchings is a pizza hoarding, coffee swilling, beer guzzling, karate loving book geek with a love of all things creepy and obscure. She lives in America's Hometown of Plymouth, Massachusetts with her hilarious husband and two genius children.

Prologue

HAVE YOU EVER found yourself in an unfair position, dealing with someone who's insane? That's what every year of high school was like for me. My abusive stepfather, who I called the Drunk, was one such person. It's not always the victim's fault. Sometimes you don't have a choice but to spend your time picking up the pieces and trying to avoid most of the fallout. However, innocent people are often the ones who suffer. In my senior year he was hauled off to prison, not to be released anytime soon. The family was trying to get their lives back in order, but it was hard when such a large part of my life was missing. Gloria—my young, golden-haired stepsister—was one of those innocent victims. I suppose you could also say that Frank, my older stepbrother, was a victim of circumstance and problematic upbringing for the same reasons. Heck, living with the Drunk as a father would drive anyone to drink, and Frank suffered the consequences. It's kind of like growing up and running through life in a straitjacket; your decisions and choices are limited to what you can do with your hands tied. Eventually you learn to get out like Houdini, or you drown.

For me... I'm still missing another large piece of my heart. My real father, Terry Drummond, died when I was in eighth grade. It wasn't a secret. People knew, but they didn't talk about it. Grandpa, my dad's father, had Alzheimer's and was in a home up the road a few hours. That first year we visited a few times, but Mom had a hard time reminding Grandpa that Terry was gone and who we were. The visits stopped not long after that. A while after I graduated I bought a car, an old Buick; I stopped by from time to time. Unfortunately, he didn't know me. One time I convinced him I was a vacuum salesman for the hell of it. He wouldn't remember after a few minutes anyway, but boy was he excited about the prospect of getting a Supersucker—at least for the ten minutes or so his memory held out.

At home with Mom and the girls, things changed; we were coping. However, my life was never to be the same. I wasn't what you would call normal. I didn't grow a second head or anything, but I couldn't help the grotesque things I saw. I had a few run-ins with victims, people speaking from beyond the grave. And I know what you're thinking... don't get me wrong; I'm not crazy. I thought I might be at first—crazy, not senile—but enough truth came out of those first few visions that there's no doubt in my mind anymore. There is one question that still bothers me at times, though: is this ability, these visions—are they a blessing or a curse? Father Gilbert said the future is whatever we make it. I think he might have stolen that saying from some sci-fi flick, but I came to agree with him. It doesn't matter *why* I can see these horrific murders. What matters is what I do with the ability.

The summer after those awful events flew by faster than I could have imagined. Graduation came and went. Madessa High School was finally just a speck in my rearview mirror. I still keep in touch with a few friends like Jessie and Paige, of course. The time I spent at Dad's grave resting under that old, familiar pine dwindled, though. Every once in awhile I make it by and spend a few hours by his side. The bark on the tree is still smooth and comforting like it used to be, having conformed itself to my constant company. Now Jamie, my only son, has taken to sitting under those comforting limbs. I can only hope it isn't for the same reasons. His life is better than mine was back in high school—I made sure of that, but he's quiet, much like I was. Guess he's got a lot on his mind.

Like him, Glory is always present in my mind, too. I can't always keep the feelings at bay. She's still with me. There are even times when I think she's whispering through the leaves in the wind, but it's as if the words are a blend of the many voices I've heard over the years. They come to me when I least expect it, and sometimes I still wonder if it might be a curse. But, it's my responsibility. These people need help. They've been beaten and bloodied, left with no one to speak for them—no one but *me.*

Chapter 1

Fallen Friend

September 20, 1996

THE DOOR CHIMED as I stepped into Sammy's Shop Smart.

"Alex, where've you been?" asked Vivian, a woman I'd begun to call *Mom.*

"At the community college. I stopped by to see Dad for a few, though. You need somethin'?"

Mom punched a few keys into her register, and it shot open. Glancing at the woman in front of her, she grinned and said, "Thank you. Have a nice day."

The customer took her change, patted her small boy on the butt, and hissed, "Now quit begging. No more candy this week or your father'll have a fit." She ushered him out the door as Mom came around the counter to give me a hug.

"How was school?"

"College is different from high school. The classes are a bit more grueling. Mr. Tanner's Intro to Environmental Science is taking more time than I thought it would, especially with everything else."

She nodded, understanding the implied *everything else* better than most people. Vivian and I had been getting along a lot better since the previous year's incident. Even my stepsister Abby seemed to have turned a corner. She took Gloria's passing hard, maybe as hard as me, but lately she'd focused on school a bit more. She even made a friend or two in high school.

"Yes, but *I* needed a hug," Mom said, after releasing me and my book bag from her grip. "How's Abby? Still doing better?"

I nodded. "Yeah, she's just taking it day by day, like the rest of us."

"Good." Her lips trembled, and her eyes glistened with unspoken words, but after a shake of her head, she grabbed a box from the end of one of the small aisles. "So Abby made it home alright?" she asked, unpacking the box and hanging bags of peanuts and trail mix on the assorted pegs.

"Yeah, Mom. I walked her most of the way home from school before stopping by the cemetery. What is it? What's on your mind?"

"It's nothin' new, hon," she said, averting her eyes and using the edge of her red work apron to wipe away some tears. "Just still gets to me, is all."

I nudged the edge of the box with my shoe, giving her a moment. "Look, I know I said I'd stay and help out like most days, but Mr. Tanner gave me a boatload of homework. You mind if I skip out today?"

She nodded. I slipped out as quietly as I could, brushing past a group of teenagers who had just made their way from school. Backpacks in tow, they were jabbering about movies and video games. I caught just a snippet of their conversation, but it was enough to trigger a few memories. The childhood joy of no responsibilities and familiar, loving parents had haunted me for years. Dad was a good man, but since the wreck when I was in eighth grade, my family had been through a lot.

At least the Drunk is out of our lives, but was it worth the cost? I wondered. A shiver ran down my spine, and I pushed the question from my mind. There was no use contemplating what couldn't be changed.

I trekked over the concrete sidewalks, past the black, iron fence surrounding the late Brogand Manor, and under the tall trees shading the street. The wind was calmer, but the leaves still rustled overhead. I was careful not to touch the fences. You never know what might have happened in the past. I didn't mind helping out when the ghosts found me, but I wasn't gonna go looking for trouble. I barely had enough time to finish my homework as it was.

I crossed the railroad tracks in thought and unconsciously followed my daily routine toward our new trailer. It was by no means new, but none of us could stand the thought of staying in the Drunk's old one. Even in prison he held the deed, and we wanted nothing more to do with him. It didn't take more than a few weeks to convince Mom that our combined income at Sammy's would more than pay for the rent on another trailer. At first I'd pushed for a house, something more like what I'd grown up in with her and Dad. It would've been good for Abby, and probably for the rest of us too, but those meager paychecks were more than enough to demonstrate what we could and couldn't afford. All the beer the Drunk and my stepbrother Frank used to consume took up most of the income they brought in, but with Mom and I both working full time over the summer, it still wouldn't have been enough for anything more than what we already had. We found a place a few rows over. It was a little newer, probably no more than a dozen years old, and wasn't infested with the putrid, lingering smell of stale cigarettes.

The memory of stepping into clouds of rolling smoke assaulted my senses. Even with him gone it was sometimes difficult to get the man out of my head. His slurred, drunken voice echoed in my ears, drowning out the squeak of his recliner and the vague chatter of a street chase radiating from the television. "Stupid, disrespectful kid. Cants even call me, Dad."

A shudder ran through me. Then I stepped over a curb, and a wave of knee-high grass whisked along my jeans, jolting me back to reality. At one end of the vacant lot was a wooden fence where someone's house butted up to the lot. It had been mowed in the search for Helen, Abby and Gloria's mother, but the grass had again grown up. It wasn't to the same height as before, but was still high enough to partially cover the white cross we'd placed in the field.

After receiving my first paycheck that summer, Abby and I went to the florist and picked up a memorial cross for Abby's mother. The pink Delphiniums she chose, Helen's favorite color, still ran across its arms, marking her first burial place. The flowers seemed to have taken root and peered out between blades of grass. *At least something's growin' here,* I thought. *Hopefully it won't be completely lost as nature takes over again.*

Seeing the lot in daylight was easier to handle, but the memories were difficult to overcome. The vision again assaulted my senses: the bed of the truck clanging shut, the feel of being dragged through waist-high grass, and the *chook—shiff, chook—shiff* of the shovel carving the hole in the ground, then slinging the dirt aside. I stepped onto the street's edge and followed it to Tranquil Heights Trailer Park.

The large sign at the entrance was faded, with cream and brown paint chipping and weeds growing from the mulch at the base of its wooden posts. The green moss may have taken over more of the sparse shrubbery than last year. At least I no longer dreaded coming home each day. Although the visions haunted me, the familiar, forlorn sense of impending doom was absent from them.

"Hey, Alex," Abby said as I entered the trailer. "What're you doin' home so early?" She sat at the kitchen table, her school texts spread before her.

"Hey, Black Mamba," I hissed with a teasing smile. I'd recently given her the nickname since learning about the snakes in science class.

"Alex, cut it out," she said, frowning. "You know I hate when you call me that."

I slung my bag into my room down the hall and made a beeline for the refrigerator. "I can't help what your hair reminds me of." She'd recently taken to partially braiding some of her jet-black hair.

"Well, I'm not gonna stop for you," she said, without much

conviction. "It's what a lot of the girls at school are doing."

"You don't have to. It's your hair, but since when do you go along with what everyone else does? I've never known you to be a follower." While digging through the fridge, I noticed her running fingers through one of the braids, unconsciously loosening it. I smiled at the milk, grabbed the carton, and poured myself a glass. "Listen, I've got a bunch of homework, so I'll be in my room if you need me. Just give a yell."

"Mmmm-hmmm," she murmured back, not bothering to look up from her books.

The remainder of the evening was dull, uneventful, and consisted of me, a couple ham sandwiches for me and Abby, my CD player and headphones, a desk lamp, and school books. I'd never studied so hard before. I spent high school in a daze. Now life was different. When people are depending on you, you can't give up.

Mom came home late and disappeared into her room, saying she had to be up early yet again. Flicking the light off at close to midnight, I slunk out of my heavy metal t-shirt and jeans, and slipped into bed.

* * *

The next morning was much the same. I escorted Abby to Madessa High School, my alma mater. It was her first year there, and I normally didn't stay long.

"Hello, Mr. Drummond," said Mrs. Easely, spotting us as we approached the clock centered in the courtyard. Her face and tone were grim, like she'd just bitten into a rotten prune. This was why I avoided good ol' Madessa when I could. I ignored her.

"You good to go?" I asked Abby.

She nodded. "Yep, have fun at school."

I forced a smile under Stone Face Easely's accusing gaze and focused on Abby. "I'll try."

I turned to leave as Abby walked away, but my old Trig teacher's voice echoed through the yard again. "I know you heard me, Mr. Drummond."

I stopped and slowly turned to face her. "Yes... yes I did, Mrs. Easely. Is there something I can help you with?"

By this point, my blood was simmering, but I couldn't speak my mind for fear of what she might do to Abby in class. They say the sins of the father will be visited upon the son. Well, there's a good many years between a father and son, and only the summer between Easely's classes with me and those with my stepsister. Considering the rumors going around after Coach Moyer vamoosed, some people—faculty included—think I had something to do with it. While they're right, I certainly wasn't the one to blame. But telling that to Stone Face Easely would be like trying to coax a viper over for a cuddle.

"I hear tell that you're in college."

"That's right."

"So what do you want to do when you drop out?" The question came out with such nonchalance I stalled for a second, rewinding her words and running them through my mind again.

"I'm sorry. I don't believe I heard you right."

"You certainly did, Mr. Drummond. You're wasting your money on school right now. You barely scraped by in my class last year, and that was solely due to my giving nature. You can't cut it in college. We all know it, and you won't be able to pull the same thing you did with Mr. Moyer. Your professors won't run away just because you threaten them."

My jaw dropped... threaten? My face flushed and I had to clench my fists to keep from shaking some sense into her. "Mrs. Easely, I've never threatened anyone for a grade, but I will make you a promise: I will graduate. And to answer your question, I'm working on a degree in Criminal Justice. In fact, I'm sure you'll be seeing a great deal of me, because I'll be the one pulling you over and watching you stumble over a sobriety line while trying to find your damn nose!" By my final word, my voice had risen about twenty decibels. Clusters of students throughout the courtyard were all turned toward us. Abby stood by the waist-high, rock wall that encircled the tall, narrow clock and flowers. What little color her skin possessed had drained from her face, but a smile twitched at the edges of her lips. "And another thing," I continued, my voice returning to a more reasonable volume. "If I hear so much as a peep about you treating Abby different than the rest of your students, I'll have your job." I wasn't sure how I'd do it, but I meant every word.

My old Trig teacher paled and seemed to shrink a few inches. A few students clapped, but as soon as Easely resumed her composure and turned to find the culprit, all sounds stopped, leaving barely an echo resounding off the buildings. She turned back to me with eyes blazing. "You unethical, irresponsible child. You think you can threaten me and get away with it?"

A momentary pang of regret shot through my gut. "Actually, I think I just did." Breaking into a grin, I turned on my heels and left the sixty-five-year-old teacher fuming. A swift glance back at Abby told me she shared my happiness. "Have a nice day," I shouted to the math teacher. Then I waved. Considering the monotony of how I awoke, the day was turning out better than expected.

* * *

A finger tapped my shoulder as I stepped into the college cafeteria. "Hi, honey. How're things going?" asked Paige, as beautiful as ever.

The cafeteria was more like a mall's, with six or seven small fast-food joints arranged in a semicircle. The windows covering the far side of the cafeteria were enormous and made up the entire circular wall, filling the large room with light. The sun shone through the windows, and the rays played off her brown curls.

I couldn't help but smile as I stared into those honey-brown eyes. "Hey, beautiful. Going great now that you're here. How'd I get so lucky?"

She blushed and averted her eyes, then glanced up at me from under long eyelashes. "How can I resist that sweet talk?" Brushing by, she whispered, "Keep it up and someday you might just get lucky."

Her affectionate tone anchored my feet to the semicircular pattern of tiles below, and I was forced to catch back up in line.

She'd elected for Chinese food, which we both enjoyed, and grabbed a tray.

"You know I love it when you tease me like that," I whispered in her ear as she ladled noodles onto her plate. I grabbed some Kung Pao Chicken, rice, and eggrolls, then paid for our dishes. As we slid into a booth, I said, "You'll never guess who I spoke to today."

"Who?" she asked, slurping a noodle with a smile.

"Stone Face Easely."

"Oh yeah, how's she doing?" Her tone was more affectionate than I expected.

"Well, fine I guess, but she's really got it in for me."

Paige paused. "What do you mean?"

"The old nag blames me for manipulating Coach Moyer into leaving."

"You did."

"No I didn't. I... I spoke with him and revealed the truth about what *he* did. I may even have insinuated that people might find out. But I didn't do it for the grade or to be vindictive."

"I know that. Are you telling me she thinks differently?"

"Yep, Easely said I was going to drop out, couldn't hack it, and wondered what menial job I had in mind for the future. Then she had the gall to say my professors won't skip town because I threaten them. She even said I only passed her class because of her good graces."

"Well, you have to admit that you didn't do much in her class," Paige contended.

Every time she spoke, she blew my thoughts out of the mental water. She was my girlfriend. Why was she supporting this horrendous woman? "I know, and maybe she was lenient toward me. Compared to any other teacher, that should still have given me a B+, but saying I threatened Coach Moyer, and insinuating that it was the only way I could've passed, was too much."

She shrugged mid-chew, swallowed, and said, "Maybe, but look at it from her perspective. The only things she has to go on are rumors. You know the truth, but aside from me and Jessie, you're the only one. You should be used to people not understanding by now. You're the only one that experiences these visions, so the only thing other people see are your actions."

My shoulders slumped. She was right. I'd only managed to get the nerve up to tell my best friend Jessie over the summer, and I wasn't always sure he believed me, but at least he didn't act like I had some disease. "I know. She's wrong though, and I'm afraid she might take it out on Abby."

"She might, but life isn't fair. You can understand how she came to that assumption though, can't you?"

"Yeah," I muttered, "here you go again, always acting as my voice of reason."

"That's what a second opinion is good for, an unbiased way to look at a situation. Now quit yapping and eat your food. Your eggrolls are getting tough. They've probably been under that heat lamp for long enough to cure beef jerky. If you wait too much longer, you'll break your teeth."

I nodded. "'Kay. Where were you this morning when I needed you?"

Paige's brow drew down in confusion. "What do you mean? I was in class."

"Yeah, but I wasn't the nicest to Easely."

"Oh, no," Paige whispered, leaning in. "What did you say?"

It wasn't like anyone around cared about our conversation, but I played it up and leaned in, too. "I was kind of a smartass, said a few things, and told her that if she treated Abby any differently I'd have her job."

Paige chortled and about choked on a stray noodle. Then she shook her head. "You shouldn't have done that."

"I know. Like I said, where was my beautiful conscience when I needed her?"

"Around," she answered with a teasing smile. "And how on earth did you expect to pull off that threat?"

It was my turn to shrug. "Not sure. Sounded good at the time though. Besides, I think it meant a lot to Abby to see someone sticking their neck out on her behalf. She hasn't had a lot of support over the years."

"That's true."

The rest of the meal went by like normal with grins, laughs, and moments that I'll never forget. Unfortunately, on the way out of the

cafeteria, things changed. I wasn't searching, but a victim found
me. As we stepped through the foyer, I spotted Jessie on the
veranda outside. Telling Paige I'd catch up, I walked over to him.
He was the same old Jessie, but a bit more cleaned up in jeans and
a long-sleeve polo. However, his hands were stuck deep in his
pockets like he was searching for some hidden route to
Wonderland.

"Hey, Jess, what's happenin'? I thought you were supposed to be
up in DC trying out for the Nationals."

He nodded and put on a forced smile. "Yeah man, I was. I even
made it. I'll be pullin' stakes and movin' there for a while. Gotta
play triple-A first, but I'll make it to the big time. Maybe it'll
actually turn out that going to school is plan B for me, but I'm back
for a different reason." His smile faded. "Did you hear what
happened to Junior Lee?"

Junior Lee was a couple years behind us at Madessa High. He
played football with Jessie and was a good guy all around, nothing
like Grant Brogand used to be. "Nah, I haven't heard anything.
What happened?"

Jessie scoured the concrete pavement for a minute with his
eyes. "They found his body and the remains of a ritual."

"What ritual?"

"Well, someone drugged him and tied his wrists together. Then,
and this is the worst part, he was burned alive."

"Jeez... and they're sure it's Junior?"

Jessie nodded.

"Man, that kind of thing just doesn't happen in Tranquil Heights," I commented, to keep him talking.

"I know," he mumbled. "Junior's mom and mine are good friends. We were over there when the police arrived. His dad was freakin' out. I spent last night with them. He was never into drugs or anything, so they've got no idea what might have caused this."

"Junior was a good kid. Do they have any leads?"

"A couple things from what I can tell. The police mentioned this tattoo of an ankh on his forearm, but that's not much to go on. Lots of people have that," Jessie explained while staring off into the distant mountains. "What's even weirder is where they found him."

"Where was that?"

"The cemetery," he muttered, "opposite side from your dad's grave, across the road."

"Jeez that's weird. I was just there yesterday."

"Yeah, they say it happened sometime in the night, probably early morning."

"How about you? Got any ideas what he might've gotten into?"

Jessie shook his head, fighting tears that were struggling to flow. "Did you know I used to babysit him when his folks went out?"

"No, I didn't."

"Yeah, the little man shouldn't have gone out like that... well, I guess he wasn't so little anymore, playing linebacker on the varsity team as a junior and all. But still, it ain't right."

"I know. Want me to take a look at some of his things? See if anything comes to me?"

Jessie nodded and his chin fell to his chest, eyes closed tight. I rested a hand on his shoulder, and then gave him a minute. I caught up with Paige, who was seated on the grass beneath a dogwood to the side of the walkway.

Chapter 2

New Lead

September 14, 2011

JUNIOR LEE WAS only the first. The years since college when those murders began have been educational and fraught with easy lessons while faced with embarrassment. After the second year and a second murder, the mayor issued a public declaration that the killer would be caught by any means necessary. Unfortunately, even up to now the police force hadn't found the appropriate *means necessary*. Who would've guessed that it would take fifteen years to finally catch a break and find a new lead?

The Tranquil Heights Airport could never be considered large. It consisted of one long, cigar-shaped building that looked more like a metal-paneled warehouse than an airport. The entrance and ticket counter on the far end, Benji's Cuisine and a few waiting rooms for boarding in the center, and one small room at the opposite end where the baggage handlers dropped off your luggage. There wasn't much need for more because most flights that traveled there were no bigger than commuter flights, seating around twenty people, like a Beechcraft 1900. A handful of flight enthusiasts had their own hangars and small-engine planes. It wasn't what you would call an international airport.

Being such a small town, there wasn't much call for security, but they had one guard with a nightstick and taser at the security checkpoint before the terminal—that is, unless he was on break at Benji's. I had a few occasions to go there over the years.

I slipped out of my Lincoln as the dark-haired woman, who looked like a modern Mary Poppins, crossed the semi-vacant street to the waiting terminal. The gathering clouds overhead left the morning sun dim, and rain began to fall. She quickened her pace, her wide heels clopping on the asphalt as she lugged her bag over the curb and under the safety of the airport awning. Irene Harris was a *person of interest*. I'd been following her for the past two weeks, since she'd flown in from DC. Tilting my fedora to block the now-slanting droplets from my eyes, I crossed and leapt into the shelter. An escaped droplet ran down my spine, and I shook the collecting water from my long, black overcoat.

Irene was at the counter, picking up her ticket. She was chatty and had an easy smile, talking up the ticket agent. Mrs. Harris was smooth—well I guess Miss Harris or Widow Harris would be more accurate after the loss of her husband last year. He had been a businessman up in the big city, an accountant in a small practice. Over the past year, I'd looked into her and every person she associated with. A judge had let her off with time served for the three-month stint she spent in jail and four years of probation. Although the justice system gave her a slap on the wrist, I was certain she was getting away with a hell of a lot more.

I slipped through the automatic doors and drifted toward Benji's, perusing the menu until she walked past to her flight. A glance at the digital display of flights said she had fifteen minutes till boarding. I followed, leaving some distance and people separating us. She walked with purpose, dragging her luggage along the white-tiled section of building. A squeaky wheel on the bag made her easy to track, even in a public place. Once on the carpet of the terminal, she weaved through the zigzagging, retractable-belt barriers. It was an overdone maze that led to the security conveyor belt and imaging terminal. I stifled a laugh. The airport and runway couldn't handle jets or anything of size, but by God, they had enough retractable security barriers to direct crowds of people to a Rolling Stones concert in New York.

The passenger ahead of Irene passed through the metal detector and began putting his shoes and belt back on while gathering his briefcase and items. Miss Harris stepped up and pulled her ticket from the pocket of her purse. Unbeknownst to her and the security guard who was directing her through the detectors, a small, silver Zippo fell from her pocket to the carpet and bounced a few feet away.

I occupied myself reading the list of banned conveniences on a sign to the left, behind a portable wall that may have been standing longer than the building itself considering how dilapidated it had become. Once she'd passed through and started down the length of the building, I slipped under the retractable barrier without a second thought and grabbed the lighter. Larry, the security guard, watched me quizzically as I assessed the Zippo; the edges and cracks appeared scorched. Then the telltale aroma of oiled leather assaulted my senses, but this time mixed with the disturbing smell of burning flesh. I'd grown accustomed to these visions over the years, even expecting them at times, but that didn't make it any easier when you were immersed. My eyes blurred as I became someone else.

* * *

I flicked the silver, brushed-metal lighter and it illuminated the shadowed room. Puffing the end of my cigarette to life, I lay back in bed, naked except for a pair of brown, striped boxers. I set the lighter back on the nightstand with a contented sigh.

"Hey, Vic, you want a drink?" asked Irene, slipping a skimpy nightgown over her bare body.

"Sure, love," I answered as she made her way across the room and around the bed. With a mischievous smile and a giggle, Irene snatched my crutches from where they were leaning against the dresser. I leaned forward, shocked at her audacity. "Hey wait. You know I need those."

"Don't you go anywhere, honey," Irene whispered with a glint in her eye. "I'm not through with you yet." As though she were the worst thief in the world, she tiptoed out the bedroom door with my crutches in hand and a mischievous smile on her face. Her slender shape disappeared behind the closing door.

The door clicked shut and I leaned back against the wooden rails of the stained headboard. Letting out a puff, I followed it with small, circular smoke signals. "What a good woman... What am I doing to her?" *I asked the room. Thoughts passed through my mind unheeded.* Pam's a good woman too, but she isn't my wife, Irene is. What've I been doing? I'm an idiot. If not for Irene, that damned store sign would've taken me out last week, or anyone. It might have even fallen on Pam. I could have her blood on my hands, yet Irene stood by me. I have to call Pam—end this before it goes any further.

With a shake of my head, I reached for the nightstand where I always set my phone to charge, but only felt the end of the chord. My fingers fumbled through the receipts and change I had left piled near the phone. Where is it? Finally, I jerked on the lamp chain. The faint light chased the shadows from the moonlit window to the far corners of the room. I scanned the bedside table and then hoisted my pinned and braced legs over the bedside, propping myself up with each hand and searching the dim floor—nothing. Peering around the room, I found no blinking light, no glowing digital clock, nothing to indicate I had even brought it in. I absentmindedly grabbed for my crutches, but found only vacant space where they'd stood. With another shake of my head and a subtle smile, Irene's words echoed through my mind. "Don't you go anywhere, honey. I'm not through with you yet."

"Woman, what are you up to?" I asked with a chuckle. Sucking at my cancer stick, my stomach did a cartwheel, anxiously awaiting the upcoming events of the night. I'll end it with Pam. I promise. No matter what it does to the business partnership, the tax firm, and the company's future, I'll end it with her tomorrow, *I thought to myself.* I want to spend the rest of my life with you, Irene. *If she*

only knew about the affair, I would have said those words aloud. However, this wasn't the time or place for that, not when things were going so well. Besides, she didn't know. Why hurt her?

Then, the ebbing, red glow of another cigarette caught my eye from outside the iron security bars we'd had bolted over the window years ago after a break-in. At the edge of the yard, just before the forest line, Irene stood, her slippered feet standing so near our small koi-pond's fountain that it must have been splashing them. Her figure was radiant under the moonlight, the translucence of her nightgown revealing a silhouette of her trim curves. The trembling glow of her cigarette lit again as I leaned closer to the window. She waved with something in her other hand.

I hobbled to the edge of the nightstand and lifted the window, maneuvering most of my weight to a hand on the dresser. "Baby, what're you doing? Ain't you cold?" I asked, raising my voice to carry across the yard.

She shook her head. Taking one last puff, she flipped open the object she was holding and her face lit from below in the glow of a cell phone—my cell phone. The new light illuminated her smile, but it had changed. It was malicious... vindictive.

Something fluttered in the base of my gut. "Honey, what're you doing out there," I yelled again.

She didn't answer, instead flicking her burning cigarette butt to the ground and pressing one button on the phone with an extended, purposeful finger. Then she pressed another, and the subtle glow allowed me to watch her eyes glance up to meet mine. It was a look I had never seen on her face, two-thirds grim determination and a double shot of pure hatred. The look seemed to last for eons.

However, a few seconds later, the glowing ember of her discarded cigarette erupted, engulfing the surrounding grass in flames that coursed toward the window with intent. Leaning closer, I caught a whiff of something different, something that overpowered the smells of dew, grass, and the forest outside, something I should have smelled moments earlier—lighter fluid. The flames met the side of the house, but rushed around the corner and out of sight, leaving the remaining, rising flames to lap at the house's cedar siding.

My legs trembled through their fragile, pinned bones. "Babe, what the hell's going on?" I shouted, but then I spotted it. At her feet, just outside the growing flames, sat my old, five-gallon jerry can, the one I kept in the shed to refill the lawnmower. I stumbled backward and collapsed to the floor. "No, no, it can't be. Why would she—?" But the answer came that instant and stopped my rambling. She knows... but what about this evening, how great it was going, her not being done with me yet—

Suddenly the pieces came together. Oh beloved Jesus! She wasn't done with me, not yet, but it wouldn't be long. Fear flooded my gut and flowed through my useless legs, but anger followed it, warming me from the inside out, aided by the rising temperature of the room.

Looking up, I spotted the door a few meters away and pulled myself across the carpet. I stretched for the doorknob and gripped it, but it didn't turn. I gripped it harder and pulled. It jiggled, but did nothing more. "Bitch!" I shouted. It felt good to let it out, but the knob in my hand was growing hot, and quickly. I peered between the door and carpet, but gray smoke was now billowing through, causing my eyes to tear up.

My animosity for Irene was growing. I wasn't sure if it was the inferno building behind the door or my own hatred, but it spurred me on. I gripped the corner of the long dresser and pulled myself to my feet. The words, I gotta get out! reverberated through my skull. I grabbed the porcelain change tray in the shape of two hands with fingers intertwined. It had been a wedding present. I flung it at the window with relish. Change scattered, but the tray flew true, shattering one pane of glass. An alarm clock, the lamp, and Irene's makeup mirror followed, finishing the last of the glass panes, but the security bars and wooden frame remained.

I stumbled through the room, coughing with each smoke-filled breath, and then savored the limited fresh air that made it through the flames circling the window. "You bitch! How could you?"

Irene's voice answered through the flames, but I could barely make out her figure. "You should have thought of that before you went and stuck your little member where it didn't belong, Victor. It's not like I didn't give you hundreds of chances to come clean and fix it."

"I'm sorry. I just wasn't happy and didn't know what to do."

"I'll bet you are... now."

The walls blackened in places and began deteriorating before my eyes, revealing gaps of the skeletal structure beneath. Then fear settled deep within my chest. I'm going to die.

"I know I did wrong, but I was going to tell you. I was. But—" I coughed. Air was becoming a rare commodity, even at the window. After taking a shallow breath and hacking for a moment, I wheezed out, "Better than that, I decided to call it quits with Pam." Another coughing fit seized me. "I didn't want to hurt you anymore. I loved you, and you didn't—" My chest struggled to free itself of the clogged air, and I gasped, coughing again as I fell to my knees. Bones snapped under the pressure, and pain shot through my lower appendages. A glance down told me that they weren't on fire, but the edges of my boxers were singed and the carpet beneath my fingers began to melt.

The walls were caving in, the ceiling loomed closer, and I could only move my arms. Rather than flinch from the pain, I dug my fingers into the melting, plastic weaves, mingling the burning ache with my anger. I was running out of time. I took a deep breath. It came somewhat easier in my lower position. "I didn't think you deserved it before, but now I know you did. You sadistic, twisted lunatic! You deserve every misery that comes your way," I screamed.

Another fit of coughing gripped me. Then, the memory box Irene gave me last Christmas shone through the growing smoke, beckoning from the nightstand. Using my free hand, I threw it through the window, this time avoiding the bars and aiming for the ghostlike figure past the fog of smoke. It fell short.

"Oh, you didn't like that present, I guess," came Irene's taunt.

"Screw you, you bitch!"

"Yeah, I think I've heard that one before. Know who I'm dialing?"

"I don't give a shit!" I yelled as flames inched their way up my supporting arm. I grabbed my silver lighter off the burning side table and flung it out the window. It flew true, and Irene jerked backward.

"You little bastard! You shit!" Irene screamed, lifting a bloody hand from her forehead. "You know, I think I'll wait a little longer before dialing the last digit. I don't want them arriving in time to save you. You gotta burn for your sins."

"You arrogant, sick, heartless wench!" I cried. "You'll go to hell for thi—" But another round of coughing assailed me. Ragged gasps were all I could manage—no words, but the lengthy list of curses rattled on in my thoughts, slowly being overwhelmed by the anguish of blistering skin and the smell of burning flesh.

Minutes passed like years, but Irene's feigned words of panic filtered through the roaring blaze. "Help, I just came home and found my house on fire... Yes, my husband's inside!"

I screamed once more, hoping they would hear me, but unsure whether the sound made it beyond my lips. Spots were clouding my vision, and the roaring flames began mixing with her voice, like loud white noise that permeates your very mind.

"It's too far gone," she wailed. "I can't get... him. It's getting too... Oh no... screams. I can't take... help, help... please!"

Over the lip of the window, I watched her vague shape vanish as pain flooded my thoughts. The thought of dying had passed, leaving me only with the horrific, throbbing agony. The ceiling collapsed and the dream became etched into my memory forever.

* * *

The smell of aged leather and burnt flesh drifted away, leaving me to rotate the brushed-metal Zippo in my fingers. *For Victor Harris,* the engraving read, *my darling, my savior, my life. With love, Irene.* Thinking back to the horrific end, the irony of the gift wasn't lost on me.

My thoughts turned back to the job at hand. Irene was dwindling down the long, tiled corridor, passing makeshift rooms of linked chairs at each flight gate. This woman was certainly guilty, but she'd served her time in the eyes of the law. Could she really be guilty of the other murders? I didn't have time to think on it further. Everything pointed to her. Too many times killers are let off scot-free, but not this time. She might have gotten off easy because of politics before, but not in my town. Around this time of the year, Mayor Dihler always became touchy. However, this year he'd taken off the gloves, saying, "Use every means possible to catch this bastard." And yes, he used those words.

I had no bag. In fact, I hadn't planned on leaving, but a glance at the flight schedule on the wall told me I had ten minutes to grab my briefcase from the car and make my flight to the capital. That might not be enough time. "Shit!"

"Can I help you?" asked Larry from his counter.

"Nah, just think I'm gonna miss my flight. Gotta hurry."

Larry nodded, and I turned toward the counter. "Yep, probably should." His words echoed in the large corridor as though he'd shouted in Canterbury Cathedral. "You know, you really need to try and get here a couple hours before the flight—that way this doesn't happen to you."

I stutter-stopped and spun back around. "Two hours! Whatever happened to one?"

"Well, since 9/11, all the airports have beefed up security," he said with a wave of his uniformed arm, as if the metal detector, screening machine, and the maze of retractable barriers were evidence of that fact. "You never know how long it will take to get through security. We're usually much busier than this."

"I'm sure," I replied, trying to keep the sarcasm out of my voice. His bushy eyebrows scrunched together. Evidently I hadn't restrained myself enough. Turning back toward the ticket booth, I dashed to get my ticket.

I think he would have given me a cavity search when the metal detector went off on the way back through. I undoubtedly would have missed the flight had I not flashed my badge and given up my gun before rushing to the gate.

"You'll get it back when you arrive at your destination, Detective Drummond," he assured me.

Shaking my head, I ran to the gate and slipped into one of the last seats after spotting Miss Irene Harris Poppins sliding into a window seat a few rows up. I'd never been to DC before, but I had the feeling this trip was going to be memorable. *At least I know someone there.* Before the announcements came to turn off all electrical equipment, I pulled out my phone and sent a text to Jessie:

Gonna be in town in a couple hours. Pick me up?

Thankfully, Jessie replied in seconds, *Sure. Where?*

Will take Metro to Branch Av. Pick me up there.

I knew it was out of his way, but that was the station nearest to Irene Harris's new house. The phone beeped as I was shutting it down. I ignored it with a smile. *Good ol' Jessie. He'll be there.*

Chapter 3

A Capital Welcome

September 14, 2011

WHEN WE LANDED, I grabbed my briefcase and slipped out just as the stewardess opened the door. I tried to casually walk down the extended hallway, but wanted to be out of sight when Irene reached the gate. My heart thumped with the beat of my footsteps. I restrained myself, even though the adrenaline pumping through me was enough to outrun a surging freight train. Tracking someone while remaining hidden was something I'd honed over the years; it was a must in my profession, but the thrill had to be controlled to remain inconspicuous.

I stepped off the platform, onto the solid floor of the airport, and scanned the terminal. Scooping a magazine off of one of the bolted rows of chairs, I sat down and immersed myself in its pages, glancing back at the gate with periodic interest. Irene exited, rolling her carry-on luggage behind her, the telltale squeak of the wheel announcing her. She walked with purpose, not stopping to window-shop or eat. When she'd passed one of the eateries a few shops down, I folded the magazine under my arm, gripped my briefcase, and strode after her.

Thank the maker for uncomfortable women's shoes. Although hers weren't high heels, the height slowed her down and allowed me to stop by the customs office and pick up my gun. I would have lost her by the time they finally brought it if she'd been in sneakers and without the squeaky wheel. Irene would have blended in with the crowd like the rest of the unremarkable strangers in the large airport. It worked out this time. I would have to speak with Martinez back home before the return trip though.

Unfortunately, the pedestrian traffic exiting Reagan National and entering the Metro station across the way was less accommodating. Mrs. Harris paused for a second to remove her Metro pass and then slipped through the turnstile to vanish into the mix of people heading below.

"Shit!" I stepped up to the security booth, flashed my badge, and said, "I've gotta get through."

One guard leaned closer, then crossed his arms. "You're a little out of your jurisdiction, aren't you?" Both men chuckled and shook their heads.

Cursing them under my breath, I grabbed a handful of coins and sped to the pass dispenser. I deposited the bunch and scanned the machine. *What pass do I need? How far is it?* "Crap!" I took a deep breath. *Remember, she's heading to the Branch Avenue stop,* I whispered silently. *No worries. Just catch up before the Metro comes.* Hitting the button, I snatched the day pass and followed down the escalator. Fortunately it seemed proper etiquette in DC for people to stand to the right, allowing those in a rush to pass by, using the escalators like accelerated stairs. After one changeover onto the green line, I spotted Irene in the dimly lit underground as she boarded a front car. My heart slowed its panicked beating as I stepped through the nearest entrance and took a seat for the remainder of the ride.

Shifting in the uncomfortable seat, I pulled a file out of the briefcase and propped a foot on my knee as the Metro sped through the underground passage. Elongated, white lights flickered through the side windows as I flipped through the paper-clipped pages of a thick file. Gruesome pictures peered at me, accompanied by officer's notes, witness statements, and coroner's reports. Each victim was another knife sliding deep into my heart. I hadn't been able to save them, but maybe I could find them justice.

The tinny sound of someone's headphones gave off a *ricka— dum—chink* over and over, echoing throughout the narrow cabin. A large woman in a black-and-white, floral-patterned dress came in at the next stop, directing her five children into the row of seats in front of me. The youngest two continued an argument from earlier in whispers across the aisle. The smallest, a dark-skinned boy with a crooked cap, pointed at his slightly older sister and said, "You's scared of the tunnels."

"Nuh-uhh," mumbled his sister, hiding behind her water bottle.

"Yes you is," he persisted, "and I's gonna tell Momma." Their mother and oldest sister chuckled at the two.

I tuned them out. *What on earth could this arsonist be trying to do? Why burn someone while they're still alive?* Over the years Tranquil Heights had become much less tranquil, but it still wasn't a place where you expected to see things of this nature. Family photos of the three victims stared back from individual pages. Even the victims seemed to be staring askance, awaiting some clue to the murderer... for answers, something. Each victim had gone off to school or work elsewhere in the world, one even went all the way to Alaska to become a crab fisherman. Yet somehow, they all wound up back home and burnt to a crisp. It was obvious there was a serial killer on the loose in Tranquil Heights, but more questions kept knocking at my mental door: *Why only one victim a year?* The more irksome issue was the lingering connection with September 20th and a murderer from my past.

* * *

September 22, 1996

"Hello, Alex," said Mr. Lee, taking my hand in both of his, just inside his front door. "I-it's good to meet you." His voice cracked and his eyes were red and irritated. He and his wife were both having a hard time with it, but he was handling it better than she. Mrs. Lee sat on the far end of the couch, refusing to look at us, her head buried in a blanket. "Please excuse my wife," he continued. "It's been very difficult."

"I understand, Mr. Lee. I'm so sorry for your loss," Paige added, placing a hand on his shoulder. "It was horrible, but at least he's safe now. Whoever it was can't do anything more to him."

Mr. Lee nodded and his wife burst into another fit of sobs. He led Jessie and the two of us to the dining room, out of sight of

Susan, but not out of hearing. He pulled out a seat like an elderly man, as though he'd aged forty years overnight, then lowered himself into the chair. "J-Junior was a great athlete, a great student... great at everything he did," Junior's father whispered, trying to fight off a fit of sadness.

"I remember Junior from high school. He was a few years younger, but he was a good kid," I said. "I'm sure he would've made his mark in the world."

Jessie added, "Everyone that knew him was affected by his positive attitude and upbeat approach to anything he put his mind to. He already made a mark on many people's lives, and he won't be forgotten."

Mr. Lee nodded again, but was unable to meet our eyes. "Now, I appreciate you coming. I know Junior would too, but Jessie told me that you might be able to help where the police couldn't. How's that?"

Jessie didn't say how much he'd told the Lees, but he had to give them some reason for bringing us in. Fortunately, I was prepared for the question. "Well, I'm in school to become an officer of the law and have an uncle in the department. Something I've noticed in dealing with them is that, while very thorough, they sometimes miss things because they don't always know where to look. They're good; don't get me wrong. I'm sure they're working very hard to find Junior's killer, but maybe if I had a look at Junior's room, things they might have thought unrelated could be the needed clue to solve the case."

Junior's father nodded again, his shoulders slumped as though carrying the weight of the world on them. "That's fine. Junior looked up to you, Jessie, and if you trust Alex, then that's good enough for me. Please, just try not to move anything if you don't have to." At this, he looked up at Jessie and me.

"Not a problem, Mr. Lee," I assured him. "We have Junior's best interest at heart here, too."

Without another word, the brokenhearted man returned to scanning the table for something he'd lost... something he might never find again: his will to go on.

Jessie directed Paige and me past Mrs. Lee and down the hallway to Junior's bedroom with the silence of a mosquito walking on water. During the somber walk I remember thinking about a lesson I learned not long before: the victims often aren't just the ones that have passed.

Once my friends and I were inside, Jessie closed the door. "Man, Mr. Lee is rough. At least it ain't as bad as the day we found out, but did you see those wrinkles at the corners of his eyes?"

"They're called crow's feet," Paige said, correcting him out of habit. She winced after the words passed her lips. It was obvious that Jessie was hurting too and didn't need her added irritants.

"Crow's feet, right."

"Yeah, Jess. I saw them," I replied.

"Mr. Lee didn't have them yesterday. I can chalk a good bit of it up to the stress and a long night, but those ain't goin' away," he continued. "It's like he's already an old man. Hell, he's barely forty-two, and Junior always took after his father. That's why he was such a good guy to be around."

"I know," I mumbled, glancing around the room. Jessie was just saying whatever came to mind at this point. He must've been real close to Junior. "Look, Jess, can you give me a hand?"

"Yeah," he said, his tone anxious.

"Where're Junior's things, his possessions that the police recovered?"

"They should be in a box," Paige interjected, "and it might have tape—ah, like this." She rose and tapped a finger on the black and white lettering of the tape strapped across a cardboard box on the dresser. It said, *Evidence.*

"Yep, Mr. Lee put it right there," Jessie said, as though the search was over and his task done.

"While I look through that, do me a favor and—wait, was he a smoker?" I asked as a thought struck me. Jessie shook his head. "Then look to see if any of his clothes smell like ashes or fire. Check the hamper."

With a task in mind, Jessie leapt to the challenge and found a wicker hamper in the closet.

I returned my attention to the box. It could have been the same one we searched through less than a year before, Frank's box from when he died. The Drunk's words again echoed in my mind. *"Just give it back when you's done."*

"We'll make sure to leave everything as it was before we got here," I whispered, answering both Mr. Lee and my absent, hateful stepfather once more.

"Don't worry, we will," Paige said reassuringly. Then, she sliced through the tape with a pocketknife, the one I'd gotten her when we went to the Luray Caverns over the summer. An image of one cavern was burnt into the wooden handle. I rolled out Junior's desk chair while Paige lowered herself and the box onto the edge of his bed. Opening it, I peered in.

The contents were sparse and nothing special, but had significance to Junior. In addition to his charred wallet and blackened cell phone, a burnt rabbit foot was attached to his keys. The fur on one side was rubbed clean, leaving the shriveled and charred bone and skin revealed. *He must've been pretty stressed,* I thought, *or hopeful.* Each item was labeled with a tag by the police department.

I grabbed the cell first when a green light flashed from beneath the grime; nothing appeared to me.

"Oh wow, how can that still work?" Paige asked, leaning closer, but she scrunched her nose when she got a whiff of the acrid smell.

Flipping it open, I managed to wipe off the screen and manipulate the buttons to scroll through his contacts. I recognized most of them, but the last call was to a *Shelley.*

"Jessie, got any idea who this Shelley girl might be?" I asked.

Jessie dropped the shirt he'd been holding to his nose with a grimace. "Oh man, that's bad. I think I found his gym clothes."

Paige snickered.

"Nothing smoky yet?" I asked.

"Nope, not yet."

"How about Shelley," I prompted, nodding at the image again.

Jessie leaned in. "Oh, that's just a fish who's been hanging around this year. Junior took a liking to her. She's a sweet girl, really. That's a picture of them there on the desk." He picked up the glass-framed picture of Junior and a young brunette with a tight-fitting, pastel sweater that accentuated her maturing body. She looked small and innocent next to the strapping jock, but part of that may have been the carousel of painted horses behind them and the fair booths in the distance. They were sitting on the lowest platform, at the feet of the running animals, and it was as though the childish machine had paused just for this picture. He handed it to Paige.

"A fish?" she asked, staring at the glass-framed image in her hand.

"Yeah, a freshman," Jessie supplied.

"So, how long have—I mean, had they been an item?"

Jessie's shoulders slumped at the reminder of Junior's passing, and he lost a bit of his vigor. "Not long. Maybe a couple weeks. Just since the school year started. They hooked up pretty quick."

"Hmmm, we may need to talk to her," I said.

Following my logic, Paige said, "She might have been the last one to see him alive."

I nodded. "Too bad he didn't get a picture of the murderer and get it framed. That would've made this a lot easier. Keep looking, Jessie." Turning back to the box, I reached for the decrepit, hairless lucky rabbit foot. The smell presaging a vision wafted through the air as soon as my fingers touched it, as though drifting up from the furry keychain.

* * *

"Wait, stop," I demanded, attempting to force the great beast's boot off me, but my hands were bound, and my head felt like an oversized balloon. The world swam in slow motion, and my mind was sluggish. As the situation gradually dawned on me, my heart skipped a beat and tripled its pace. "Y-you can't do this."

The beast stepped back with dark, unintelligible eyes.

A headstone stood near, crumbling under the moon's rays from years of neglect, but it was something solid and present. A corner flaked off and tumbled to the damp grass below. I wiggled my body along the ground, mixing with the smell of dew, grass, and dirt. The decrepit stone drew closer as I progressed, but only by mere inches. A glance back at the hazy beast sent a shiver through me.

The lifeless eyes of the hairy, elongated head stared down like dark, skewed orbs, and an odd, feminine voice that didn't match the figure declared, "I am doing this!" In a hoarse rasp, she continued, "You are the first, the chosen, the answer to my prayers. You are my golden bull, my flesh sacrificed in her honor. Don't flop around. Rise to your knees. Be what thou art, and accept your fate!"

The shiver grew to a tremor, beginning in my feet—somewhere below my ankles where the lack of circulation had numbed any feeling—but it travelled upward. Using my elbows, I struggled to sit and then rise, overcoming the fearful wave travelling through every appendage. "P-p-please, I'm doing what you say. N-now, please, please let me go. I'll get you a bull. I p-promise."

A whip lashed out of the creature's hand. Where it landed, it slashed my shirt and tore the flesh beneath. "Speak when I say," ordered the voice. This behemoth seemed to be a cross between an animal and a woman, like a monster from ancient myth, but its mouth did not move. My mind was sluggish and couldn't come up with a name. Can there be a person beneath that? I wondered. Who would do such a thing? Summoning the courage to speak again, I voiced my second question.

A whiplash answered me, adding a second stripe to the first. Then, the creature began chanting in a language I'd never heard.

"Wait, what are you doing?" I asked, my pitch rising as the creature encircled my neck with the braided leather in one stroke and threw me onto a concrete slab. The moon and stars appeared overhead, calmly holding their place within the universe. Tree branches stood above, waving in the wind as though in a failed attempt to block my only light. "God, please help me," I begged as the lash tightened, crushing my throat. A dark fog approached, obscuring my starry witnesses from view in black, swirling waves.

* * *

I opened my eyes to dim light trickling through the shades of Junior Lee's room. The scent of oiled leather was only a hint of what it was moments before, but the shiver coursed down my spine more freely now that I was not bound.

"I... I always forget who I am. It's like I almost lose myself in the dream," I muttered.

Paige took my hand in hers and tossed the keychain back into the box. "It's okay. Did you see what you wanted?"

"Wanted?" I spat. "That's an interesting question. I never want to see these things, but if I'm the only one who can, who am I to reject the visions?" I knew I shouldn't take it out on her, and her eyes reflected my pain. "I'm sorry. I... I still haven't gotten used to them, but yes I saw what happened."

"So why the ritual burning?" Jessie asked in a moment of reprieve from his chore at the laundry hamper.

"I don't know. I was—I mean, Junior must have been a sacrifice for something. She called him her 'golden bull.' Hopefully he'll be the last." I didn't believe it, but maybe it would give Jessie some hope.

"That's a blessing," he muttered, going back to his task.

A blessing? I think not, but I couldn't bring myself to say those words. Jessie didn't need to know the details. Instead I asked, "Was there anything about lash marks on his chest in the report?"

Jessie shook his head. "I don't know about the report. They didn't show me that, but no one mentioned anything about them."

"They must be keeping that part quiet."

"Why? What marks? What happened?" asked Paige, squeezing my hand.

Shaking my head, I whispered, "Not right now."

"It's okay, man," Jessie interjected. "I can take it."

"I know you can, Jess. This isn't something I want you having nightmares about. I have to deal with it, but you have a choice. Don't let your curiosity lead you to things you're better off not knowing."

He accepted my recommendation with solemn dignity. We'd been through this before, and he knew to trust my judgment, as did Paige.

* * *

September 24, 1996

A few days after our visit with Junior Lee's parents, I caught up with Shelley in school. Mr. Broaderick waved when he spotted me in the hall, but I tried to avoid most of the others.

Mrs. Easely's voice echoing from behind an open locker stunned me, and I ducked around a corner. "Mr. Roden, what did I tell you about those naked pictures?" she shouted. The constant chatter echoing throughout the hall ended the instant her voice boomed.

"Ah, come on," pleaded a youthful boy. "She's got a bikini on."

"Those kinds of thoughts lead to alcohol, drugs, and Satanism. I know you don't want something so awful on your conscience." The sound of tape ripping from the metal locker resounded through the hallway. Then her heels clopped back the other way.

Peeking back in the hall, I found the coast clear of any Stone face obstacles and breathed a sigh of relief. She would've had me kicked out or worse, being a graduate. The kids' voices grew until the atmosphere had returned to normal and students began milling about again.

I suddenly spotted the girl from Junior's cell phone waltzing down the hall with a condescending smile on her face. "Hey, Shelley. You got a minute?" I asked, grabbing her hand and pulling her out of the crowded hall, into a vacant alcove. Paige was on my heels.

The young Shelley was brunette, short, skinny, and had freckles speckling her cheeks, but curves in the right places for someone so young. Her brown eyes looked me up and down from six inches below. Her face still held the innocence of childhood, but her body looked to be maturing at an accelerated rate.

"Uh, yeah, I guess. What do *you* want?" she sneered and appraised Paige with raised eyebrows.

Paige looked shocked at first, but then hid a smile behind a balled hand. I hadn't expected the condescending attitude from what I would classify as a child. Considering all the rumors going around about Coach Moyer's disappearance and Grant Brogand's confession about his parents, I guess it shouldn't have surprised me. People fear what they don't understand. "Well, first off, you can stuff the attitude."

She huffed and stomped a foot, her full book bag jiggling on her back. Overall, she was so small and wiry, it looked like she could've curled up inside it. I stifled my laugh.

"Fine, what do you want?" she asked. "I'm gonna be late for

history."

"It won't take long. We just heard that you and Junior kind of had a thing, so I was wondering if you'd seen him that night." I didn't mention that we'd also found a picture of her on his phone, but it wasn't anything scandalous. It did, however, put her in connection with him shortly before his murder.

"Yeah, so? We dated, but I date a lot of guys." She tossed her head, and her long hair caught on her backpack, destroying the intended effect. It was almost comical, like a child readying herself for an imaginary beauty pageant.

"So... did you date him that night?"

"If you can call it that, but it wasn't anything special. We ate dinner at Bayside Pizza. Then he dropped me off. I've had much better."

I couldn't tell if she was just forced to look up at me or her nose was permanently stuck that way, but she was sure full of herself. "So, you weren't with him later that night."

"Oh, no! If I had been, who knows what would have happened to me? I got out just in time."

I nodded. "That's true. You were lucky." *And heartlessly selfish,* I wanted to add. Instead I settled for, "Who knows what that beast would've done to you?"

Shelley paused for a moment and glared. "I can take care of myself. Is that it? The bell's about to ring."

"Yeah, that's it. You can go."

"Great," she said, turning on her heels and giving a hop to hoist her backpack back onto her shoulders. "And please don't talk to me again; you're going to ruin my reputation."

Paige snorted once Shelley disappeared into the crowded hall. A chortle followed, and Paige bent over holding her knees, a few random tears even finding their way down her cheeks. "My-my, Alex," she said behind pursed lips as she tried once more to hold in the giggles. "That girl is a hoot!"

I finally allowed my own amusement to show and shook my head. "I almost laughed in her face. I practically couldn't help myself."

"I know. When she tossed her hair, I almost collapsed. It was just too funny."

The momentary thought sent my mind to thoughts of Glory, my stepsister that had died from internal bleeding earlier that year. My smile immediately disappeared as I remembered her glowing face smiling into the mirror as she tried to put Abigail's lipstick on, only to smear it all over her chin and upper lip. She even got a dot on the end of her nose. Other memories came back to me, ones of a childhood innocence that had never been lost, but never allowed to flourish. The ache for a missing part of my world returned, and I bit my lower lip, staring at the floor.

"What's wrong?" Paige asked, seeing my abrupt change.

I shook it off and muttered, "Nothing. Just remembering Gloria."

The concern in Paige's eyes turned to pity, and she wrapped an arm around my waist, pulling me to her as we meandered into the dying traffic and out to the parking lot. To change the subject, she asked, "So what's your gut telling you? Did she do it?"

"She isn't nice, but I didn't get anything when I grabbed her hand. I don't know for sure, but I doubt she's behind it. Did you see how small she is? How could she? Junior could've manhandled her in his sleep."

Chapter 4

Complications

September 14, 2011

THE MEMORY OF Junior's murder haunted me. There was a connection there. I knew it from the visions, but where was the evidence? The police and our justice system required it. There had to be more to the murders... something I missed. I read on, scanning the pages on my lap as the Metro sped to the next stop. A recorded, female voice announced the Waterfront stop as we slowed, and I tuned it out once more. There were still plenty of stops before Branch Avenue, where Jessie was waiting.

I'd looked over the files time and again over the years, but still felt like I was missing something. The locations were different, but each spot seemed to be moving closer to the center of town. The boys weren't the same age, but they were close, and I'd known each of them. It was a small town, and they were about my age, graduating classes of 1996, '97, and '99. So far, all of the victims were male athletes or had been in the past. The day was quickly approaching when one more name might be added to the file: September 20. If only the Tranquil Heights Police Department knew where to look. There should have been one last year, but the department never found a body.

I flipped to the photo of the last victim: *Timothy Sterling—born*

May 10, 1978—died September 20, 2009. We found him because of the smoke, but there wasn't evidence implicating anyone for the murder. Even with my visions, I didn't know who was behind them, but I at least knew they were connected. *How to prove it, though?*

Fortunately for the department, most of Tim's body was still intact. They'd gotten to him sooner than the others, but nowhere soon enough. His clothes and possessions had turned to ash. Enough damage had been done that they had to resort to dental records for confirmation of his identity. The only thing that remained was a piece of the plastic zip tie used to bind Timothy's hands in front of him.

After fifteen victims, it was the only clue I'd found. It told the department nothing, but the autopsy revealed a shard of wood grasped under his wrists and an impression of a large staff. Give one up for science. However, I couldn't say anything about my visions; if I had, they would've kicked me off the force. Not even Lieutenant Tullings could have stopped it. He would've tried, but there's only so much even a superior can do if it gets out that one of your lead detectives has gone loopy, accusing people of heinous acts without a shred of evidence. The zip tie was a simple item used in every household to bind cables and cinch trash bags, so as scientific proof, it didn't go far. Even the staff imprint on his burnt body didn't lead to anything.

Thinking back to the moment, I recalled reaching down to run a finger over the black, plastic binding protruding from the man's charred hands. Timothy looked like he'd been killed mid-prayer, just like the last few victims, but this time in the middle of a vacant parking lot. The familiar aroma of old, worn leather drifted near, as it had that late night, mixed with the disturbing odor of burnt flesh.

* * *

"Don't do this. You don't have to do this," I pleaded in a masculine voice that wasn't my own. I couldn't make out much because the world swam through my vision. I'd obviously been drugged. Rocks dug into my knees on the asphalt parking lot. I tried to stand, but another tie bound my feet. "Please stop. It hurts. I never did anything to you." My body ached from heel to head, and the skin crisscrossing my right forearm was blistered.

"How do you know?" demanded the woman's voice from a few feet ahead. I could make out a dark, fuzzy shape, but that was all. Suddenly, something hard slammed into my collarbone. "I asked, how do you know? Do you even know who I am?"

I raised my hands, pleading. "No, but please—"

Another blow to the opposite side sent me to the ground. Pain flared in my neck and shoulders.

"I don't," I mumbled. "Please stop." Bile inched its way up my throat and mixed with the metallic taste of my own blood. At some point I'd bitten my tongue.

"My blessed bull, you need not worry," her voice intoned. "You'll be in a better place in the afterlife. It will be glorious. You will see."

Whatever did I do to deserve this? *Something pinched the center of my back, and a horrendous shudder ran through every inch of my body, slowly immobilizing each appendage: first my left hand, then my right. Soon I couldn't move a muscle.* Thoughts of my family, the faces of my son and daughter passed through my mind: Travis, age six and just entering school with blond hair, a wide grin, and shining, blue eyes, and Sarah, not yet eleven, her hair a tangle of brown curls... my sweet children. I'll miss so much. Please forgive me.

Something coated my running shirt and pants in a spray, weaving back and forth over me. A whiff of lighter fluid assaulted me. Please make this quick.

The woman's stiff shoe sole found my shoulder, rocking me onto my back. I would have winced if I could. Next, something was placed between my palms—something long and wooden. Then, the sound of a match striking echoed into my void like a dark beast. "No... no, please!" I tried to shout, but nothing worked.

A warmth began at my feet, sped up my body, and over the wooden handle in my grip. My murderer's voice began chanting, but it was impossible to distinguish over the signals flying to my head from every agonizing limb and the roaring flames in my ears. Screams echoed through my skull, the anguish in my head and body building to a crescendo. It felt like I would pop, but still the flames ate at my flesh.

"God, nooo!" I screamed, but it never pierced the silence beyond my blazing thoughts.

* * *

Timothy's smiling face looked out at me, and I slapped the file shut as the Metro halted at another stop. The murders, and my failure for so many years, created a feeling of grime and dirt that could not be washed away. It was as though my head, heart, and lungs were coated in motor oil, making it hard to breathe, live, and grasp the thoughts that seemed within reach. I was close. No one else had to die. But who was perpetrating these murders, and how was she picking her victims?

Then a tart, young voice caught my attention. The nine-year-old girl ahead of me replied to something I missed with a sarcastic tone and vivid imagination, saying, "I'll turn you into a girl."

The youngest boy spun on her, yelling, "Nuh-uh, I'll turn you into a boy."

"Nuh-uh. I'll turn you into an elephant," she shot back. After a thoughtful pause, her tone changed as she added, "And I'll turn me into an elephant too so we can be huge!"

What I would give to be something else.

* * *

When the Metro finally stopped at Branch Avenue, I stepped from the cabin to see a tall, young man in his twenties; he had jeans, a white undershirt, and dreadlocks that reminded me of Bob Marley. He was punching keys on his smartphone. Thrust out to see his phone, the dark ink of a large, ornate ankh was visible on his forearm.

Jessie's words echoed in my mind: *There's this tattoo of an ankh on his arm, but that's not much to go on. Lots of people have that.* A few of the victims had that same tattoo, or at least some version of it, on their bodies. Past visions of the case from the years following my graduation sped through my mind. The victims of that killing spree were drugged, but Junior, the first victim, was more cognizant than the others. Every subsequent one was left barely aware of the world around them, as though the dosages were getting stronger. It was like she was learning from her mistakes, getting better... smarter. Plus, I'd been a simple student. I didn't have access to the bodies at the time, or the bone remnants in the case of the earlier murders. Before we learned the different kinds of places to look, the only things the department had been finding were spent candles and bone-mixed ashes. Although the Drunk's brother was on the force, he was the sort of guy more inclined to give you a kick in the keister than a leg up. I made my way through school and helped them to find the bodies sooner, before they'd been fully reduced to ashes.

The tattoos I knew about were mostly reported by friends and family I spoke with. Others had photos of their recently deceased friends with the tattooed skin visible. One man had a small illustration of it on his calf with rose stems wrapping around its base. Another had a Romanesque depiction of an ankh on his forearm like the Bob Marley clone. The third victim had one emblazoned across his back with Celtic knotwork. The picture was etched into my mind. In it, Robin Gemanc was shirtless and hunched over the engine of his old Pontiac in the front lawn, his tattoo staring into the camera. When I first saw the picture, my eighteen-year-old mind clicked and sent me to the Internet for a quick search.

Jessie was right. It was a common Egyptian symbol, and tons of people across the nation had begun using it to decorate their bodies. Thinking back, even with it so prevalent in society, how many people in my small hometown of Tranquil Heights were likely to have one? The common thread linked those four victims, but were there others?

I pulled myself from my thought-filled immersion and glanced around for Irene, but she was nowhere in sight. *Did she get out before me, or is she still on the Metro?* I peered at the exit, but found no one matching her modern Mary Poppins description. The squeak-squeak of her wheel echoed through the covered Metro station, but then the subway began moving, the clack-clack of its tracks drowning out the sound. "Dammit!"

I headed for the exit, gazing into the milieu of people. *At least there're less of them than outside the airport.* Jessie spotted me outside the fenced wall of the escalators as I came up. He waved, hardly having changed a bit since I last saw him more than a dozen years ago. I slipped my ticket into the machine and walked out into the sunlight. Irene was nowhere to be seen.

"Alex, how've you been?" he said, wrapping me in a one-arm hug while taking my briefcase with the other. "Where's your bag?"

"Oh, I don't have one, but I've been doing pretty good. It's great to see you."

"You too, my boy. Looks like you might've put on a couple pounds," he added appraisingly.

I scoffed. "You've gotta be joking. I still have a pair of jeans from high school I wear on the weekends."

"Seriously?"

I nodded. "Yep, but you look like you're in the best shape of your life."

Jessie grinned and curled one arm up, posing like a bodybuilder with the other lifted toward the sky, my briefcase dangling from his thumb. His dark-blue, long-sleeved shirt fit snugly enough that it showed off his bulging muscles. "Yeah, I like it." A few people glanced at Jessie posing in front of the Branch Avenue Metro Station, and a passing woman in a miniskirt and high heels smiled, then giggled. "You know you like what you see," he said as she wandered away. However, she did glance back, lips in a tight smile, but whether it was in appreciation or laughter, I didn't know. "These chicks up here just can't get enough of me," he added, eyes sparkling with glee.

Over the years, Jessie had become more outgoing, and I'd discovered that he had very little humility. We talked on the phone a good bit since he left. Much of what he said was in jest, but discerning which half was jest and which serious was sometimes a difficult process.

I shook my head, and we started for the car. "Jess, you never would've gotten away with that in high school. What's gotten into you?"

"Life. I was a pushover in high school, but coming here opened my eyes. I played ball for years, and it taught me one thing: there're always people watching. You either hide or put on a show. I got guns now, so why not show them off? The worst they'll do is laugh, and even that ain't a bad thing."

I couldn't help but chuckle. In a strange way, it made sense. While we walked and talked, I scanned the parking lot, but the blazing sun glinted off of too many car windows to make out the people in the distance. Seeing my distractedness, he asked, "You waiting for someone else?"

I shook my head. "Nah, just tracked someone here. That's why I don't have a bag. She should be around here somewhere. I watched her get onto the subway, and she always gets off here. I even heard her luggage squeaking, but it could've been anyone's." *Maybe this was the one time she didn't,* I thought with a shake of my head.

"Maybe she got off early."

"Yeah, maybe, but can we do a couple circles around the lot to be sure?"

"Sure, Alex. No problem."

Once we were in his beat-up, green-and-white pickup, I asked, "Jess, you remember what happened to Junior Lee?"

Jessie's smile vanished with the change of subject. "Yeah, what of it?"

"Well, I can't help but think there might've been more to those tattoos."

"Is that the case you're working?" The lingering edges of a smile crawled back to his lips. "And I thought it was just to come visit little ol' me."

We both chuckled. "Nah, it's not that. As much as I've missed you, bud, what began with Junior is still going on."

"You've gotta be joking. How long's it been now, ten or twelve years?"

"No. More than that. We're up to fifteen—well, fourteen for sure, but I'm pretty certain about the fifteenth victim."

"And you never caught the guy? What about your... you know?"

"Visions," I mumbled. "They still come to me. As much as I'd like them to stop, I can't ignore what these people have gone through. Morally, it would just be wrong, and it's impossible to turn off, so I really can't stop."

"Dang, bro. I can't believe you've gone all these years and still can't tune it out or somethin'."

I shook my head. "It doesn't quite work that way. I came here following a killer. She commutes back and forth once a month from Tranquil Heights."

Jessie turned back to circle the lot a second time. "Now you've seriously gotta be joking. That's a seven-hour drive one way," he said, taking his eyes off the road to glance at me.

"Yeah, but she flies."

"That's a lot better, but it still gets expensive—wait, did you say 'she?' So, you came all the way out here to follow some chick?"

"Well, when you say it like that, it seems like something Paige would kick my butt over, but it's nothing like—"

"Whoa, hold on!" shouted Jessie, throwing a hand in front of me and stomping on the brake. A pale woman clad in a dark shawl, dress coat, and skirt rolled a case of luggage across our path. Her black hair was curled in a bun that had seen better days. The squeak of her luggage drifted through the truck window. "Man, that girl almost lost her license to live."

"That's her," I hissed, pulling another file and flipping it open to Irene Harris's prison photo. I tipped the brim of my hat lower.

"What's that on her neck?" Jessie asked.

I quirked my head, trying to make it out. The edge of a tattoo peered over her collar. "I... don't... know." I looked back at the picture. "Come to think of it, she always wears high-collared shirts and jackets. I don't know how long she's had that tattoo, but it isn't in the prison photo. It has to be fairly new."

"If she hides it, maybe she's ashamed."

"Could be." I nodded. "Follow her."

"Dude, she's walking. We're in a truck. I think she'll notice."

"Jessie..." I shook my head. "Sorry, I'm used to operating with Martinez. Just pull into that gas station like you're gonna fuel up. I'll keep watch."

"Martinez?" Jessie asked with a teasing smile. "That your girl on the side?"

"Nope," I replied, not taking my eyes off Irene in the side mirror, "my partner."

"Ahhh." He pulled in and followed my directions, but he actually got out and began gassing up the tank.

"Uh, Jess, what are you up to?"

"Filling up. Might as well, you know."

I shook my head. "And how are we supposed to leave if she vanishes down a side street?"

"Alex, she's walking. It's not like she's got a teleporter or nothin'."

I nodded. "True, but have you ever heard of parking a car? She could be heading to one."

Jessie looked at me through the window with a stunned expression. Evidently that hadn't occurred to him. The gas pump clicked off and he returned the nozzle, screwing on the truck's gas cap.

As I feared, Irene stopped next to a silver coupe in the long-term parking lot. She threw her noisy luggage in the trunk, then got in and started her car. "Jessie," I whispered. He didn't respond. "Jess."

"Yeah?"

I pointed at Irene in the distance. "She's getting in her car. We've gotta go. Come on."

"Dang!" he said. "Be right back." He loped past the car toward the store.

"Where're you going?"

"I gotta pay."

"Ever heard of a credit card?"

"Of course, but I don't trust 'em." The greeting bell rang as he stepped into the store, and I thrummed my fingers on the window

ledge of the door. Irene pulled out and passed us just as Jessie
returned and jumped in.

"She went that way," I said, pointing.

Jessie gripped the wheel and pulled to the curb, bouncing over
it with hardly a glance at traffic. "Which lane?" I nodded to the left,
and he pulled over, cutting off the black, dually truck behind us. It
honked angrily, but Jessie was jazzed for action and didn't seem to
take notice.

"I appreciate you trying to get there quickly, but could you play
it cool? We don't want to cause a commotion and have her take
notice. We need to remain incognito."

Jessie let out a tense breath and chuckled. "Right. Gotta stay
cool," he whispered more to himself than me.

"Just remember. We're the law. She's the criminal. That's good
and bad, though. We have to obey the law while she can make a
run for it and disappear."

"Yeah, but you can pull records: credit cards and everything.
You can find her... I mean, if I lose her."

I shrugged. "Maybe. I can have my department pull her reports,
criminal records, and transactions, but it takes time. We aren't the
NYPD or the FBI. We don't have jurisdiction here. Hell, Jess, I
couldn't even get through the turnstile when I got on the Metro.
The security guards wouldn't let me through without a day pass,
even after I flashed my badge."

"I could be wrong, but I don't think they hire security guards for
the Metro," Jessie said as we came to a stoplight. "I think they have

Metro police or transit police or somethin'."

"Well, I was in a bit of a rush and didn't check their credentials, but if you're right, how helpful do you think the local police department's gonna be? No one here seems to trust outsiders, even the police."

"Yeah, that's pretty much the way it goes," Jessie said with a nod. "Never know who might have an explosive diaper strapped to his ass."

I looked at him in shock. I'd heard about the attempt to blow up a plane wearing explosive underwear, but didn't consider it affecting places around the nation.

Seeing my wide-eyed expression, he said, "You heard about that, right?"

"Yeah, yeah I did, but that wasn't here, was it?"

"Doesn't matter—"

"Wait, she's turning. Keep left here."

"Yeah, I got it. Look, this is DC, Alex. This is the capital. If anything like that happens, what place do you think is gonna get the best, most updated security?"

"DC, right." Everything he said made sense. I just didn't realize the extent of things. "Guess living in Tranquil Heights for so long kept me isolated from the real world."

"Yeah, bro. When I got out of that piddly town, I didn't know what hit me. The big city was different."

"I guess, when you grow up in a small town, you take certain things for granted."

"Yep, but at least I don't have Old Lady Selma looking through my bedroom window every night to make sure I was in bed."

"Oh, man. I forgot about that."

"And it all started when we went to check out that murder at the zoo. I got home late. The parents got mad, and lo and behold, I was grounded for the last month of school my senior year."

"I remember. Sorry about that."

"No worries."

"I still don't know why they had Old Lady Selma from next door come and check on you at night."

"They didn't. They were even a little freaked when I told them, but just said, 'Serves you right. Better get home before curfew next time'."

"So she took it upon herself to look in?"

"Yeah," Jessie said, taking a turn onto a residential street lined with condominiums. "Mom had been gossiping to the neighbors and word got out. Before we knew it, Old Lady Selma was checking on me each night in her nightgown, just peering through my window with that wrinkled face of hers. That's what I mean about small town livin'. Everyone's in your business. It's not like that here—"

"Whoa, hold up. She just turned into that complex there. Pull over. We don't want her to see us."

"Is this where she lives?" Jessie asked, spinning the wheel and pulling up behind a burgundy SUV parked along the curb. Irene parked in front of a brick condo that was almost a twin of every other one connected in this neighborhood.

"No. I've got her address here. She lives on this side of town, but not here."

She approached the door and knocked. A man with a long ponytail in a polo shirt answered. They chatted for a moment before he invited her in, slapping her butt with a grin. She jumped, but smiled back. He grabbed her luggage as though it were empty, lifting it without a problem.

"That's one buff dude," Jessie commented. "She was working to lug that bag."

I nodded. "Evidently he's her suitor up here."

"What do you mean, *up here*?"

"Well, she's dating a guy named Otis Simmons back home, an African-American that works at Crandell's Used Cars. He's a local boy, a little older than us."

"Don't remember him, but I know Crandell's. Is that the place that used to be Buddy's Auto?"

I nodded. "Yeah, Crandell's moved in there when Buddy's closed down."

"So what do we do now?" Jessie asked.

I took a deep breath and let it out. "Now, we wait." Taking off my hat, I laid it on my lap.

"Well, I hope this ain't gonna take long. I've got work in the morning. It's bad enough I had to drive over to pick your ass up," he said with a chuckle. "You're stayin' at my place right? I got the guest bedroom ready."

I nodded. "Yep, and don't worry, Jess. It'll be okay." I handed him my cell and credit card, then planted my skull against the headrest for a little shut-eye. "Do me a favor and call the rental place. Give them my card number and make sure they deliver. Just keep an eye out. I'll take over in an hour or so. If she doesn't show by then, my rental should be here and you can head out."

"Dude, you've got a dumb phone," he complained after flipping open the cell. It bounced off my leg and landed atop the fedora. "I'll use mine." A few beeps later, he asked, "Yeah, this is the Pizza Café right?" There was a pause. "Do y'all deliver?"

Always gotta be a pain in my butt, I thought, but said nothing. Then his conversation faded from my mind.

Chapter 5

New Friends

September 16, 2011

OVER THE NEXT twenty-four hours, I checked in with Paige, but she didn't have much time to talk. The hospital had her assisting in the emergency room. I followed Irene Harris from her lover's condo to work, out shopping, and to a local martini club called Snookers, snapping a few photos with my cell phone along the way. There wasn't much to do between times. I snacked on some leftover pizza, littering the gray sedan's passenger and back seats with printouts from the file, my coat, and pages from a local newspaper.

I finally tailed her to her recently acquired home. It was nothing special, just a ranch-style one-story a little farther out in the suburbs. The front lawn was green and well landscaped, with a few garden gnomes littering the mulch-covered ground around the shrubs. The figurines were well equipped, and all seemed intent on building their own little homestead. It was as though they'd posed for a snapshot with wide grins and had frozen that way. The entire façade was quaint and too pristine for a woman with such a gruesome past. I ran a finger along the edge of the lighter in my pocket.

Ahh, the skeletons that must dwell just beneath the surface of this city, I thought, remembering how many I'd uncovered in my first few years in Tranquil Heights. A shiver ran through me at the thought of living here, encountering so many people each day, and undoubtedly being drawn into their horrid secrets.

I wanted to sneak in and see what Irene had hidden inside, any treasures she might have kept from so many gruesome murders. If she had kept the Zippo, she must have taken souvenirs from the others.

The frosted-glass front door opened, and Irene emerged into the setting sun. Pink and orange coated half the sky, mixed with swirls of wispy clouds, but there was still plenty of light to see her. The modern rendition of Mary Poppins had vanished. A skin-tight shirt covered almost to her midriff, and a short miniskirt that would make any man stumble left nothing to the imagination below. I shook my head. *And the skeletons come out at night.* Then, a subtle breeze lifted her curls off of a bare shoulder, revealing the ankh tattoo beneath. The arms of the ankh seemed to embrace both sides of her shoulder in a hug, while the lower portion snaked down her arm. The broad, upper end of the ankh was what we'd seen the day before, peeking over her neckline. The details were impossible to see at this distance, but it definitely coincided with the other victims. *This ties her to the victims, not the murderer. Maybe her husband had one, too.*

Irene pranced to her car, her high heels clicking on the cement. Folding her slender legs and body into the small, silver coupe, she started the car and pulled out. *To follow or not? This is my best chance. The way she's dressed, she's probably headed to scout for another victim.* But the house called to me, beckoning me in for a sneak peek. *Wait, what's today?* I glanced at my watch. *The sixteenth—she never kills until the twentieth.*

As her car sped through the neighborhood and out of sight, I fought the urge to start the sedan's engine. Instead, I grabbed a clipboard I kept for just such occasions, stepped out of the car, and strode toward her door, leaving my hat and coat behind. The button-up and slacks I was wearing would be enough. I walked up the path to her door and knocked, peering through the window like any salesman might. Seeing no one, I walked around the house, subtly peering through the windows as I checked the backyard. The gate was unlocked and no pets seemed to be present. Slipping in, I strode up to the sliding-glass doors. I pulled on the door and it slid open with a swish. Peering around for any casual observers that might be able to see over the fence and finding no one, my heart rate slowed.

I stepped inside and was instantly assaulted by a horrid stench wafting from the kitchen. I crept through the dining room, grimacing as I approached the plastic trashcan. It was overflowing with banana peels and chicken bones. An entire chicken carcass sat on the island separating the two rooms. The meat had been gnawed off, leaving only gristle for the flies to feast upon.

While not a jailable offense, it seems Miss Harris might want to consider hiring a maid or picking up after herself. I breathed a sigh of relief as I left the noxious room and entered the hall. A brief glance at the living room revealed a tidy space filled with the scent of fresh potpourri. The most visible room to guests was on show, and that told me I would find nothing there. She'd want to keep her precious mementos for herself, more likely hidden in a basement or bedroom.

I continued down the hall, my shoes squeaking on the laminate-wood flooring. When I opened the bedroom door, I expected to find another smell, especially with her present love life. However, her bedroom was stagnant. Dust even floated through the air from the rapid movement of the door. It was as if the bedroom hadn't been slept in for months. The comforter and pillows were arranged neatly, but had a few wrinkles where she sat on the edge of the bed.

Probably putting on her shoes, I concluded. *There's gotta be something here though.* I began sifting through her drawers, careful not to misplace her possessions and only touching one thing at a time. I hated that I couldn't use the surgical gloves in my pocket, but I'd discovered long ago that without actual contact, no visions would come—meaning there was no way to avoid leaving fingerprints. Because of this, there could be no reason for her to suspect someone had been here—none.

Shelf after shelf, drawer after drawer, and even her jewelry boxes came up empty. She had plenty of possessions, but nothing linked her to the past murders. "Dammit!" I glanced around the room once more until the repetitive vibrations of my pocket scattered my focus.

"Hey, Jess," I said after seeing the caller ID.

"Alex, you haven't gotten caught by that woman yet, have you? You know, she'll probably beat you with a pair of those clobberin' heels she wears if she catches you. Being a Peeping Tom is against the law."

I rolled my eyes. "No, she hasn't yet, Jess, but I'm pretty familiar with the law. When you've got a badge and reason for suspicion, the rules are a little different."

"Dude, you aren't even in the same state. Don't you think your ass might be hangin' out a ways, being so far from your jurisdiction?"

I couldn't help but chuckle. "You mean, out of my jurisdiction. Yeah, but there's nothing wrong with following a lead."

"Oh, right. So you're not doing anything wrong?" Jessie asked.

"No, not while we were surveilling her," I replied. Then, a rapid movement caught my eye out the window. Not ten feet away, a young girl stood at her own house window, waving. My heart leaped into my throat, but I clenched it, smiled, and waved back.

"Wait, what do you mean? Aren't you watching her right now?"

"Well..." I glanced at her dresser where a photo of Irene and her new crush, Otis Simmons, sat. They stood embracing in a gazebo, competing to see who could smile widest. "You could say that," I finished.

Jessie's tone turned stern. "Alex, what're you up to?"

"Nothin'."

"Al," Jessie replied as though he was my mother, Vivian, and she knew I'd just gotten into something. "What's going on?"

"The less you know, the better."

"You *aren't* breaking the law are you, Alex?" he intoned.

Seeing that the girl was still waving, this time with such enthusiasm that her pigtails wagged in the window, I left the room and closed the bedroom door. "Don't you worry your little head about it, Jess. I just had to find out a few things."

"Oh man, Alex. You're gonna get us in trouble, man."

"No, I won't. Besides, I needed to drop by the police department, anyway."

"Wait, you're gonna waltz in and give yourself up."

"Not a chance," I assured him. "I need to pick their brains a bit about this Irene character."

"Right, like your Peeping Tom act hasn't gotten you enough info on her."

"Actually, no, it hasn't. There's nothing here to connect her." I strode through the hall and toward the front door. Leaving out the back would be too conspicuous with my new ticker-tape-parade child watching. I wouldn't be able to lock the deadbolt, but Irene would probably think she forgot to lock it herself.

"*Here?* What do you mean *here*?" asked Jessie.

"Don't worry," I said, stepping onto the driveway. The girl was at her door, waiting and waving. I smiled and waved back before making straight for my car. "I'm out now."

"Dude, what were you thinkin'?"

I shut the car door, slipped the clipboard back in my briefcase, and breathed a sigh of relief. "I was thinking our good friend Irene might have kept a few mementos. She kept the lighter, so I figured—"

"You figured you might do a little B and E," Jessie supplied. "Man, is that how you guys operate back home?"

The reality of the situation set in as I remembered the home I'd left and my family: Paige and Jamie. "No, it's not," I replied as the shame of what I'd done settled on my shoulders. "You're right, Jess. I just got anxious. It's the sixteenth. There's only a few days before the murderer strikes again."

"Yeah, I know, man, but you've gotta rein yourself in. If you go down this route, there won't be any coming back."

"I know," I spat, allowing the frustration to get to me. "You got a point rattlin' around in that brain of yours? What'd you call for?"

"Well, I was goin' to ask what you were doing for dinner. I just got off work here at the site."

My stomach grumbled at the mention of food. "Nothing right now," I replied, taking a bite of my leftover slice of pepperoni pizza from lunch. "Like I said, I need to run by the local station and check some things out before it gets too late, though."

"Sure thing. There's this great taco place on Madison. You've gotta experience it. There's nothing like it. We can drop by the station afterward."

"Alright, sounds like a plan. Don't worry about a thing. Irene left dressed like she was heading to an S and M club or something, and following her around is getting a little old. It's like watching Women of the Suburbs on the Estrogen Network. She's got a few hidden habits, but nothing like the vision I saw. I didn't get to look at the basement. She doesn't seem to stay in the house much though."

"I said it once, and I'll say it again," Jessie said, mimicking a famous comedian. "Are you sure she's the one?"

A chuckle found its way across my lips. *Good ol' Jess. Sometimes he can get right to the point. Other times... not so much. Guess he's over the B and E.* "I'm beginning to wonder. That's why I want to stop by the local department."

"Will do. Meet me at home?"

"Sure. Be there shortly."

"'Kay, over and out," Jessie replied, even imitating the static.

Shaking my head, I closed the phone. *And I wondered why you weren't married.*

* * *

We walked into the Taco Hut to a roar of cheering construction workers who'd just gotten off work. Their jeans, denim work shirts, and hair, or in some cases balding heads, were still dusted with wood shavings. The sight lit Jessie's face. "Hey, boyos," he shouted. "You've gotta meet my good friend. This is Alex." Jessie pummeled me on the back, ushering me forward. Many of the guys rose to shake my hand.

A large, burly fellow was closest, and he reached out a meaty hand and took mine before I could extend it. "Good to meet ya. I'm John," he rumbled. His crew-cut hair and stature reminded me of every retired military man I'd met.

Another coworker who stood reached across the table and took my hand next. "Hey there. Any friend of Jessie's is a friend of ours."

A third man with long, graying hair pulled into a ponytail was next in line at the aligned picnic tables. "That's too true. If not for Jessie, Groucho over there would've bit it a few years back." He nodded at the balding man next to him who was eyeing me excitedly and waiting his turn.

"Fred's right," he said, clutching my hand next and pumping it like it was a jackhammer. "I would've surely taken a dive when that crane flew loose."

A questioning look at Jessie told me that the story was far more complex than they made it sound and that Jessie had played a smaller role.

A behemoth of a man noticed the silent exchange and Jessie's shake of his head. The dark-skinned brute almost bowled Jessie over with a friendly shove. The man's deep baritone belted out, "Now see here, rookie. You know wha'cha did. Don't even try to say climbin' that crane was nuttin'. Groucho was about to pee his pants and jump ta his death if not fer you."

Jessie caught his balance and smiled sheepishly before taking the seat that they'd shifted to open up. "It wasn't nothin', Anton. Any of you guys would've done the same."

"For his lazy ass?" Anton said with a wide, dark smile and a bulbous thumb extended at Groucho. "Not a chance."

The men I'd met sat down while a few others rose from the red, wooden tables to greet me. Each time I came into contact with someone else, my eye twitched, expecting a handshake or slap on the shoulder. Trey, Sly, and Paco introduced themselves, finishing the group. Trey and Paco were smaller, wiry like Jessie, but the pressure in their friendly handshakes spoke volumes about the conditioning their jobs brought on. Paco was a jolly sort with a chubby face and a bit of a gut, but his arms were strong, contradicting the apparent age the streaks of gray in his wavy, black hair portrayed.

"Anton's right," Groucho said with a smile that creased his bushy brows. "I didn't know what I was gonna do. Couldn't believe it when the little rookie shimmied up that crane and onto the steel beams I was hangin' onto. Somethin' malfunctioned with the damn thing, and it pulled away from the building when I was unhooking the first chain."

"Good thing you're slow, G-man, or you would have spilled with the beams," Jessie said. "As it was, things were still intact and it was just a matter of time till they got you down."

The guys laughed.

"That's true. It's a blessing you hadn't unlatched that first chain when the crane went nuts," added John.

"So what did you guys do up there?" I asked.

Jessie shrugged. "Talked."

"And played Xs and Os," Groucho added.

The others looked at him with the same silent question.

"You mean tic-tac-toe?" Trey asked the silent table.

Jessie nodded with a smile, and the group roared with laughter.

"So tha's where that crap came from. I noticed a bunch of tic-tac-toe games on one of the beams I was working next ta awhile back," he said and burst into another fit of laughter, his smile stretching from one side of his face to the other under his broad nose.

"Hey, Rayson, glad you could make it," said Fred as another straggler appeared in the entrance to the indoor patio.

"Yeah, had some things to take care of," Rayson said with a nod. A crown of short, brown hair blessed the thin man's head. He had to have been in his forties, but the years had not been good to him. He appeared almost twice his age, slightly frail, but more agile and mobile than an eighty year old.

Jessie whispered, "Something's happened to him recently. He looks bad, but he's really a great guy. He must not be sleepin' well." Turning his attention to the newcomer, Jessie said, "Rayson, this is my good friend, Alex, from back home."

The man nodded to me and extended his rough hand. I hesitated for a moment and then took his hand in mine. The soft feel of braided leather and beadwork was clasped under my index finger, and the world suddenly shook as though rocked with a vicious tremor. The smell of aged, massaged leather wafted to me as I looked in Rayson's gray, mournful eyes. *Ahhh, not again!* was all I had time to think.

* * *

The broad, night sky spread itself above as though orchestrating a symphony within the stars to accompany "Brick" by Ben Folds Five as it echoed out the open windows of the car a few yards away. A smile creased my face and giddy laughter bubbled inside me. The night was dark, and the city spread out below us, dotted with phosphorescence and zooming headlights as though the entire panorama were simply a tabletop model city.

"So how's the wine?" asked a husky, male voice.

I turned to face the sound and found Greg returning my smile, his eyes dancing in the shadowed night, lit only by the glass-encased candle centered on the blanket. I wasn't sure if it was the light playing tricks, but he looked healthier, happy... younger. "It's good," I whispered in a youthful, female voice tinged with a Mexican accent. I tried to stifle the subsequent giggle with a hand. "S-sorry, Greg."

He shook his balding head and brown crown of hair. "Nothin' to be sorry about. It's the wine, is all."

"My mom would hate you if she knew."

"That's why we aren't gonna tell her." His smile remained and seemed genuine. I couldn't find any ulterior motives hidden deep within his gray eyes. They were almost silver in the moonlight.

I nodded, unable to control my response, only to watch as though sitting in one of the new 3-D theatres. "I w-won't. I-I'm having too much fun." My head swam with the alcohol, flushing my cheeks and sending tingling sensations down through my knees, legs, and into my toes. Even the fingers of the arm I was leaning on tingled numbly, almost threatening to give way and send me to the ground. But it *was a pleasant tingle and seemed to carry out into the soft blanket beneath us. A cool breeze wafted by as more notes and a gentle, male voice sang out of the car window, reaching us in our evening picnic. Sensual thoughts streamed through my mind, flushed with warmth that might have been hormones, the wine, or both.*

"Good. You know, I still feel kind of weird about this," Greg said, swirling the half-filled glass of dark liquid in his hand. "I-I don't know. I tried to stop myself from asking when we first got together, but I couldn't."

"Well...," I said, trying to remember the thought that had come to mind and then flitted away as quickly as a starling. "You know, all my friends say I'm mature for my age, and I-I've got my driver's license." I set down my empty wine glass and caressed his knee with the tips of my fingers. "It's what I want."

Greg nodded. "I know you do, hon. That's why I'm still here." He leaned in for a kiss, and I met him halfway, although somewhat shakily. The feel of his five-o'clock shadow on my lips and cheek was unnerving, but a rush of emotions sent me in for another, longer, less-restrained connection. His hands caressed me gently and a moan escaped my lips.

After a few minutes we parted, the stars above me spinning and swirling. "Whoa, is it always th-this way when a girl kisses you?" I asked in a sultry, somewhat slurred combination of words.

Greg's brows knit in curious confusion. "Like what?"

"The world and s-stars spinning."

"Oh, no—no, that's probably not me, or at least not all me. Do you

need to move back to the car?" Greg rose to a knee, his arm extended in concern.

I shook my head, but it made the world spin faster. "N-no. Just give m-me a m-minute."

He nodded and plopped back down. "Sure thing."

After sitting for a few minutes, a nauseous surge blossomed in my stomach.

"Oh, Evie. You look a bit green. Here, honey, try and focus on me. I'm sitting very still, but if you need to let it out, just turn to the side. Don't worry about the blanket. I'll take care of it."

His words seemed to warble. I tried to focus on the car and then Greg: his flannel shirt, jeans, and work boots, but what drove away the squeamish feeling within me was his gentle smile. It even looked cute with the few strands of hair up top that remained. His smile was wider, although a little worried. "I'm okay n-now," I whispered. "You have a wonderful smile, you know that?"

He blushed so deep that even his forehead reddened in the pale starlight. "Not as beautiful as you. And thank you for the bracelet," he said, turning his attention to his wrist. A glimmer of grief seemed to twitch behind his eyes as he looked at it. "You know I can't wear it at work, though, right? They all know who you are."

The edges of my lips tweaked up in a feigned smile, knowing the truth about the secret romance, but wishing it could be different. "I know." The words came out as a mumble, and Greg glanced down at the blanket.

"I wish it were different, and it can be later, but you've still got

two years." He met my gaze again. "Besides, you can wear yours. Greg's a common enough name that you can get away with it without letting anyone know." He winked.

I brightened at that. The urge to tell Kimmy and brag to my BFF emerged like a tiny bird of anticipation. She won't tell. She'll be happy for me, *I assured myself. Turning my attention back to Greg's caring smile, the thought faded and the warmth of the wine and shame washed over me once more.* I can't. It's too risky. He could go to jail, or at least lose his job. *I silently cursed the world and the politicians that had forgotten what it was like to be sixteen and lonely. I peered down at my own bracelet, the twin to Greg's, and straightened the small, white cubes with pink letters, fighting the swirls that entered my vision. The cubed, plastic beads were woven into the strands of leather, each one held in place. Mine spelled out* Evelyn loves Greg, *while his had the names reversed. It had taken me two entire evenings to make them. Memories of the frustrating process, the weave, and embedding the beads passed through my mind like one of the flipbooks I'd made in kindergarten, each page a scene accompanied by emotions: those of frustration and the wonderful reminder of Greg's affection for me. The few times he'd said, "I love you, Evie," fluttered past like a soundtrack of leaves whispering in the wind. The words rejuvenated me, and I'd forced my pained fingers to continue on, anticipating Greg's smile when I gave it to him--the symbol of our love.*

"I love you too," he whispered, seeing me fondling the tiny beads between a thumb and forefinger. At those words, the warmth

overcame me and darkness overwhelmed my vision.

"My little niña," tsked an older voice I recognized as mi abuela, my grandmother. Yet her face didn't appear. Instead, darkness pervaded. "You know, señorita. He's no good for jou."

"But, Abuela, I love him."

"He's too old," chided the aged woman's voice.

"But he loves me," I whimpered into the void.

"No. You stop this foolishness, niña," she demanded.

A surge of anger rose from inside. Unable to see her, I pushed and shoved, fighting to get away. "No, Grandmamma. No. I love him. I will be with him."

Something strong slapped my face, and the sting remained, but still I couldn't find mi abuela. "Stop this foolishness, Evie. Stop it now," came her voice again, harsh and direct. Now, something strong gripped my arms, pulling me to her, cradling me like a baby.

I struggled harder. "No, leave me alone! It's my life."

"Evie, stop it!" came the voice once more, but accompanied by another slap. This time, the voice was deeper.

"No, Abuela. No!" I shouted, struggling out of the grip that held me. The star-filled sky flashed above again, finally, but slipped away as I overturned and plummeted to the ground. The impact knocked the breath out of me and sent new stars into flight, but they drifted, shifting in my dizzy head. Now free, I stumbled to my feet. Trees flashed around me and a hazy figure approached. I stepped away, planting a foot behind me, and then another.

The figure said something, but the words were mumbled. The

voice was deeper, but caring like mi abuela's.

"No, Grandmamma. I love him."

The stranger came closer and I took another step back, but my foot slipped on the dew-covered grass. "Evie, no," came Greg's fear-filled words as the ground vanished beneath me and I dropped over the cliff.

Strong fingers wrapped around my wrist, and the jolt of my body stopping slammed my head against the rocky cliff face. I blinked away the blurriness and tried to look through the murky liquid leaking into one eye. Greg lay above me, his arm extended, gripping mine, his face contorted, each wrinkle of strain illuminated in the pale moonlight. His grip was strong, but the sweat and dew between our skin caused me to slip an inch further away.

"No, Evie. Don't—leave me," Greg panted. "Please, Evie—I love you."

A look into his fearful, silver eyes and the wide whites around them brought me to my senses. "No, don't look—"

I glanced down at the forest below and the scattered lights of the city in the distance.

"Shit," he muttered as my panicked eyes found his once more.

Terror thrust itself into my gut and twisted up my torso and out every limb. "Help me," I pleaded through the blood distorting my vision. Salty tears came unbidden. "Greg, my love, please help me."

Tears flushed his silvery orbs as I slipped another inch. My bracelet twisted around my wrist, digging itself into the back of my hand as Greg clutched at me. He tried to reach me with his free hand,

but his shoulder slipped over the edge and he began to flail,
struggling to anchor himself. "Help us! Please!" he shouted, but even
the crickets and frogs silenced themselves to his tormented cries. He
never took his eyes from mine. They begged for mercy, for
compassion... for love.

"Please, Greg," I croaked, trying to grip his wrist with my other
hand, but it seemed like even nature was working against us. I slid
another inch until my fingers were crushed in his vice-like grip, and
the leather strap, the symbol of our love, clung to my thumb, pulling
it from its socket.

"Evie... Evelyn, please, no. Don't leave me."

"Please. I want you. I love—" But my thumb slipped free, and the
tips of my fingers flew from Greg's grasp. My words turned to a
bloody scream as the compassion, love, and anguish in his face
dwindled in the spinning night.

* * *

A thump echoed in my ears as the familiar smell of leather,
much older than the chord under my forefinger, drifted away on
the patio breeze.

"You okay?" asked Greg Rayson, placing his other hand on my
elbow. The sadness had returned to his eyes, but it was
accompanied by genuine concern—for me. Jessie took a moment to
peer sidelong at me, and his eyes widened. "Here, have a seat,"
Rayson continued, motioning me back toward my spot on the
picnic bench.

I shook my head. "Nah, it's nothing. Don't worry about it."

"You sure? You look like you've seen a ghost."

I chuckled and took a deep breath. *Something like that,* I thought to myself, but let it go unmentioned. "It happens. Not to worry. I got them pretty regular. See, it's gone now," I finished with a halfhearted smile, but the vision remained pooled in my lower gut, fighting to bring up my leftover pizza from lunch as though it were a defective toy to be returned to the store. I fought the bout of nausea for a moment more and waved Rayson off. "It's okay, Greg. Thanks for your concern."

He quirked an eyebrow. "Have we met before?"

Chapter 6

Dilemmas

September 16, 2011

I SHOOK MY HEAD. "No, sorry. Jessie's just mentioned you from time to time. I feel like I already know you."

Rayson looked from me to Jessie. "Hope it was all good." The older man smiled and laughed, but it was obviously feigned.

If he feels this guilty, why'd he even come out? If it'd been me, I'd probably be holed up in a room of my house, refusing to step into the light.

Jessie interrupted my thoughts with one of his characteristic smiles and a hearty, "Rayson, you know what's what. It's always a chipper place when you're around, but don't let the compliment go to your head." Slapping the scrawny man's shoulder, Jessie turned around and seated himself, but gave me a look that meant, *You're gonna tell me what you just saw... but later.*

Rayson followed Jessie's lead and took a seat across from us.

"I think I'm gonna grab a plate of somethin'," I announced to the group. "What's good here?"

"Good luck findin' a plate, bub. Everything here comes in a basket," said Anton, motioning at the red, plastic baskets littering the picnic table, each one lined with a red-and-white, checkered wax sheet, just like you'd find at most local country restaurants.

John chimed in. "Yeah, but just about everything's super here. Just pick your meat, a few veggies, and how you want the tortillas, and *bada-bing*—you's got a meal for champions." A few men grunted their agreement through stuffed mouths.

"I'll come with you, then," Jessie muttered, getting back up. "I gotta get me some beef-tip tacos, deep fried. Oh yeah!" A couple coworkers chuckled at his enthusiasm.

The restaurant service counter was more like a mobile-lunch trailer that had been converted to stationary status with a green, plastic patio roof casting a green hue over everyone and thing within ten feet of the vendor. Even with the dim bulbs strung beneath it, the reflection was somewhat crude. "So what's the deal?" Jessie mumbled as we approached the counter.

"What do you mean?" I asked, avoiding the subject. Greg was a good man; I could tell. They say that the eyes are the windows to one's soul, and living with this blessing—or curse, depending on how you look at it—for over sixteen years had proven the saying true time and again. Greg Rayson had been a victim of chance. He'd certainly made some bad choices, quite a few, but he was suffering for it. *Did he turn himself in, though?* I wondered, the ingrained detective and upholder of the law coming to mind instinctually. *Did they find her, bury her, and help her find peace? How long ago did it happen?*

"You know exactly what I mean," Jessie shot back. "Don't play dumb. I know that look when you see something. After Junior Lee, Rosie, that nurse from the Civil War, and everything else we did after high school, how could I not?"

The mention of the other dead we encountered the year following graduation before Jessie went off to try out for the Capitals sent a shiver down my spine. Each name was a vision, a memory of death, murder, or worse. I shoved the thoughts aside. "Look, Greg's dealing with a lot right now, but until I know more, just keep in mind that he's a good guy." *Unfortunately, bad things happen to good people,* I added, but didn't voice that thought.

Jessie tilted his head, his eyes peering out from under his eyebrows at me, which should have been difficult considering the few inches he'd grown and how much taller he was, but the look was knowing and somewhat intimidating, at least it would have been had it not been coming from one of my oldest friends. "Alex, you and I both know you only get those visions when it's really bad, murder and whatnot. So, give it up. How can he be a good guy if you had one of those dreams, and he's alive?"

"Remember," I said as we stepped through the line and up to the counter, "bad things can happen to good people." I gave the older woman behind the aluminum counter a smile.

"Hola," she said, brushing her hands on an apron that had managed to remain mostly white throughout her shift. "What chu want?"

Jessie's charming smile was back on his face. "Hola, Mrs. Sanchez. You got any good beef tips tonight?"

"For jou, Jessie, always," she said with a forced smile. The look in her dark eyes was frightening and familiar. It held a pain I'd

seen too many times, much like the depression Greg was hiding.
"And jou want the same?" she asked, turning to me.

"No thanks. I'll just have fajitas, chicken, with everything and
two drinks."

She raised her eyebrows. "Everything?"

I nodded.

"Sure thing," Mrs. Sanchez said, copying down our order on a
pad, ripping it off, then slipping it under the heating counter
behind her and rattling off a few more instructions to the cooks so
quickly I wouldn't have understood, even if they'd been in English.
We moved down the counter. A young woman with tanned skin
and raven-black hair handed us two cups and punched in the
order. We paid and stepped aside to wait for our orders.

"Look, I know bad things happen to good people," Jessie said.
"You're the epitome of that."

"Yeah, trust me. I know." Flashes of the Drunk, my ex-
stepfather, passed before my eyes. The memories were never
good: beatings, slurred conversations, and even murders that my
real father never would have allowed—that is, had he been alive.
"Just leave it be until I find out more. Okay?"

Jessie hesitated, but nodded. "Alright. Have it your way, but
you're sure there's nothing I need to know."

"Yes," I hissed, my frustration beginning to show.

"Fine then. I'll just take my food and go." Jessie took the tacos
the woman slid to him, and I grabbed my basket from the brushed-
aluminum countertop, but with the aroma of seasoned fajitas and

peppers came another draft of scented leather.

* * *

The sound of the portable meat grinder echoed through the confined walkway behind the counter. The morning sun's rays peered through the slatted lattice over the far end of the patio. I pressed more of the large package of meat into the grinder's opening. It growled, but ground the raw meat, spitting out bloody strings as though they were threads of spinning yarn. I swapped metal pans as the accumulating mound of meat reached the top and pressed the large lump of plastic-wrapped meat further in. The machine growled deeper as the pressure inside grew, but the threads of ground meat continued to stream out.

"Louis!" came a woman's shout from out back. "Louis!"

"Si, Señora Sanchez. I'm here," I shouted, turning toward the open back door. At that moment, something seized my hand, tearing through my fingers and jerking my arm further in. I spun around as the gears and blades of the grinder continued their work. Streams of bloody, threaded meat emerged from the other end with interspersed flecks of white. I screamed, trying to pull my hand free while blood—my blood—leaked from the machine's cracks like flowing oil, coating the counter, my apron, and floor around me. However, the gears turned on, sucking my arm deeper, the edge of the aluminum housing meant to hold the slabs of meat now anchored against my bicep. "Help, Señora Sanchez! Help!" I shouted through the pain. The machine pulled again, its gears growling for

more. I jerked harder. "Please, p-p-please," I begged as tears streamed down my cheeks.

A shriek came from behind me, but it was drowned out by the pain and grinding blades squealing and gripping me harder, pulling my arm deeper into its maw. More screams echoed and two large hands gripped my shoulders. Suddenly the machine hemorrhaged and squealed one last time as its motor ground to a halt.

Someone pulled what remained of my mangled hand and forearm from the machine. I let out a bloodcurdling scream at first, but then, numbed to it all, I watched as though through a muted tunnel. I tried to cling to the counter, but instead toppled a stack of plastic baskets over top me as I collapsed to the bloody floor.

"Louis, stay with us. José... get... hospital," said Mrs. Sanchez as darkness began clogging my senses. She fell to her knees next to me, her words garbled and unclear.

"But, señora, they will... no... card. They... deport...," interjected José, a fellow cook who stood on my other side with a similar white apron to mine, yet his was stark white, having been cleaned for yet another day at the Taco Hut. It wasn't covered in pulpy blood. The contrast seemed odd, yet intriguing in this state of mind.

As my vision faded and the silence of the small food trailer pervaded my thoughts, Señora Sanchez mumbled, "Ah si, ah si. Try Señora Tegura."

* * *

I stumbled as I took my first step to follow Jessie and winced at the feel of my fingers grasping the basket of food, but the pain vanished. "Jesus," I whispered. *There's so much going on here that no one even knows about.* Taking a moment to regain my balance, I steadied my breathing and glanced around. It was as though the world had gone on, ignorant of Louis's death. I looked at the basket, one from the stack that must have fallen on him, and then glanced at the counter behind me. *He has to be dead, or else the memory wouldn't have imbued itself.* As another chill ran down my spine, I returned to my seat lost in thought.

As I passed Greg's downturned face, his wrist caught my eye. He sat fondling not one, but two matching leather bracelets in his lap with one hand, rotating them around his wrist and caressing the messages beneath his fingers: Evelyn loves Greg and Greg loves Evelyn. I forced myself to go on and took my seat. The others smiled as they munched on their tacos, burritos, quesadillas, sopes, and various other dishes. Jessie chortled a few times, boasting about one thing or another while Greg nibbled at his own food, but maintained his focus on the bracelets he clutched beneath the table.

"Ain't this great," Jessie said through a mouthful.

A few of the men around the long table even had ground beef in their orders, and each bite they took tweaked my stomach. *Could they have reported it? Would they use the same meat?* The thought of it disgusted me, and each glimpse of the ground product I got appeared to have white flecks of what must've been bone peeking out. I closed my eyes and looked again. The flecks were gone. *Gotta be my imagination.* Shaking it off, I stared into my filled tortillas; thankfully none of it had gone through that machine. I waited for a moment, calming my nerves and my stomach.

"What are you waiting for?" asked Jessie with brows furrowed. "This place is the best."

"Yeah, so long as you stay away from the ground beef," I muttered and took a bite.

"What, nah that's great, too. You can't go wrong here, man."

I leaned into him and whispered, "No, seriously, don't eat the beef."

Jessie paused mid-bite and stared into his. "Mine's steak tips. They're alright, right?"

I glanced at them and nodded. "Just don't get anything that's ground up, just in case."

Jessie quirked his head and looked me straight in the eyes. "In case what?"

The question sent a shiver through me. "I'll tell you later."

Jessie continued his silent look for a moment and then turned to Rayson. "So, how's yours, Ray?"

"It's Greg, Jessie," he replied, narrowing his eyes. He took another bite, and a tattoo peeked out from under his shirtsleeve.

"Hey, Greg. Is that a tat?" I asked.

The question caught him off guard. He turned a quizzical eye to me until I pointed at his arm. Understanding dawned on his face, and he lifted the short sleeve to reveal an ankh, but more statuesque than most I'd seen with doubled, three-dimensional walls on its sides. A decorative, forked flag wove itself over and around the arms and the ankh's circle. On it, a woman's name was scrawled: Sandy. He took another bite and let the sleeve fall.

Jessie gave me a sidelong look and said with comedic sarcasm, "I just can't take you anywhere."

Rayson chortled, almost choking on his burrito, and waved off Jessie's admonishment. "No, it's fine. I got it when my ex-wife Sandy and I were together. She was big into those things."

"Ah, I see," I said, curious about Sandy, but unsure how to ask without prying too deeply.

"Yeah," Jessie added after swallowing a large bite. "Rayson's from Tranquil Heights, too."

Greg nodded, and I'm sure my eyebrows rose into the sky. "Oh really?" Tranquil Heights was a small town, and such a coincidence wasn't likely.

"Yep, born and raised. I haven't been back in years though."

"Yeah, he was obviously there some years before us, Alex, but it's his old stomping grounds, too."

"I'm sure things have changed a bit since you were there," I added. "What class did you graduate in, if you don't mind my asking?"

Greg shrugged. "I ain't no lady. Don't care if you know. I'm forty-two. You do the math. I never was any good in that subject."

Jessie and I both laughed at that. Even Greg joined in, cracking a smile at his own comment. "About the same here," I replied. "I'm pretty sure my trig teacher—ol' Stone Face Easely, we called her—

was about ready to hog-tie me by the time I left the school." I didn't mention the reason, or the way I'd treated her. A part of me regretted speaking to Mrs. Easely that way, but every part of me knew she deserved it.

"Yeah, she was pretty bad," Jessie said.

Rayson made a face as though considering something, then nodded and said, "I think we've all had a couple of those."

Then, movement in my peripheral vision caught my attention. Greg's head swiveled to the TV mounted to the post in the upper corner of the patio. A picture of Evie with a wide grin appeared on the television. She stood amongst the trees in a floral-patterned dress, looking innocent and beautiful as the sun's rays shone off her midnight-black curls. Below the picture was *Evelyn Cervantes—Missing since September 10th. If you have any information call....* I glanced back at Greg to find tears streaming down his cheeks. It took him a moment to notice, but he wiped them away with a bare arm, glancing at the others in fear of being seen until his eyes settled on mine. The others were all enthralled by the television. We exchanged a look. In Greg Rayson's eyes, a moment of panic fluttered to life before he calmed himself.

He didn't tell anyone. The thought sent a pang through my gut, and I sat the half-eaten taco back in the basket. *She's lying in the forest at the bottom of that cliff, been there for a week, and he didn't tell anyone.* It felt like I stared at the wooden table so long that it should have withered before my eyes. *What to do?*

"That's just horrible," exclaimed a voice, interrupting my

thoughts.

"Yeah," Groucho said, "Mrs. Sanchez is heartbroken over it. When I asked her if there'd been any word, she almost broke down right in front of me. I didn't know what to say, so I just ordered. She wrote it down, and I moved on."

"Yeah, it's a shame," Fred added, his long hair brushing across his back as he shook his head. "That's a good woman in there. She don't need her grandchild abducted. There's no telling what's happened to her."

Greg didn't say a word. Instead, he stared at the photo until it vanished from the screen and then turned his attention back to his lap.

"So Evelyn Cervantes is Mrs. Sanchez's granddaughter?" I asked, curious if I had heard him right. Jessie and the others nodded. *Mi abuela.* Evelyn's words echoed through my thoughts, and the pieces in the puzzle began to come together. *Was she remembering a conversation she had with Mrs. Sanchez? No, she hadn't told anyone. A dream—it must have been.* "And she used to come around here?"

"Yeah," came a couple deep voices in chorus, but the question caught Greg's attention and he looked at me as though considering my measurements for a tailored suit... or a coffin. The look in his eyes was wary, considering, and still pained, but now contained an element of fear.

He's... somehow he's onto me.

Chapter 7

Metro Police and Sergeant Rollen

September 16, 2011

DURING THE RIDE to the DC Metropolitan Police Department, Jessie asked, "So what's the deal?"

"What do you mean?" I continued staring out the window of the rented sedan, following the GPS to Indiana Avenue Northwest.

"Don't give me that. You know exactly what I mean. Why do you always treat me like I'm an outsider? Since you got on the force, it's been that way. What happened to your good ol' trusted friend, Jessie, the guy you used to take with you and Paige to investigate murders and ghosts?"

I sighed. "Look, Jess. It's not like that. I'm not trying to keep you out, but you have to understand. You're a civilian, and these people could go out of their way to hurt me, especially since I'm not even sure Irene's still our girl."

"Then don't you think I should know what's going on, especially if someone might be gunnin' for me?"

"You're probably right. I just don't want you getting hurt. I've already gotten you more involved than I like."

"That never stopped you before," Jessie shouted.

"It did... you just didn't know about it. You moved up here and things were going well for you, so I didn't want to mention how bad things got with the arson murders."

"So, it got worse than you said?"

I nodded. "Yeah, people were freaked out, but it always calmed down by the end of the next month. Later on people accepted it, but knew that it would only be *one* of them, so they'd mourn the victim and for the family that next week. Basically, life went on. It's pretty bad when a town accepts an annual sacrifice and believes the police are inept and unable to stop it."

"Well, weren't they?" asked Jessie, but it was a rhetorical question.

I flinched. "Yeah, but even I couldn't find the person responsible. The mayor hounds us this time of the year like clockwork. I've tried everything I can think of, but this murderer is smooth. She never reveals herself to her victims, always appearing in that damnable costume. She's so slippery, she'd hold her own in a pond full of eels."

Jessie chuckled. "You know, my dad used to say things like that, too."

My thoughts turned to the few memories I had of my father and the smiling picture of him in his trucker cap. "Yeah, mine too," I whispered. "But the only links I've found so far beyond the tattoos are the arson and body positions."

"What is it with these tattoos? You keep telling me there's some connection with them, and I'm telling you, there's not. They're just really common. Hell, I've seen a few people with ankh tattoos today alone."

"How do you know there isn't a connection? It can't just be a coincidence." Slipping the file out of my briefcase between us, I tossed it into his lap. "Take a look at them. They all have one."

"Yeah, so?"

"Jessie, you can't be that stupid." I shook my head. "And here you were telling me to stop acting dumb." *He's not this stupid, never has been and never will be.*

Through my peripheral vision, I watched as Jessie searched for his voice. Each time he opened his mouth, it snapped shut before a word could escape.

Maybe there's more to this than I thought. Something's going on.

As we rolled to a stop in front of the large, glass-walled police station, I parked on the street and shifted the car into park. "Look, Jess, I love you like a brother, but if you've got somethin' to tell me, do it now. I need to know."

Jessie glanced at me and our eyes met, but only for a moment. Then he shook his head. "Nah, it's nothin'. I just know you're chasing your tail on this one. It's..." But he couldn't finish.

"Fine, save it for later. We gotta have a little powwow with the local department here."

"You still think Irene might have somethin' to do with these murders?" Jessie stepped onto the curb and closed his car door.

I shrugged. "Maybe. I have a few other questions, too."

* * *

Jessie loudly sipped at his cup of coffee as we left the detour to the coffee shop and entered the department office. Behind the marble counter sat a slender but well-framed, black man in uniform. His gold nametag read Rollen and the three chevrons on his shoulder labeled him Sergeant. "Can I help you?" he asked over the ringing telephones and chatter of background voices.

"I really hope so. I'm a visiting detective and thought you might be able to help me with a case I'm working. Seems my town and your city share a few citizens from time to time."

The man nodded. "Doesn't surprise me. We get people from all over here. Where are you from?"

"Tranquil Heights," I replied.

The officer looked at me quizzically. "Where?"

"It's a small town in southwest Virginia, in the mountains."

"Yeah," Jessie interjected, "one of those places most people don't hardly notice when they're passing through."

The officer nodded. "I gotcha. Never lived in a place like that myself, but I know what you mean. Born and bred in NOVA here."

Jessie and I both nodded. I was aware of the differences in perspectives. To people living in northern Virginia—or NOVA for short—the rest of Virginia could be an entirely different state.

"Things are a bit different here from what you're used to, I'm sure."

"So I've noticed," I replied. "But we've got a serial killer that I think may have come to your fair city."

"A serial killer?" the man asked. He lowered his voice. "You gotta be joking. Don't tell me we got another redneck sniping the highways again, pardon the term."

I stepped up to the counter. "No worries. Most country boys would take the name as a compliment. They're survivors, most of them at least, livin' off the land. But no... no sniper. In fact, our murderer seems to have an affinity for a particular date— September 20—and only murders annually. She's killed fifteen people over the last fifteen years."

"At least it's not thirteen," he whispered, obviously somewhat superstitious.

Jessie breathed a sigh of relief. "At least there's that. It could be worse."

"I think any murder is bad. These are horrible." I grimaced as scenes from the last seconds of past victims' lives came to mind: the monstrous treatment, the fear, the smell of lighter fluid, and the pain as the flames torched every inch of skin. I shoved the memories aside, but the lingering smell of burnt flesh still coated my nostrils. Shivering, I said, "Look, Irene Harris used to live in Tranquil Heights. She grew up there, but she's since moved here. From what I can tell, her travel arrangements over the years pretty well match up. I was hoping you might be able to tell me more, do a search on her past, things she's been caught doing, Sergeant."

"You got credentials and a department number I can call? I gotta look into things a bit first. You know how it is."

I removed my card from my jacket pocket and laid it and my badge wallet on the counter between us. He scanned my ID and badge, then took the card and picked up a phone on a nearby desk, just out of earshot.

"Damn, Alex. I gotta take you with me the next time I encounter one of these fellas. It's like you're long-lost buddies."

"I wouldn't say that, but there's a certain respect we have for one another…" My thoughts turned to the two policemen in the shack at the Metro entrance. "Usually."

After finishing one call, Sergeant Rollen dialed another number, spoke for a few minutes, and finally dialed a third. Eventually he sauntered back to us. "Mind if I keep this?" He waved the card between two extended fingers. "Just in case I need to get hold of you."

"Sure. I'd appreciate it. So what'd you find?" Grinning wide, I asked, "Am I the same Joe Shmoe I flew in with, or did someone knock a few screws loose?"

Jessie and the sergeant both smiled.

"Yep, I spoke with Lieutenant Tullings. He was a little pissed to hear you'd skipped town, but vouched for you. He said to be sure and call them, hurry back, and somethin' about his coattails poppin'."

I nodded. "Yeah, just a little local lingo. You get used to it down there."

"What's it mean?"

Jessie answered with a chuckle. "That he's pissed."

Sergeant Rollen smiled. "Yeah, I got the gist of that. That explains the last thing he said. He wanted me to remind you that this wasn't what the mayor meant when he said by any means necessary."

"They'll get over it," I said, waving away the warning. "The mayor's son was one of the victims. So what can you tell me about our fair lady?"

Rollen's eyebrows rose. "Well, she ain't necessarily a fair lady."

"That much I know."

"She got in some trouble a while back with her husband. He died when their house burned down. She pled to involuntary manslaughter and was granted time served for the three months she spent in jail and four years of probation."

"Yeah, I figured that much out from the reports our office came up with. That's a pretty light sentence."

The officer nodded. "Yeah, I thought so too, so I dug a little deeper. I'm really not supposed to tell you this, but I called Moten, the DA that worked the case. He said there was some speculation from her lawyers about treatment when they hauled her in at the local PD. I'm sure they didn't have nothin', but after the scandal last year, none of the government offices want a whiff of media attention, especially the department. So, with things not lookin' so rosy, they cut a deal. According to the law, she did her time."

Jessie looked stunned; his jaw hung open until he managed to say, "You can't be serious."

Sergeant Rollen looked at Jessie with the same expression I knew mine held: pity. "That's the way the world works. We just manage where we can while the people with power walk around with the keys to the kingdom, worryin' about stocks, multi-million-dollar bank notes, and election funds."

"It's the world you live in, Jess. I don't like it, but get used to it."

My tall friend shook his head in shame. "But this is the police department. You guys can't cater to the bad guys or let people off for murder. Who'll protect the innocents?"

This time my pity turned to skepticism. "This isn't news to you, Jessie. Think about years ago, my uncle, and the way the police's hands were tied. It's no different. If anything, it's worse now. Like Rollen said, we just roll with it and do what we can."

Jessie's eyes found mine and this time held them.

I said, "What more can we do, but try and uphold the law, bring a little justice to those in need when we can."

His shoulders slumped. "I know," Jessie mumbled. Turning away, he dropped his half-finished coffee into the trash and said, "I'll wait for you in the car." Then he quietly slipped out the doors.

"Wow, how old is he?" asked Sergeant Rollen.

"Old enough to know and still young enough to dream."

He nodded.

"So what about these other murders?" I asked. "She's been in my town for every single one of them."

Rollen punched a few keys on his keyboard and printed the results, motioning me around the counter. I came around and leaned over his shoulder. Scanning the monitor, his head twitched for a moment. "September 20, you said?"

"Yeah."

"Then why's she back here so soon?"

I pondered the question. It was valid. This was early for her. *Does she know we're onto her? She couldn't have just stopped,* I concluded. Everything I found in my research said that serial killers don't just stop. It's like an addiction. That's why her location changed last year. It was her husband, and she couldn't just fly him back to her hometown to die.

"What about her alibi?" asked the sergeant.

"Family; they claim she was with them the whole time. She flew into Tranquil Heights September 1 and stayed with some family, but she visited a man and stayed the night more often than she stayed with her sister or parents. The guy's a car salesman at a local dealership, Crandell's Used Cars, in Tranquil Heights. His name is Otis Simmons."

"What's her motive?"

"Workin' on that," I replied halfheartedly.

"Soundin' less than solid then. Why would she change locations after fourteen murders?" Rollen replied.

I thought for a minute. It was the same question I'd begun asking myself since taking a sneak peek through her dirty laundry. "Yeah, I'm starting to wonder about that myself. The date lines up though, and the method. She's been in town for every one until her husband's death, and one of the victims was living in DC."

"You sure you got the right person?"

"Pretty sure."

He turned his head and arched an eyebrow at me. "You don't sound sure at all. Why hasn't BCI been called to get involved?"

"I was sure enough to hop a plane on my own dime up here chasing after her, but you'd have to be from down there to understand why no one called BCI. When outsiders come into town, everyone clams up. This is where tons of moonshine was made during Prohibition. A lot of them still make it, and none of the locals speak with outsiders. That's a surefire way to lose any cooperation or respect the public still has for us."

"I can see your point," Rollen replied. "Seems kinda insane... paranoid even, but if that's how it is down there, then you do what you've gotta do. I can tell there's somethin' nagging you about your suspect, though." Rollen grabbed the printouts off the printer.

"Well, I haven't found the kinds of things I'd expect to. Irene certainly got away close to scot-free on the murder of her husband, and some of the characteristics are the same: arson and such. However, I expected to find more mementos of her murders—you know, souvenirs."

Sergeant Rollen took a deep breath and sighed. "Yeah, most serial killers do. Maybe you just haven't looked closely enough," he added with a shrug.

I looked close enough to tell what size undies she wears, I wanted to add, but didn't.

"Where'd you hear about this woman anyway?"

"Anonymous tip," I answered, knowing those were always less than reliable and didn't help my case.

"No wonder," was all he said. A moment later he continued though. "However, that isn't your biggest problem." My face tightened as he slid one of the sheets to me, a flight report. "Last year, she left town early to burn their DC house down."

He was right. According to the flight statement, the ticket was for September 20, at 12:53 a.m. *How did I miss this?*

"Do you know when the murders took place on the twentieth?"

"Yeah," I replied with a disheartened nod, "the night of. The time and location varies, which is why we haven't been able to catch her, but it's always the night of the twentieth—Shit!" I hissed, crumpling the paper in my fist. "She couldn't have been there."

"Nope, not if she really murdered her husband. You said the locations changed, but they're always in Tranquil Heights, right?"

"Yeah, except for her husband's murder. I figured that was number fifteen, but you don't think she did it, murdered Victor?" I asked, intrigued by the idea, although my own memory of the murder confirmed that she had.

"I didn't say that. I worked the case—that's how I know there wasn't any bumbling going on—but leave it to the bureaucrats to run in fear whenever someone with a high-powered attorney steps up. She did it, but that means she's not your gal."

Taking a stab in the dark, I asked, "Did her husband have any tattoos, by chance?" *Maybe we lucked out. Maybe the tickets weren't just for her. Maybe it was her husband all along and I've been chasin' a ghost all this year.* The thought stirred me with excitement, but also seemed hollow and unlikely.

Rollen perused the documents and autopsy report before saying, "Nah, nothin' that I know of, but he was pretty charred up.

It would've been hard to tell. Why do you ask?"

As the feminine voice echoing from the monster's snout in my past visions came to mind, my shoulders slumped as though mimicking Jessie's earlier. "That's just one of the few things I've found that tie the murders together, an ankh tattoo, but the serial killer couldn't have been Victor Harris."

"How do you know?"

Closing my eyes for a second, I pondered telling the truth, but knew it would end any hope of future information. *Yes, Rollen's superstitious, but will he buy my story?* "I can't really say, but a reliable witness told me it was a woman's voice he heard."

"You're sure?"

I nodded.

"Okay then. Seems like you're back where you started. You know there's more women in this country than men, right? You've got a long way to go, and a new question to answer: if Victor Harris wasn't victim fifteen, who was? Worse yet, was there a murder last year, or did she take the year off?"

"Yep," I said with a frown as the added uncertainty piled on. "I've got one more question for you, though. Can you look into Greg Rayson?"

Rollen spun his computer chair to fully face me. "Why? Didn't you just say you were sure it was a woman?"

I wanted to tell Rollen about Greg Rayson and Evie Cervantes, to expose him, to mention her *abuela*, Mrs. Sanchez, and Louis's needless death, but none of these were callous murders. The living were suffering, and there was no one to avenge, no justice to serve. The deaths were so closely linked that it would rip apart all of their lives and end their livelihood if the health department found out. The Taco Hut couldn't be using the same meat, no matter how vivid my nightmarish imagination was. Weighing the costs against the suffering of the living, I stood in silence. Rollen just stared until I finally said, "Yeah, but there might be a connection. It's a hunch."

The sergeant's eyes said he knew there was more to it, but he said nothing and turned back to his computer. Pulling up another screen, Rayson's rap sheet appeared. "He's got some priors, a B and E as a kid, a couple DUIs, and a domestic disturbance with his ex-wife, but their addresses are separate now. It appears they divorced and are living in different states. There's nothing to implicate Rayson, though. We're pretty hooked up to things, but without giving me more to go on, I can't fully investigate the guy. Your department might be able to though."

I nodded. *Just a man in the wrong place at the wrong time who made some bad decisions.* The inner turmoil of the decision whether to fess up ate at me, and Rollen's face turned quizzical.

"What's on your mind?"

I shook my head. "Nothin' I can say until I've got more to go on. You got a card? I'll let you know if I come up with anything."

Rollen pulled one from his breast pocket and handed it to me. "Alright—Alex, was it?"

"Yep." I gave him a half smile. "Alex is fine."

He reached out a hand. "Keenan Rollen. My friends call me

Keen."

I shook it.

"By the way, keep your investigation on the down low. Not too many guys on the force up here like outsiders traipsin' through. If you get something, call me. The last thing we need is a fiasco with cops working out of their jurisdiction. At least if I'm involved, we can keep things legal and from becoming a thorn in the bureaucrats' asses."

"Sure thing, Keen. You have my word on that."

As I turned away, he added, "And if you finally come to a decision about that other stuff or just want to run it by another professional, let me know."

I nodded and stepped out from behind the corner, heading to where Jessie sat waiting in the car. Flipping out my cell, I called home base and got Taylor, our only dispatcher. She said she'd look into Rayson further, but it was really just a shot in the dark.

* * *

"Find anything worthwhile in *big brother's* office?" asked Jessie when I ducked into the driver's seat.

"Only if you call having to start at the beginning worthwhile."

"So Irene's off the hook?"

"It appears that way."

"That's what I'm talkin' about!" he shouted, breaking from his distraught expression. "Now don't get me wrong, I ain't tryin' to get people off. But I've been sayin' those ankh tattoos really aren't connected for years."

I nodded, sullen with the lack of prospects after years of investigating and so many murders. *Maybe he was right.* Something tickled the back of my brain, telling me the tattoos were still important, but thus far they'd gotten me nowhere.

"So where to next?" he added, a bit more cheery than before.

I shrugged. "Home, James." I turned to shift the car into gear and spotted an assortment of flyers and advertisements in the center-console shelf. "What's up with the flyers? You trying to clutter up the car and get me charged for cleaning?" I grabbed the handful and scanned them.

"Nothin' much. Just got a girl I've been dating for a while. I thought I'd take her out. She's into that kinda thing."

"What... food?" I asked, holding up a flyer with a pizza coupon advertising two-for-one. "Most people are, Jessie." I grinned, but the look disappeared when I saw what was on the back.

"Nah, not the pizza. The stuff on the ba—"

"Yeah, I see it," I mumbled, lost in thought.

"She's into that Egyptian-mythology stuff," he added, but the words seemed distant and muted. "GW's got something going on..."

On the color flyer was an advertisement for George Washington University's Archaeology department. However, what caught my eye was the brown bowl pictured below the title. In jagged hieroglyphics was a line of symbols and connecting lines in black ink. A stick figure seemed to be moving around as though it were an ancient flipbook. In one hand it held a large key in the shape of an ankh, and in the other was a staff with an angled, oblong head and a forked base. I couldn't decipher the text, but the key and creature's head brought back a particular vision of the first victim, Junior Lee. Vague images of the woman's mask had been silhouetted at times by torchlight. In my drugged state I hadn't been able to make out more than partial figures, but piecing them together the image began to take shape. The depiction on the bowl was of a man with a wolf's head. I hadn't been able to make out the creature in the visions before, but this couldn't be coincidence.

"Alex, what is it?" Jessie asked, pulling me from my thoughts.

"Give me a minute," I said, holding up an index finger. The tug in the back of my mind wouldn't let up. My research and the Internet had been pretty reliable, but maybe there was more to it. I tried our local college years ago, but unfortunately they shut down the archeology program due to budget cuts. "You know, you may be right about the tattoos, but I've got a hunch that there's more to it. I think the ankh's the key." I flipped over the flyer and slapped the image. "See, it's a key, literally, and that's exactly what I saw."

"What, Anubis?"

"Yeah."

"It's a dog-headed god. He was over life and death or somethin' back when Egyptians ran things."

"I ran across him in my past research, but it just hit me what that creature was."

"You know, you could have mentioned that before: like years ago, before more than a dozen people were murdered."

I lowered my head. "I didn't realize it before. You don't understand how hard it is to interpret these memories, especially when the victims are drugged. I barely realized the glimpses I got of the wolf and ankh were one and the same."

"Dog."

"Right." I paused, squinting at my friend. "Wait, how come you never mentioned you knew about this?"

"Because everyone does." He made a wide circle with his arms. "It's nothing new. Didn't you see *Stargate*? There were ankhs and Anubises all over in it. It's about different worlds, somewhere people still worshipped Ra and the ancient Egyptian gods. It came out years ago."

I shook my head. "No, I haven't, but I know someone who can tell us more than we ever wanted to know." I pointed at the bottom of the flyer where Dr. Mohammed Kamal's name was listed as a guest speaker, a visiting Egyptian historian.

"Alex, you gotta get a hold on yourself here. You're grasping at straws. Irene, the only reason you came up here, is innocent. You've got nothing left to go on, so you're gonna barge in on a visiting professor from Egypt based on a hunch? Does that sound sane to you?"

"Yes, it does," I agreed immediately. "I can't believe you didn't tell me about this before. The ankh tattoos might be the key to breaking open this whole case."

The astonished look on Jessie's face was almost comical, except for the ounce of fear hiding behind his eyes.

What's he hiding? I thought as I pulled into traffic.

Chapter 8

Present or Past?

September 16, 2011

PULLING INTO THE GWU campus, Jessie spotted the sign first. "There! Over there," he said, pointing at a large, red-brick, two-story building with unique cornicing and window air conditioners hanging out upper-story windows. The look of it was quite interesting compared to other buildings on campus.

"Anthropology, right?" I asked.

"That's what the guy on the phone said," Jessie replied. "The Anthropology department hosts a bunch of the exchange students and visiting professors for the other departments. I couldn't believe it when Dr. Kamal said he'd see you. You know he probably never sees anyone outside of the school faculty and students."

"That may be exactly why he agreed," I said, grabbing my hat off the backseat and stepping out.

"Maybe. I still think you're chasin' your tail on this, though," Jessie added.

I waved him off and locked the car. "We'll soon see who's right."

"Hold up a second," Jessie said, walking around to my side, eyeing me up and down. "You gotta stop wearing that hat, Alex."

"What do you mean," I asked, taking the fedora off my head and flipping it over in my hand. "It's nice. It looks good."

"You ever seen those gangster movies set in the forties? If you were wearing a suit you'd look just like them," Jessie explained. "You've gotta get rid of it. I'm tired of seeing you out of the corner of my eye and thinkin' any second you're gonna pull a tommy gun on my ass. Talk about conspicuous." He snatched the hat out of my hand. Opening the door, he tossed the fedora inside like a Frisbee.

"Come on, Jess. It's my style."

"Dude, you look like the stereotypical dick, and I do mean that in both possible ways."

I frowned at him. "It's not that bad. I like it."

"I know, Alex. I know what you've been doin' over the years. You don't want to be that kid you were while growing up. You've even created this whole persona—"

"No, I never—" I interrupted, but Jessie didn't stop. He was on a roll, and this time he was being serious. It was one of those rare conversations where I could tell.

"You can't stop being who you are. You're a good guy. You're not your stepdad."

I breathed a sigh of resignation. It wasn't snowing yet, but winter was certainly on its way. Feeling an anticipatory chill as a cold wind swept past, I pulled at the collar of my black overcoat. "This gotta go, too?"

Jessie smiled and glanced at the fall leaves on the large oaks and maples around us. "Nah, that looks cool. Now you're stylin'. Plus, it's a bit too chilly to go without a jacket. Let's see this mad professor of yours."

I shook my head and ran a hand through my black, wavy curls as we headed into the building. "Paige likes that hat," I mumbled.

"Good for your wife. When you're in the bedroom, wear it for her. Till then, keep it in the trunk."

* * *

It didn't take long to find Dr. Kamal, just three wrong turns through the corridors of the building and a confused stop in a random secretary's office for directions. The Anthropology building was much larger than it looked from the outside. I knocked on the door to the office they had supplied the visiting professor and entered at the request of the deep voice inside.

The room was dark and without windows, reminding me a little of our local jail cells, but that's where the similarities stopped. A desk lamp and two wall sconces brightened the otherwise gruesome atmosphere. A battered skull sat atop the mahogany desk, and a wide, matching credenza spanned three-quarters of the back wall. A few pieces of ancient pottery were enclosed in luminescent glass cubes and spaced appropriately on top of it. A dark-skinned man in his fifties with a scraggly beard and charcoal eyes rose to meet us, offering me his hand. "Good to meet you—Mr. Drummond, yes?"

I nodded and shook his hand. "That's me, and this is my friend Jessie Arturo. Thanks for taking the time to see us."

"No problem. This murderer, or serial killer you spoke of on the phone, seems very unusual," he added. He spoke perfect English, but his accent inflected every word. Motioning to an occupied chair at the side of the office, he said, "And this is Dr. Mayna."

The woman was about our age and wore a black business skirt and white blouse. She rose and nodded, shaking both of our hands in turn. "It's nice to meet you. I hope you don't mind, but I'm the local professor at GW on Egyptian history and wanted to sit in."

"The more the merrier," I replied, draping my jacket over the arm of the chair Dr. Kamal indicated and lowering myself onto the leather seat. Jessie took the other one facing the desk. "This is actually more than I could hope for. I've been investigating a serial killer for years, but our local resources are a bit sparse. I've had to rely on the Internet."

Dr. Mayna grimaced as soon as I mentioned the Internet, but Dr. Kamal just nodded. "The net can be helpful, Mr. Drummond, but you really should have come to us sooner. There are all too many misstatements online," Dr. Mayna chided in her perfect, college-educated speech. However, I thought I heard a hint of southern drawl subtly clinging to her words. Dr. Kamal nodded again, but had nothing to add. "Now," she continued, "why haven't we heard anything about this serial killer, and how many years has it been going on?"

"Well, you haven't heard because the mountain folk in southwest Virginia are a bit tight-lipped, especially when it comes to things they find embarrassing. Fourteen or fifteen years of unsolved murders can be a little embarrassing."

"So the murders aren't happening here?"

"No, down in Tranquil Heights, about seven hours from here."

"I see—wait, how many years?"

Jessie chimed in then. "It's complicated. Alex followed a woman up here to DC who he thought was the murderer, but we just found out she's not. Big surprise there."

I shot him a look that would boil water, but he ignored me.

"Now, there may or may not have been a murder last year," he continued. "She did commit a murder, but she did it here. Plus the timing wasn't right."

My eyelids grew tired as he piled on the complications and setbacks, and I slumped against the back of the chair. "Yeah, that about sums it up."

"Okay. So what brings you here? What can we do to help?" asked Dr. Mayna.

Dr. Kamal placed both elbows on the desk and rested his chin on his interwoven fingers, intent on our answer.

"I found out a few things when I first began researching years ago. I'm pretty sure the information is reliable, but am beginning to think there might be more to it.

"The murders began just after I finished high school. By the time I made the police force, the murders had a mystique about them. Officers and detectives tried for years to find the killer, but couldn't. I've come the closest, but I still don't have the proper evidence. When I first came across the remnants of a staff in one of the victim's hands, it helped to focus my research. We'd known they were ritualistic killings, but not what kind. What I found left impressions on the body in the shape of this." I unfolded the flyer from my pocket and pointed at the depiction of Anubis's staff.

Both professors nodded again. Dr. Mayna mumbled, "A Was staff."

"A what was a staff?" asked Jessie, his brows furrowed.

"No, a Was staff. That's what they were called. It used to be spelled differently, obviously, but that was the Egyptian name for them," Dr. Mayna added. "They represented the power of the gods. Lots of gods were depicted with them throughout Egypt on artifacts, clothing, tombs, and a variety of other places."

Dr. Kamal nodded once more, but said nothing. His silence and dark eyes hiding under bushy eyebrows were beginning to unnerve me.

"Yeah, that's what I found."

"So you found an actual staff?" Dr. Kamal interjected, curious.

I shook my head. "No, not quite. I felt it—" I stopped myself and reconsidered my words. "I think it's a Was staff. The autopsy report even showed a burn pattern and gave me its approximate dimensions."

"How big was it?" Dr. Kamal asked, his interest piqued.

"About five feet tall with an angled head, like in the picture. I think the bottom forked."

"The head is normally an ornate carving of an animal head," Dr. Kamal explained. "The Set head, people often call it."

"Whoa-whoa-whoa, what in the world? What's a Set? Is there a set of these things? Do they, like, come in a package you pick up at the local corner store?" Jessie asked.

Dr. Mayna waved a hand. "No, nothing like that. Set is another Egyptian god. The Set animal was his mascot. It was a kind of wild dog from the deserts of North Africa."

"So do you guys think this thing that's been attacking people is a god?" He looked from me to them, waiting for an answer. After searching for the murderer for so many years, the question seemed at first to hold possibility.

"No," Dr. Kamal answered. "The gods don't meddle in human affairs."

"Wait, but they do exist?" Jessie asked.

Both professors looked at Jessie like he'd just asked what color underwear they were wearing. The question was one I'd pondered for years—not in relation to the Egyptian gods, but considering my gift and how unexplainable it was, I couldn't fully accept or reject the idea. I'd more or less just learned to deal with it and take my future into my own hands. Dr. Mayna answered first. "Mr....," she said, drawing out the word.

"Arturo," Jessie supplied.

"Look, Mr. Arturo, it's complicated," she continued. "Whether gods actually exist or are just figments of human imagination doesn't matter here. What matters is who's behind the murders." Dr. Kamal looked like he had something to add, but rather than do so he simply nodded at Dr. Mayna's remark. Turning her attention back to me, she asked, "Detective Drummond, what else do you know?" I considered the few conclusions I'd been able to come to, but before I could answer, she said, "Before you mentioned that the killer was a 'she.' Are you sure about that? You said yourselves that you were wrong about the woman you followed here."

How to answer? I can't tell them how I know. "It... It's a hunch, a solid one."

Her eyelids drew down in a look that spoke volumes about what wasn't being said and her silent opinion of my leaving it out.

"Look, you wouldn't believe me if I told you. Just trust me, it's a woman," I added.

"Okay, let's say it is," she said, an undercurrent in her tone showing her skepticism. "Is there anything else you have to go on? For instance: how often do the murders happen, is there any regularity to it, what's the murderer's motivation for the ritual sacrifices?"

It wasn't the first time those questions had tumbled through my mind. For years I'd wondered. "Every year on September 20. I'm not sure about her motivation. The whole department's tried to find an answer to that at one time or another, but all of the murders have occurred in and around our little town, aside from the last one."

She cocked her head at my final comment.

Jessie said, "We assumed the last one was Irene's husband. She burnt him alive in their house here in DC, but we've pretty much decided she didn't do it. It's a good thing, too, because that woman was hot!" Turning his attention to Dr. Kamal, Jessie hissed, "You should have seen her when we first arrived. Even after the flight she looked like the hottest school teacher you've ever met with an added dose of *good-God!*"

Dr. Kamal smirked. "I went to a religious school. My teachers were all nuns."

I bent my head into my hand, massaging my temples.

"So, about the motivation issue," Dr. Mayna said, trying to hide the look of disgust on her face. "It probably is a ritual sacrifice, like you mentioned. There has to be some significance to September 20, but nothing stands out in my mind that would be relevant. Maybe it's something personal? But there has to be more to it. The Was staff ties it to Egyptian culture and a couple others. Is there anything else that will help us narrow it down?"

Clearing my throat, I said, "The ankh symbol."

Jessie bowed his head at the mention, but Dr. Kamal's eyebrows shot up. "The ankh? That's fairly common. It exists in ancient Egyptian religions and goes back to others. It's very big even now, although its meaning has become somewhat distorted."

"Yeah, I know. In my research I found that it was supposed to symbolize the unity of man and woman. Supposedly it meant a blessed union or something. I couldn't make heads or tails of it. Why kill only people with ankh tattoos?"

Dr. Kamal's face contorted in thought. "So, all of the victims had this... this tattoo?" His words were still thick, but thankfully easy to comprehend.

"I'm not sure about all of them. Like I said, a few people had already died by the time I came onto the force. I was interested in it before then, but wasn't privy to the information firsthand. I was just a kid. I'm pretty sure they did though. Unfortunately, the bodies were burnt beyond the extent that we could tell. I looked at some pictures of the victims and saw the tattoos. Other times friends and family corroborated the story. That accounts for most."

Dr. Mayna now seemed much more interested, and she leaned closer.

Dr. Kamal said, "The ankh isn't just used for unions. It is symbolic of truth. It is on tombs, too, throughout Egypt. There are a variety of beliefs, lots of speculation." He waved his hand in a circle, indicating that the discussion was still ongoing in research circles.

"Dr. Kamal, is it possible that people still participate in the old religions of Egypt?"

"Oh yes," the visiting professor answered without hesitation. "It's called *Kemetism*. Many people still practice the rituals, although not including human sacrifice. That's a rarity."

"But it happens?"

"Yes, on occasion."

I mulled over his answer for a minute before moving on. "Well, one of the last clues to the Egyptian connection is how they were killed."

"Burnt," Dr. Mayna supplied for me.

"Yeah," I replied, my silent question visible on my face.

"That's very common for human sacrifices," the visiting Egyptian professor supplied, "in many cultures on many continents, from the Aztec to the Celts. Although, most scientists would say ancient Egyptians wouldn't make that list."

I stared at the floor, wondering what else I could tell them without winding up coming off like a crackpot loony.

"I know there's more," Dr. Mayna said, her tone softer and more understanding. "We can't help if we don't know."

I glanced up at her. "You won't believe me."

"Try us," she said, a simple smile playing at her lips. Dr. Kamal just look intrigued.

I took a deep breath and let it out. *What do you care?* I asked myself. *You're gonna be gone in a couple days anyways. Even if they do blow you off, at least you've confirmed your research.*

Jessie elbowed me and shook his head, mouthing, "No."

"Okay, fine—"

"Jesus, Alex!" Jessie shouted. "You know, I've gotta live in this town after you leave, right? You want me to be the laughingstock everywhere I go?"

"You do a good enough job at that on your own, Jess. You don't need my help."

He clenched his jaw.

"I know for a fact that the murderer's a woman," I continued, "because—"

"You are one," Jessie shouted sarcastically and gave a forced laugh. I glared at him. Turning to Dr. Mayna, Jessie asked, "You mind if I walk around a bit? This rooms a little stuffy, and if Alex is going to embarrass himself, I don't need to be here for it."

She nodded. "There's a small exhibition on loan from the museum down the hall if you'd like to wander through it while we talk."

"Sounds freakin' spectacular!" he growled, lifting the back of the chair and slamming it down as he got up. The door hissed closed as he left.

Both professors raised their eyebrows to me once in the same silent, curious question once he'd gone.

I licked my lips, counting the seconds while trying to resummon the courage to admit to my visions. "Look, I can... do something. Most people don't understand it, and really neither do I, but it works and it's real. That's about all I can say to justify it though." I took another breath. "The truth is that I have visions. Some might call it being psychic, but I can't read people's minds—at least not living people's minds."

They both look confused and somewhat skeptical now. *At least it's not the other way around. When strangers learn about it, they're normally pretty sketchy and think I'm nuts as soon as they hear the words "visions" and "psychic."* I decided to run with it. "I've had the ability since I was in high school, and basically it allows me to relive people's murders."

Dr. Mayna's mouth dropped open and Dr. Kamal perched his chin on a closed fist, thinking with eyes that seemed to be reassessing me. I guess it made sense. He was the one that seemed to believe in Egyptian gods. If they're real, why not unexplainable abilities?

"So, how does it work?" the local professor asked in a whisper.

I shrugged. "Basically I have to touch something someone was holding when they were murdered. It's like the things people touch are imbued with a memory of something so traumatic. I can somehow trigger that memory. Then I see what happened through their eyes."

"So, you die—you experience their death?" she asked.

I nodded.

"How many times have you... died?" asked Dr. Kamal.

I tried to count, but various visions came to mind, flooding me with images and sensations that were too overwhelming. "God, I don't know. Honestly, too many to count."

A twinkle appeared in Dr. Mayna's eyes. "Can you change it?"

"No," I said with a shake of my head. "It isn't time travel. I can't change what's happened. I can't even control what's going on. I hear what's said and see through the victim's eyes. I even hear their thoughts as though they were my own. It's really hard to distinguish between them at times and gets confusing. I feel their pain. I know what it's like to be shot, stabbed, drugged, bludgeoned, whipped, and even fall to my death. It's never pleasant."

"That's horrible," Dr. Mayna said, the truth of my experiences finally dawning on her. "How can you stand it?"

"I don't have a choice. I can't control it besides watching what I touch and staying out of battlefield museums..." The mention of that Civil War trip with Paige so many years before dredged up the memories—the visions of the cannonier Able, the families lost, and soldiers that died. A shiver ran down my spine. "I just stay away from places where lots of killing and murder occurred. It can all be pretty bad."

"So how is this relevant to the serial killings?" asked the visiting professor.

"Well, there wasn't much left of the victims for me to touch and actually get a vision. However, Junior Lee, the first victim, somehow managed to keep a few of his belongings from burning too much, probably a rookie mistake on the killer's part. We never found evidence remaining like that in any of the other murders. The positive thing about it, and the later twist tie I found between a victim's bound hands, was that I was able to relive their murders. I heard her voice and got a couple brief glimpses of her."

Both professors were again leaning forward, Dr. Mayna almost to the point of falling out of her chair.

"The killer wears a costume, a dog head like in this picture." This time I pointed at the figure.

"Anubis," Dr. Mayna whispered. "It's a ritual to Anubis and Osiris."

"And it is not a dog," Dr. Kamal interjected. "It is a jackal."

I couldn't help but laugh. Both Jessie and I had been wrong. "Thanks for the clarification."

"It's Egyptian then," Dr. Mayna whispered to herself, staring at the floor in thought.

"A ritual sacrifice of resurrection," Dr. Kamal added. "It was done in ancient Egypt to help ensure the dead passed Anubis's test of worthiness and were resurrected into paradise, or *Aaru*."

I digested the information for a minute, deciphering his thick speech combined with the few unfamiliar terms. Thinking back to the few encounters I'd had with the murderer, I remembered her words: *You are my golden bull, my flesh sacrificed in her honor.* "You know, in one vision she called the victim a golden bull and flesh sacrificed in her honor. That's got to mean something, but I haven't quite figured it out."

Dr. Kamal fielded the question. "Makes sense. Apis was a god symbolized by a bull. Eventually Osiris, god of the underworld, replaced him. To many, the bull is still the most important of all the sacred animals in Egypt. The animal has often been attributed to Osiris. Saying her sacrifices represent a golden bull might mean they are the best she can offer. Bulls were often seen as kings who moved on to be deities before the New Kingdom. Little is known of rituals at that time, but it makes sense that it would be a burnt offering."

"How about *in her honor?*" I asked.

Dr. Kamal's brows knit in thought. "So, she actually said *in her honor*, not *his honor?*" asked Dr. Mayna.

I nodded.

"Normally the sacrifice would be to honor Osiris, or possibly Anubis," she said in contemplation. Turning her attention to the other professor, she asked, "Could she be referring to Anput?"

"Who's Anput?" I inquired.

"Anubis's wife: another jackal-headed god, or goddess as it were. It's possible." Turning his attention to me, he asked, "Were there jars, bowls, things that might hold the mummified remains of the sacrifices?"

I shook my head. "Not that we found, and I didn't see anything in the visions."

"So the people weren't mummified at all?" he asked.

"Nope."

He paused to caress his scraggly beard, then shook his head. "I don't think she's referring to Anput then. There were spells in *The Book of the Dead* used to bless various parts and usher the dead into the underworld, helping them move past Anubis's weighing-of-the-heart test by balancing their heart and good deeds against Maat's feather. This would allow them into Aaru, but the only references to Anput deal mainly with mummified remains and organs stored in vases and pottery. She must be referring to someone else."

"But who?" Dr. Mayna asked. "I just don't know. Maybe it was something personal."

"I'm not sure either, but I remember her chanting something," I added. This caught both their attentions.

"What?" asked Dr. Mayna, unblinking.

I thought for a moment, remembering the visions, but everything was distorted gibberish, muffled and incoherent through the flames lapping at my flesh, the searing pain, and the drug-induced immobilization. I sighed in resignation. "I can't remember."

"Then try harder," Dr. Mayna urged. "You've got to remember it. It has to be—"

"You don't understand," I spat, the haunting memories whittling my patience away. "I was being burned alive. I was drugged and couldn't move. The flames were roaring in my ears, and the pain was more intense than you ever want to know. Have you ever been burned alive? Try it and see if you can focus on the words some murderer is chanting in the distance. It isn't just a matter of remembering the damn words. I couldn't hear them in the first place." I clenched my fist, trying to stifle the anger and frustration that had built up over the years. I held up a hand. "I'm sorry. You just don't realize how bad it is. Every day I wonder whether it's a blessing or a curse. It seems to be a curse that I'm forced to live with, but I can't ignore the visions. I live with them, every day. I can remember hundreds of them. I don't know how many times I've died. The only thing I can do is try my best to put killers away and find some absolution and comfort for the victims, many of which are still stuck here."

"Like ghosts?" she asked.

I nodded, allowing my shoulders to slump.

"And they talk to you?"

"Rarely, but yeah. I can't see them, but sometimes they can communicate. Normally it's just through the visions, them revealing to me their horrible murders."

"Okay, I can see that this really bothers you, and I'm inclined to believe you." She waved a finger between her and Dr. Kamal. "But we're both scientists dedicated to studying the past, finding evidence... proof."

I chuckled. It was nice to feel something that brought that emotion back up. "I know exactly what you mean. I'm a detective. Do you realize how difficult it is approaching cases and looking at them from both sides? It's a balancing act. I can never tell my supervisor or any of the officers I work with the truth, aside from my partner. And he only believes me because we've worked so well together for so many years. He's seen the results. If anyone else knew, I'd be ostracized. They'd have me drummed off the force."

"Then why did you tell us?" Dr. Kamal asked.

I shrugged. "I'll likely never see you again, and you have information I need to stop this woman from killing again. It was a shot in the dark."

He nodded, satisfied with the explanation.

"And have we been able to help?" asked Dr. Mayna with a curious and somewhat anxious look in her eyes.

I shifted in my seat, sitting up a little straighter under her gaze. "Yes."

"Then maybe you can help us."

This time Dr. Kamal and I both looked at her, a bit confused.

"I—no, here at the university we've been trying to piece together some events from the past. There are a few skeletons people have uncovered and shipped to us to investigate. We can sometimes determine whether a broken bone occurred prior to death based on bone growth, like if it's fused back together, but mortal injuries don't show those; they are often harder to determine if the broken bones were the cause of death or happened after the person passed."

"So... what are you asking?"

"I'd like you to take a look at them and see if anything comes to you. Maybe you'll have a *vision*." Her emphasis of the final word seemed like a mixture of anxious skepticism with a shot of curiosity. I didn't care for her tone.

I looked around the small office and the ancient artifacts. "How old did you say they were?"

"I don't know," she said, glancing at Dr. Kamal. "About thirty-four hundred years... give or take a few hundred."

I rose from my chair and grabbed my jacket. "You know, I think I'll pass. There's probably nothing I can do to help you anyway. It's just too old, and the likelihood of a murder weapon or something else connected to a murder surviving this long is slim to none."

"Look, Mr. Drummond," Dr. Mayna said, rising with a hand half extended toward me, "I didn't mean to put you on the spot. I just hoped you might be able to help us."

I paused while shrugging into my overcoat in an attempt to flee the two skeptics. "You don't understand, and you're not being honest. I opened up and told you everything, things I never tell anyone. You don't really believe me, which I honestly expected, but now you want to try and test me, to try and catch me in a lie. I'm not lying."

Dr. Mayna gave a hesitant nod. "You're right. I did want to test you. I should have mentioned that, but I wasn't lying. I do hope you're telling the truth. It's a bit hard to believe, but if it's true, you really can help us. You can give us an insight into a world we've all dreamed of."

Even Dr. Kamal nodded at this.

"We study ancient Egypt because we're fascinated by it. To be honest, I wish I'd lived in that time, in that culture. It's just astounding what they accomplished," she continued.

I straightened the collar of my jacket and opened the door. "Ma'am, I'm sorry, but I can't help you. It's been too long. Nothing could remain after three thousand years." *Could it?* I wondered, but chose not to voice my own curiosity. I already had enough problems and didn't need more added. Besides, I was in no mood to die again that day.

"How do you know?" she asked. This time her tone sounded desperate. "You said you relived some people's murders from the Civil War."

Maybe she does hope I'm the real deal. "Well... I don't know for sure," I admitted, "but the Civil War was barely a hundred-fifty years ago. You're talking thousands of years. Besides, what do you even have that might work?"

"Bones. We have the skeletons of the victims."

"Victims... plural?" I walked out the door.

Jessie turned his attention from the enclosed artifact he was inspecting down the hall and stood watching our argument, a pleased smile on his face that silently said, "I told you so."

Dr. Mayna followed me with Dr. Kamal on her heels, watching as though this were a newly released soap opera.

I spun on the tiled hallway floor. "Don't you think I've tried bones, Dr. Mayna? All that's left of some of the victims are bone fragments and ashes. On the last few victims we were able to find earlier, I tried to see what they'd gone through. Their charred skin wasn't even able to contain the memories. Why do you think this will be any different?"

She took a deep breath. "Because... burning changes the chemical composition of things. Our skeletons show no evidence of being burned or ritual sacrifice. These were people who may have been unjustly murdered. You said you try to bring these victims, these ghosts, some kind of satisfaction, right? Absolution?"

"Yeah."

"What if these people have been stuck here as ghosts for thousands of years, left to dwell in a world they no longer understand and can't interact with? Do they deserve your help any less? I'd think you'd want to help them, to do what no one's been able to do—to give them peace."

The thought of being stuck in limbo, as some ghosts inevitably were, sent a chill down my spine. I looked around me at the posters on the wall advertising the university's attempts to rescue lost and stolen artifacts, at the shattered pottery lining the hallway and ancient artwork adorning the walls. These were some of the few remaining pieces left from an entire civilization, thousands of people gone from this world. *How many are stuck in between, not living but not quite dead either? And this is just one culture.* It dawned on me how few people I'd helped in the grand scheme of the world. There were many more people out there, searching for a way to the other side. I wasn't sure what existed beyond our world, but if ghosts were real, which I knew to be true from previous encounters, then there had to be something. Heaven, Hell, the Duat; whatever it was had to be better than limbo. "How long will this take?"

Dr. Mayna smiled. "How long does it take to have a vision?"

"Seconds, minutes, I don't even know if I'll get one. I can't promise anything, you understand?"

She nodded. "I do. It's worth a try though."

"Fine, let's give it a shot."

Dr. Kamal watched with a curious expression. "You Americans are never boring."

"Tell me about it," I replied, following the GW professor down the hall and past Jessie, who joined Dr. Kamal and me.

"What's going on?" my old friend asked.

"*Quid pro quo.* We're gonna try and see if I can die again today."

"They bought it?" he asked.

Dr. Kamal's eyebrows rose.

"There's nothing to buy," I answered.

"I know," Jessie replied. "I know it's real, but what you can do most people view the way the Puritans saw witchcraft."

"Let's just be glad we don't burn people at the stake anymore." My thoughts went to the fourteen victims. "Well, most of us at least."

Chapter 9

Ancient Memories

September 16, 2011

WE PASSED FROM the hallway into a gallery filled with artifacts. I slipped my hands into my coat pockets and made sure to keep a moderate distance from each display. Although they were enclosed and protected, I didn't want to take chances. After walking through a few rooms, we finally entered a door marked *Authorized Personnel Only*. Inside the long room were rows of stainless-steel counters and tabletops, with short boxes containing all sorts of jagged pottery shards, bones, casts, and other assorted historic discoveries. Researchers, young interns, and a few adults I assumed to be other professors worked at the different stations with brushes or sat huddled over well-lit boxes trying to piece together the remains of hundreds of years of history as though it were a jigsaw puzzle. Windows lined the walls above the tables, but instead of looking outside, through them other, similarly designed rooms could be seen. We followed Dr. Mayna through two sets of swinging doors, past more people dressed in white lab coats, and entered a room with larger, occupied, stainless-steel tables. It was like an L-shaped morgue, but without the frosty chill. Instead, dust seemed to permeate the air from the remains, and a sterile, haunted feeling crept up the back of my neck.

Dr. Mayna took a lab coat off a coat hook behind the door and slipped it over her other clothes. It dwarfed her slim figure, but seemed to belong there. "Meet Jack and Jill," Dr. Mayna said after shooing the few researchers present out of the room. She motioned toward the two complete skeletons filling the short-walled, body-length boxes on two tables. On a third, parallel table was yet another skeleton. "And this is Curly. We have other names, as you can see by the tags, but our interns spend so much time with them that they always name them." Other skeletons lay about the room in varying conditions, some only partially present. "Jack and Jill are from Deir el-Medina, just outside the Valley of the Kings."

"So which one's been giving you problems?" I asked while Jessie snooped around the room.

Dr. Mayna's head snapped up when Jessie reached into a box. "Please, do *not* touch, Mr. Arturo!"

Jessie's hand leaped from the box as though it had been slapped. He nodded and moved on, slowly meandering through the maze of tables.

"Well, we're not going to get anywhere if I can't touch it," I whispered, somehow feeling as though it were necessary. The atmosphere was oppressive, almost as though by stepping into the room I'd set foot on the consecrated ground of a graveyard.

She massaged a crick out of her neck and shrugged her shoulders as though trying to work out the stress of such an idea. "If you have to," she said with hesitance, "but be careful. Don't pick anything up."

Dr. Kamal watched, seeming curious both about the rooms, which he evidently hadn't seen yet, and what I might do.

Having touched the bodies of victims and the remains of bones before, I doubted anything would come of this. However, looking down at Jack's skeletal remains, the bones appeared to have darkened with time and sent a deeper chill through me. The top of Jack's skull was crushed in, as though with a pick or ax. The fractures and damage were typical of trauma to the head. Looking at the victim so long after the accident was less messy than what I was used to, and it seemed clear what had happened. "So what can you tell me about Jack?"

Dr. Mayna quirked her head. "I thought that's what you were going to tell us."

I turned to stare at her, but she just returned it without emotion. "Well, first off I'd say that you're right; Jack was murdered."

"A vision?" she asked with audible skepticism.

"No," I said, shaking my head. "You can see from the stress fractures in the skull that the impact was while he was living, or at least before his body had deteriorated. If it had happened later, his entire skull would have been more brittle and collapsed under the pressure."

"Why murder, though? Couldn't it have been a rock or something large that fell on Jack's head?" she asked, still showing no emotion, but circling the table like a vulture.

"No. Something large wouldn't have pierced the skull in such a way. It would have crushed it. The murder weapon was sharp, like a small ax or pick."

"I see." She continued to walk, but lowered her chin to her chest and crossed her arms as though in thought, but again her tone lacked any of the concern or conviction she'd held when we spoke over the last forty-five minutes.

"But you already knew that," I added.

She stopped to glare at me. "Yes, Mr. Drummond, we did. Like you, I'm well trained to analyze crime scenes and the results of murder. I understand you know your business as a police officer—"

"Detective," I interjected.

She harrumphed and glared at me as though I were an intruder moving in on her turf, which I guess I was, but it was at her request. "You know your business, Mr. Detective," she continued, "but we both know that isn't why I asked you to come back here."

I nodded. "You're right."

"Are you pulling my chain? Are you even a detective, or just some actor wasting our precious time because you got the urge to look at dead bodies after watching the History channel one too many times?"

"Now look here!" I demanded, raising my voice, but keeping it quiet enough not to disturb the researchers in the other rooms. I pulled a few photos of the serial killer's victims out of my overcoat pocket and slapped the most recent onto the brushed-metal surface of the table. They were of the last four charred bodies we'd recovered. "Don't you dare confuse me with some amateur out to get his thrills. The shit I endure is nothing like your neat laboratory. What I see day in and day out is blood, guts, and rage. This!" I waved a hand at the expanse of naturally cleansed bodies. "This has already been sterilized by time and nature." Pointing at the first picture on the table, I said, "Timothy Sterling, victim fourteen, murdered September 20, 2009. Less than two years ago, he was standing here, as alive as you and me." I gave her a few seconds to approach and look at the picture, then whispered in her ear, "He left behind a son, Travis, age six, and a daughter, Sarah, age ten. He'll never see them grow up, go to college, get married... never see his grandkids."

She took a half-step back, then jumped when I threw a second image on top of the first. It was another charred corpse with hands bound in front and feet tied. "Barnie Pitts, victim thirteen," I continued, reciting information from memory, "murdered September 20, 2008. He was a widower and is survived by Marty Pitts, his eight-year-old son. Marty now lives with his grandparents and will never truly know either of his parents."

Dr. Mayna stared down at the picture. When she began to look up at me, I threw a third photo on top of the others.

"Steven Tripp, victim twelve, murdered September 20, 2007. You'll be happy to know that this guy was single––no kids to leave behind, only his parents, and four older brothers and sisters who outlived their youngest, loving sibling."

Dr. Mayna's hand shook as she fingered the image, but I wasn't done. Throwing a fourth photo down of yet another gruesome ritual sacrifice, I whispered. "Waldo Gutierrez, victim eleven—"

"S-stop," she mumbled.

"Murdered September 20, 2006. He left behind three little girls, none older than six, and a wife who'd stayed at home to raise them."

"Please stop," Dr. Mayna whimpered. When she looked up, tears streaked down her pale cheeks.

I drove my index finger down on the victims. "This is only four of fourteen. I don't have the luxury of distancing myself from the murders. For some, I experienced everything they did and even died with them, only coming to as they left consciousness. I didn't know them in life, but I know them in death, and I'm their only hope." I slid the pictures into my palm and pocketed them as I walked toward the door. "You coming, Jessie?"

Jessie seemed to jolt back to life, as though he'd been in a trance through the entire scene. "Y-yeah, Alex. Coming."

Dr. Kamal watched, as though absorbing every bit of information but refusing to interact.

"Detective Drummond," Dr. Mayna called. "Mr. Drummond, wait... please."

The *please* was what did it. I stopped. *Paige is right. I am a sucker for that pitiful voice.* I turned to face the local professor. She looked haggard.

Taking a few ragged breaths, she wiped her cheeks clean with her sleeve, smearing dust across one side of her face, but she didn't notice. "I'm sorry, Detective Drummond. I didn't mean to question your integrity. The fact that you came here looking for our help should have been more than enough to tell me otherwise. I've just been caught up in everything here. Everyone wants a piece of me—" She stopped speaking and waved away the phantom excuses exuding from her mouth. "Enough. I'm sorry. Please give it a try."

"Will you stop jerking me around?"

She nodded.

I said, "I need to know what you do. You may be right, or you may be wrong, but I need something to go on, not for the vision. If it's there, in the bones, artifacts, or whatever, I'll get in touch with it, but this is a first for me. I've never tried to go so far back. I just need some idea of what I'm getting myself into."

She nodded once more, wet her lips, and said, "From what we know, everything you said about Jack was right. Honestly, we don't know much more than that. We think he lived around thirty-four hundred years ago, but even that's just a guess based on the plant particles we found on his bones. There wasn't much left—never really is, but it was a good clue."

"Where did you say he was found?"

This time, Dr. Kamal answered. "The outskirts of the Valley of the Kings. There's a small village where the workers lived. He was found there."

"Okay... that gives me something to go on. You don't by chance have the murder weapon?"

He shook his head.

"Nah, that would be too easy," I mumbled.

I paced the tile floor around the body, glancing at the surrounding tables for anything that might somehow have made its way into the wrong box. I knew it was futile, but staring down at Jack's skeleton was creepier than I'd anticipated. I'd dealt with bodies more mutilated than his before, but the unusualness of the experience had me jumpy.

"Aren't you going to touch him?" Dr. Kamal asked, a look of curiosity on his face.

I nodded. "Soon." I made another lap, this time reaching out to touch a random bone that could have been a leg or arm sitting in Jack's box next to the remains of his feet and tiny toes. It was smooth and hard like a rock, almost as if he had become one with the foundation of our world, but no vision came. I let out the breath I'd been holding.

"That was found near his body. The type of bone hasn't been identified yet," Dr. Mayna said.

Time to get it over with. Stepping up to Jack's broken skull, I took another deep breath and placed my fingers next to the wound. The odor of tanned hide, older than anything I'd smelled before, drifted in the stagnant room until the lights around me faded to nothing.

* * *

The smooth, wooden handle of a pick shuddered over and over as I cleared stone from the large, partially made cavern. Dust shifted the handle ever so slightly in my grip and permeated the air. The sound of others chipping away at rock and stone from the side of this mountain echoed to me through the dry desert. Glancing around, the completed entrances of hewn, polished Egyptian tombs glinted in the sunlight a hundred yards across the dry ravine bed below. A voice nearby said something in a strange language I somehow understood.

"Can't keep up. I'm tired," I mumbled, wiping the sweat-infused, chalky dust off my bare chest. I took a few steps and squatted next to a wall, just inside the shade of the chiseled entrance we were working on. Setting down my pick with its copper head, I took a swig of water from a clay jar.

"You know, Panhsj, you are lazy," said the tall man who had spoken before. He took his copper chisel and hammer and continued to chip away at a large stone that sat on the rubble-strewn floor a few feet outside. Flakes flew off in rapid succession as he skillfully flattened one face of the block.

"I'm not lazy. I'm tired. We've been working on this tomb for eternity. Ra will bed himself, never to rise again, before we get it finished."

The slender man chuckled, but did not stop working. The sun beat down on his darkened skin and raven-black curls, but still he did not slow. "One of these days, Panhsj. One of these days. If they see you, you might be demoted to doing our wash with the women."

I harrumphed. "Not likely. They know I'm worth any two of these others."

My friend finally stopped, chisel in hand and stone hammer at the ready. He turned to look at me with anger in his dark eyes. "I don't understand you. You take what you want, what you haven't earned. You choose not to share with your brother... your family, and now you insult me with meaningless boasting while you drink the water Sacmis brought me." He shook his head.

"Khasek, you are taking things too far—"

"No, you take things too far, Panhsj!" Khasek shouted, his curls bouncing just over his shoulders. His dirty, animal-hide kilt quivered, dancing at his knees from the rage he barely held in check. "Just like you stole Amun's betrothed, bedded her, and left her and Amun to raise your daughter."

"Amun's my brother. We share everything. Why not women? Besides, it isn't my fault if he can't keep his fiancée's passions contained."

"You got her drunk!" Khasek roared.

"That doesn't matter," I said, waving off his concern and tipping the jar to my lips.

"Sacmis is my betrothed. She wants me and served me as a favor. That drink is flavored with her own honey."

"And it's good," I chortled.

"It is mine. I work and earn my place. Who are you to take my gifts?"

"I am your friend, Khasek, always and forever. Why are you so angry?"

My friend's jaw clenched, framing his broad beak of a nose. He stood to his full height, a good six inches taller than me had I been standing. In the entrance, his head blotted out the sun, leaving his face in darkness. "You take your brother's betrothed's flower, leaving her with your seed. You take Sacmis's gifts. Will you next bed her?" Khasek loomed over me, his hands clenching his tools as though he'd carry them into the afterlife.

A fleeting sense of fear passed through my mind, but it was gone before I finished taking another gulp of the honey-blessed water. "Well, I won't pursue her, Khasek, but if you can't keep her reined in, you never know whose bed she might wind up—" Before I could finish my joking comment, Khasek plunged his chisel into my skull and a sharp pain jolted me, but then I felt little more than a muscle spasm as he jerked the tool free. I fell to the ground, staring at the dry, cracked surface of the mountain mere centimeters from my eyes. The clay jar cracked when it hit the ground, the blessed liquid mixing in my bloody hair and washing the joking smile from my face before being absorbed into the soil.

"Dammit, Panhsj! It didn't have to be this way," Khasek muttered. The sound of his stone hammer tapping a skillful rhythm on the chisel began again until all sounds faded to nothing.

* * *

"Did you see something?" Dr. Mayna asked, her voice anxious. "Did it work?"

I nodded and licked my lips. "Got any water?" I asked, but

almost refused it when she retreated to an office and brought back two, offering flavored or regular. "Regular, please regular." The honey-flavored water had tasted good, but the memory was fresh in my mind. Finishing half the bottle, I could have sworn there was a metallic aftertaste, almost as if I could taste Panhsj's blood.

"His name's not Jack," I stated and took another drink. Jessie and both the professors leaned in like cattle drifting to one side in their sleep just in time for a cow-tipping event.

"Go on," Dr. Kamal said, unable to restrain himself after watching so thoughtfully.

"It's Panhsj."

They both nodded, but Jessie's face contorted. "What the hell kind of name is Panhsj?"

Dr. Kamal frowned and placed a hand on Jessie's shoulder. "An honorable one. It was my great-great-grandfather's name. It used to be common in Egypt."

Jessie's face reddened with embarrassment. "Sorry, professor."

"Dr. Kamal, I'm afraid Panhsj wasn't making any friends, and he wasn't too honorable. I'm sure your great-great-grandfather was a good man, but Jack here, aka Panhsj, impregnated his brother Amun's fiancée and seemed to be pretty good at pissing people off. From what his friend Khasek said, Panhsj took whatever he wanted. He was also pretty lazy and had an ego the size of the moon."

Jessie smiled. "Damn, a man after my own heart."

"I wouldn't go so far as to say that," I added. "He got his

brother's fiancée drunk in order to steal her virginity. What kind of man does that?"

Jessie's smile turned down at the edges. However, it vanished when Dr. Kamal turned a glaring frown on him.

"Jessie," Dr. Kamal said in his thick, Egyptian accent, "you and I, we will talk." Gripping the back of my friend's neck, the visiting professor forcibly escorted him out of the labs.

Dr. Mayna watched with an expression that seemed caught between horror and laughter. Then she turned back to me, and the wide-eyed, childlike curiosity returned to her eyes. "So what did he do? Who killed him? What happened?"

It took longer than it should have to answer her questions, and we wound up grabbing two cushioned stools alongside the windows in order to continue the interrogation. She was intrigued by anything and everything: the sights, smells, tastes, and especially the emotional mistrust in the relationship between Panhsj and Khasek. After the first few answers, she pulled a notepad out of her lab-coat pocket and began jotting down my answers in some version of shorthand. It took an hour before she was finally convinced to move on, saving the rest for later. Surprisingly, Dr. Kamal and Jessie still had not returned.

"So, Dr. Mayna, what do you know about Jill?" I asked, rising from my seat and stretching my stiff knee. "I'd like to move on. This is taking quite a bit longer than I anticipated. I'm happy to help, but still have a killer on the loose and less than four days to find her."

The professor nodded and strode back between the skeletons, her low heels giving a subtle click with each step. "Well, there's not much to say about Jill. She's from the same period as Jack. They were excavated at the same time and from the same worksite. Hence the connection with the names. Aside from that, we can tell she was young, but nothing else seems out of the ordinary. Sickness, maybe?" she said, speculating.

"Maybe. Not sure I can help with her. Panhsj—or Jack as you know him—was murdered. It seems the bones of the wound were able to keep the memory."

"Yes, it would seem so," Dr. Mayna replied, her skepticism all but gone, but I sensed an undertone of shock and disbelief, as though her mind and emotions were in conflict. "If you're right, and you already tried the corpses in your murders, the bones might still hold some memory of the horrible killings, but I doubt it. Fire changes the chemical composition of things."

"Yeah, you said that before," I mumbled, scanning the floor in despair. "It explains why I got nothing from the victims' charred skin and the bone fragmen—wait." I glanced at the professor and held up a hand, waving it as though emphasizing each syllable I spoke. "We got to the last four victims before they were completely burnt. What if their skin doesn't hold a clue, but their bones still do? Could that be possible?"

Dr. Mayna thought for a moment and frowned. "It's possible, Detective Drummond—"

"Alex, please."

"Fine," she replied, acknowledging the interruption with but a word. "It's possible, Alex, but from the looks of those photos, the bones aren't the same anymore."

"But they're still bones," I said, struggling to hold on to some semblance of hope.

"Yes, they are," she said with a nod, "and it's possible. You're dabbling with something few people believe and even fewer have experience with. However, it isn't likely."

My chin fell to my chest and I stared at Jill's skeleton. Only the top layer of dirt had been removed. They'd excavated the entire block of ground surrounding her body, leaving the bottom half of the bones submerged in hardened dirt and freezing her position in death better than any picture could have. Something nagged at me, tugging at the back of my mind and making the back of my head tickle. I scratched it and continued to assess the skeleton. It—she didn't look content. It may have been the low-hanging jaw or the partially bent legs, but each thing I analyzed I dismissed a moment later. Then my focus landed on her hand and the nagging itch turned to pain as something jerked a clump of hair from the back of my head. I jumped and spun around, expecting Jessie to be up to another practical joke, but instead of a person, a small clump of hair drifted to the tiled floor.

"What is it?" Dr. Mayna asked.

I rolled my head from shoulder to shoulder, popping my neck, then took a deep breath and let it out. "You're still taking in the whole visions thing, right? Not really sure about me, although, I'm pretty sure you believe more now than before."

Dr. Mayna gave an embarrassed frown. "Can you read minds now too?"

I shook my head. "No, just people. You don't want to know what that was."

Her brows knitted together in confusion. "What do you—"

I waved the question off. "You're not ready for it. Just trust me."

She shook her head with hesitance and took a deep breath of her own.

"Take a look at her hand," I said, pointing more to divert her attention back to the task at hand more than anything. "This is probably the position she died or was buried in right?"

Dr. Mayna nodded and leaned in.

"Is it just me, or does her hand look like it's clutching something. The fingers—they're not relaxed. They're positioned as though encircling something. See, her thumb isn't even visible; it just disappears on the underside of the dirt."

"Yeah, but so do most of her other fingers. How can you tell her hand wasn't relaxed?"

"Well, rigor mortis sets in—"

"I know about rigor mortis," she said, rolling a finger for me to get on with it.

"Rigor mortis doesn't go away for twenty-to-thirty hours, and it looks like in this case she was buried as is. The dirt kept her skeleton in place, and you can see that all of her fingers at the base of the knuckle—"

"The proximal phalanges," Dr. Mayna supplied.

"Yes, those are all in line. When your hand curls at rest, they aren't all aligned like that. It's unnatural."

"So you're saying...?"

"That she might have something in her hand," I finished.

Dr. Mayna's eyes widened. She grabbed a brush, a small pick, and a narrow chisel from a wooden box of tools in her office at the corner of the L-shaped room. The box was old and looked like it could have belonged to Galileo. Then she began scraping the dirt away from each side of her hand, trying to uncover Jill's thumb and whatever was inside her curled fingers.

I watched with anxious curiosity, thinking to myself, *This must be what it's like at a dig, never knowing what you might unearth.* Soon, the end of something long and cylindrical revealed itself, one brush stroke at a time. A rounded, wooden cap stuck out from Jill's hand looking cracked and petrified. "What is it?"

She shook her head and brushed away more dirt from the small cavity she'd created. "It can't be," she whispered.

Chapter 10

Jill's Secret

September 16, 2011

"WHAT IS IT?" I asked again.

"A... a container... It looks like a small, cylindrical container, although it could be a cylinder seal." Prying more dirt from the base of the cap where it met the skeleton's thumb, Dr. Mayna said, "Oh wow! It's not a cylinder seal. It really does look like a container, like a small case for something."

"Like for scrolls and old documents, right?" My hand itched to reach out and touch it. The thought of what it might reveal was both intriguing and scary. "She might have died for this."

"She might have," Dr. Mayna confirmed.

Unable to restrain myself, I asked, "Can we get it out?"

"Not right now. To do more, I need to get a camera set up and gather my team. This has to be recorded. It could be incredibly valuable. Who knows what's in it, what it might tell us about Jill's past and the culture of her time? Unfortunately, being subjected to the weather, water, heating, and freezing, it doesn't look like the wood held up that well, but the wax seems to still be in place. They sometimes coated the insides to waterproof them, so who knows if whatever's inside is still legible?"

I licked my lips and felt another tingling sensation on the other side of the back of my head. I nodded, ignoring it. "Okay, I'll do it."

"What?" Dr. Mayna asked.

"There's another way," I mentioned, "to find out right now."

Dr. Mayna glared up at me. "We're not desecrating these remains. To break any of the skeleton's bones would be sacrilege."

Another yank pulled more hair from my scalp. I winced, but didn't turn around. "I w-wasn't thinking that," I stammered. "I have a feeling there's more to this than you realize. I think Jill was murdered."

Dr. Mayna's eyes drew to slits. "Detective Drummond, everything you came up with about Jack was interesting, but I have no way to verify it. I don't know whether to believe you or not. Everything you said seemed genuine, and I have to admit that I was excited by it, but it was almost too good to be true."

"Let me try," I pleaded. The fear of experiencing yet another gruesome death had been overshadowed by curiosity and what I could only assume was Jill's ghost prompting me the only way she could.

"Look, you've been very helpful, but this skeleton is off limits now. I see no evidence of foul play. The other one I wanted you to look at is over here." She turned, gesturing to the third, most-broken skeleton I'd seen upon entering. From a few yards away, it appeared as though they had mismatched some of the bones, but my gaze found its way back to Jill's skeleton and the cylinder cap protruding from her hand. Dr. Mayna's last brush stroke revealed ornate carvings around the edge and across the top, but there was too much dirt encrusted in it to tell of what. A curious swirl caught my attention and I brushed the dirt away with my thumb. Immediately, the aroma of aged leather wafted to my nose. The pressure of a hand settled onto my shoulder. Then Jill, Dr. Mayna, and the room swirled into blackness.

* * *

"Sacmis, you can't be this way. What will the others say? All over Set Maat, it will be said that you left me for him. I will be shamed," pleaded a voice I knew.

The darkness dissipated, replaced by twinkling stars over a desert valley, the brief light of the crescent moon painting the cliffs and bedrock an off-white.

Khasek shook his head and stepped toward me, his black curls dancing around his strong jaw. The whites of his eyes bore into my soul when he loomed near, and the sweet smell from the dried clove he was chewing drifted to me. "Give it back," he demanded, holding his hand out for the cylinder. "The letter in it was meant for you, not all of Set Maat."

"I don't care. I love him," I cried in a language and feminine voice that wasn't my own. Warm tears flowed down my cheeks as though attempting to match the currents of the Nile, and I clutched the wooden object tighter. In my other hand I held a quivering knife, its blade extended toward the man.

"You cannot. You belong to me!"

"I'll show your confession to the elders, Khasek. We are not

married. I can—"

"You can do nothing without my permission!" Khasek interjected and pried the knife from my hand. I then realized the ornate curls of the engraved wood cylinder were leaving a painful impression in my right palm and knew what letter he was referring to. I tried to calm down, to loosen my grip enough to assuage the pain, but thoughts of the small case vanished when Khasek ran the edge of my knife along his own cheek, the shaped-rock blade trimming a swath of his nightly whiskers. "This is mine now," he whispered, "until you learn to use it without threatening to hurt people."

Questions flew through my brain as I tried to decipher the situation, but they were overridden by the growing panic and fear in Sacmis's mind. "Please let me go," I pleaded in a mournful whisper.

"Go where?" he asked, his eyes glazed. "Panhsj is dead. Before, I could understand you wanting to run after him, but now you know the truth. There's nowhere to go, no way to get to him."

"But I love him!"

Khasek shook his head and tsked. "I do everything right, treat you like the queen herself, as good as a goddess, and still you love him. Maybe I should have done it sooner. Maybe then even Amun's wife wouldn't have been desecrated by his touch." He paused and brought the tip of the shining, black blade to my bare shoulder. "Did you and he ever touch?"

I tried to continue looking at him, into his angry eyes, but the answer forced my gaze to turn toward Set Maat, where torches flared along the paths and the rectangular-walled borders. I didn't answer.

"You did," he said with a chuckle and pressed the point into my skin, his hand shaking with rage. "You laid with him, didn't you?"

I glared at Khasek, the truth helping me find support and keeping me from collapsing under quaking knees. "No, I didn't," I hissed. "I loved Panhsj in a way you'll never understand, and this..." I held the cylinder up to his chest, mimicking his position with the knife. "This will be my release. When Anubis weighs me, Maat's feather will prove my truth and my love. Osiris will welcome me into his home with Panhsj at my side. You will fail. The people of Set Maat, my family and yours, will know what you did."

His teeth clenched, the edge of the dried clove peeking from between his flattened lips. "I do not fail," he swore.

True fear blossomed in my stomach as he clamped a hand over my mouth and with the other slid the knife blade across my throat. Panic and pain mixed with the blood and air in my throat. I gurgled, struggling to pull a breath through his tight fingers. I grabbed his arm, but it held firm until I was coughing blood and sputtering. Stepping back, he allowed me to stumble away until I fell at the base of a large palm tree on the outskirts of the walled town, the broad leaves breaking up the moonlight streaming overhead. I felt a warm, thick fluid coating my neck and chest, soaking into my white gown.

Khasek followed at a distance and watched with a satisfied grin on his face. As my vision blurred, the stars and leaves above fading to nothing, his words carried to me. "They'll find the letter when they find your body, and I'll put it somewhere they'll never know. You got what you deserved. Now you can be with your precious Panhsj. Tell Anubis I say, 'Hello,' before he damns your soul."

* * *

In the darkness, as the breeze stagnated and the dusty aroma of the Archeology department's research lab returned, Sacmis's voice whispered, *"Dua Netjer en ek!"* The words were airy, as though carrying to my ears from a distance, but the language was the same I'd heard in the visions. *But what does it mean?* I wondered. As the fluorescent overhead lights returned, I squinted and felt the pressure of Sacmis's fingers lift from my shoulder. I breathed a sigh of relief and clutched the edge of her skeleton's box.

"Okay," Dr. Mayna mumbled. "I'm starting to get used to this, but you shouldn't have done that."

"How l-long was I out?" I stammered, trying to catch my breath.

"A good forty minutes," Jessie said, checking his watch and leaning against the office wall a few yards away.

I glanced out the window. The sun was setting, casting the horizon in orange and pink.

Jessie nodded and held up a Styrofoam cafeteria cup. "Long enough for us to get a cup of coffee, have a little chat, and even hit on a few ladies."

Dr. Kamal glared at him after the last comment. Then he took a sip from a matching disposable coffee cup.

"They're never that long," I whispered.

"Technically, the last one, for Panhsj, was longer," Dr. Kamal added. "Just for your information."

My eyes grew wide. "Holy crap! What's going on? Every time before it's just been seconds: thirty to forty-five at most."

"I can hazard a guess as to why," Dr. Mayna supplied.

I met her gaze.

"You've never gone back this far—experienced memories this old. Maybe it has something to do with that, or how deeply embedded and lost the memories have become over the years." She shrugged. "Your guess is as good as mine."

I mulled it over. It made sense, but that meant... I glanced at all three of them. "Wait, if that's true, then if I ever encounter a vision older than thirty-four hundred years—"

"You could be out for days or longer," Dr. Mayna finished. "Who knows?"

"Hell, could even be years," Jessie added.

I turned a cold stare on him. "You're not helping, Jessie. The last thing I need is to be in a coma for years reliving some ancient Neanderthal's murder."

Jessie smiled and raised his cup as though giving a toast. "Always here to help, good buddy."

I just shook my head and grabbed the nearest stool. I looked from one professor to the next when I'd calmed down and asked, "Can either of you speak Ancient Egyptian?"

Dr. Kamal nodded. "Yes, it is an Afroasiatic language, similar to Semitic."

My curiosity got the best of me. "Is it still spoken today?"

"Old Egyptian isn't the same. It has changed dramatically, to what we call Late Egyptian, then morphing into Coptic with the incorporation of the Greek alphabet. That was used for centuries. Now Egyptians speak an evolved language classified as Egyptian Arabic."

"But can you translate something?"

"I'll try," he replied, "but it would be best if you could write it down."

I shook my head. "Not an option. I couldn't understand it when she said it, so aside from writing the way it sounds, it would be of no use."

"Wait," Dr. Mayna chimed in. "I thought you said you could understand what they were saying in the visions, that the person you... possessed interpreted it for you."

My back stiffened. "Well... technically this came after the vision," I mumbled.

"What?" Dr. Mayna asked, obviously confused. "I don't—how?"

"There's a bit more to it than just visions," I said, waving the question away. "Just trust me." Turning my attention back to Dr. Kamal, I asked, "What is Set Maat?"

Dr. Kamal smiled. "That's easy. It's the old name for Deir el-Medina."

"And what does 'Dua Netjer en ek!' mean?"

The Egyptian professor stared into the distance for a moment. "That's a harder one... Thank you—no, thank God for you!" he amended.

A subtle smile crossed my lips as I looked behind me where Sacmis's ghost had stood. "That's what I thought."

"So where did you hear that?" Dr. Kamal asked.

"Before I answer, can I ask you a question?"

"Yes," he replied, staring at me intently.

"Do you believe in ghosts?"

He smiled, and Dr. Mayna's mouth dropped open. Having theoretically proposed the idea earlier, even if she hadn't believed, she was at a loss for words now.

"Yes, Detective Drummond, I do," Dr. Kamal replied, his dark eyes glittering with delight for the first time since we'd met. "In fact, I've attended some services to the old deities with groups you would probably call Kemeticists."

It was my turn to frown in confusion.

"People who practice Kemet, the religious tradition of ancient Egypt," he supplied.

"Ahhh, so it isn't so hard for you to believe, then?"

"No," he said, his bushy beard waving. "Mysticism is a fundamental belief going back to the dawn of time in Egypt. It is possible there are ghosts we can't see around, just as it is also possible that they aren't so invisible to all of us."

"Then you have your answer," I said.

Dr. Mayna asked, "But who said it, assuming for the moment that you're right?"

"Sacmis, and you aren't gonna believe this, but I'm pretty sure I know what's in that cylinder."

Chapter 11

Surprises

September 16, 2011

"SO, DO WE REALLY have to come back tomorrow?" Jessie asked once we were on the road and headed for his place, my headlights blazing an asphalt trail ahead of us.

"Yeah, I was just burnt out, and they need help—the kind of help only we can give."

"You mean, only *you* can give," Jessie corrected.

I nodded. "Yes, but, Jessie, you've been a big help."

"To do what? Get coffee?"

"I wouldn't have even thought of George Washington University if you hadn't picked up those flyers," I explained.

"True, but that wasn't help, just luck."

"Well, sometimes everyone needs a little luck. That's thinking outside of the box—my box. It was good work. Believe it or not, you helped a lost soul who'd been searching for relief for ages. We just didn't realize it."

Jessie shook his head at the unusual occurrence. "Yeah, I guess so. Who would've thought? And it was all because of Liz."

"Is that her name?"

"Yep," Jessie said with a smile. "She's great. She's from a small town in Colorado. It seems to be a lot like Tranquil Heights from how she describes it."

"That's wonderful! Both of you are island castaways," I said with a chuckle.

Jessie joined in. "Yeah, somethin' like that."

"So when do I get to meet this elusive Liz?"

Jessie shrugged. "Maybe tonight. It's Friday, so she's probably done with her route."

"Route?"

"Yeah, she's a door-to-door salesman for her own little electronics-distribution company. They deal in computer-networking products and such," Jessie explained.

"Wow, that's tough work," I said. "She's probably pretty good with rejection. She'd have to be."

"She's cool. She can take it. Let me give her a call." He pulled out his phone and punched in her number. His face brightened when she picked up and he said, "Hey, babe. How'd your day go?"

It was nice getting to see Jessie, but my thoughts turned to Paige and my fifteen-year-old son Jamie waiting at home. I missed them: Jamie's lighthearted laugh and Paige's constant support. Just hearing their voices at night over the phone wasn't enough.

Jessie pocketed his phone a couple minutes later as we exited the beltway. "We're on for nine. She's gonna swing by."

I glanced at the digital clock above the car's radio. "That gives us just over an hour."

Jessie flipped down the visor, licked his palms, and smoothed his wavy hair with his hands. "Yep, enough time to get cleaned up and lookin' spiffy," he said, charming his reflection.

I shook my head and smiled. *Same old Jessie.* "So, I've gotta ask. Whatever happened with Dr. Kamal? Y'all were gone for quite some time."

Jessie's smile faded and he flipped the visor back up. "Nothin' big."

I glanced over. His demeanor had changed, thoughts of Liz and the upcoming get-together seeming to vanish the instant I mentioned Dr. Kamal. "What's wrong?"

"Don't worry about it. It was no big deal."

Thoughts of his earlier rejection of the obvious connections and significance to the tattoos came to mind... and my suspicions. *Could there be more to this than I thought? Did they know each other before? Maybe this was a setup from the beginning, meant to pull me away from my current investigation. Maybe things weren't the same... maybe this isn't the same old Jessie.* "Look, you gotta tell me."

"Why?" he demanded. "It's nothing for you to worry about. He just wanted to talk about me."

You? What would Dr. Kamal want with you? I wondered, but kept the questions to myself. Shaking my head, I said, "Jess, it doesn't add up. You two just met. Why would he want to talk to you?"

Jessie turned to glare at me. "What, you don't think anyone would take an interest in me?" he spat. "You're so special that you get the wife, the kid, and everyone wants to be your friend, but not me. Is that it?"

"I didn't say that. You're putting words in my mouth."

"I don't see why it's any of your business, but if you've gotta know, he wanted to talk to me about how I act... what I did." His voice trailed off at the end. Then, in a calmer tone he continued. "I thought it was pretty funny at first, blowing it off and such, but he led me around campus and we talked."

"About what?" I asked. *Nothing here makes sense.*

Jessie's glare intensified. "About me. He asked so many questions about my personal life that I thought he might be hittin' on me. I told him I didn't swing that way, but whatever he wanted to do on his own time was his right."

I looked a Jessie in shock, then quickly glanced back at the road as the car began to veer toward the parked cars in front of the condos around us. Straightening the car, I asked, "And what did he say?"

Jessie smiled as he remembered the events, his annoyance at my questions dissipating. "He laughed. He's not into that kind of thing either. Did you know the guy's got three wives?"

I slowed down as we approached a red light and digested the new information. "No, I didn't."

"Yeah, talk about a playa," he added.

I couldn't help the chuckle that rose in my chest at Jessie's choice of terms. "I think we're going to have plenty of sayings for our kids to make fun of, too," I muttered, thinking back to our previous conversation.

"Yeah, I'm sure."

"So why did he want to know about you?"

"Believe it or not, he wanted to help. He took pity on me. It was like a counseling session from the good doctor of Egypt, making house calls to the States."

Again I turned to stare, but returned my gaze to the road a moment later and laughed. *Good God! How could I have thought such a thing about Jess? He's just embarrassed.*

"Yeah, I couldn't believe it either, but he explained it pretty well. He said he was happy and he saw how I wasn't. He said I had some internalized anger toward you, and... well, I can't say he's wrong. He may have a side job as a psychiatrist or somethin'. Give him five minutes with a person, and he can read them like a book."

I nodded, having gotten the impression at times that Jessie had some underlying anger issues, much like a few minutes before, but I again kept my thoughts to myself.

He must have read my solemn expression because he added, "Sorry, Alex. I don't mean to be mad at you. It's just that everything seems to go your way."

My jaw dropped. "Go my way?" I asked in disbelief. "You do realize who you're talking to, right? I'm Alex Drummond, the guy who got picked on and bullied throughout school, has to relive murders on a semi-daily basis, and can't tell anyone at work besides my partner Hector what I do or else I'll get kicked off the force."

"Yeah, but you help people. You do something no one else can. You're special. Plus, you've got a wife that loves you and a son that wants to be just like you."

My thoughts turned to Jamie and something he'd mentioned last year. As I pulled into the parking spot in front of Jessie's apartment building, I put it in park and left the car running. "You're right, Jess. I've got it pretty good. It's a hard life, but rewarding."

"Yep, something I don't have, at least not yet. That's gonna change, though."

My thoughts were still on Jamie. As Jessie opened the door, I said, "Wait a minute."

He shut it and looked at me. "What?"

"Something happened last year that I never told Paige about, something important."

"What was it?"

"Well, you mentioned Jamie wanting to be like me. That's something I've been thinking about for a long time. He's more like me than anyone knows. I'm not sure if he realized what he said or not, but last year he mentioned that he spoke with my father."

Jessie tapped a finger on the armrest. "How's that even possible? Your dad died years ago, didn't he?"

I nodded. "Yeah."

Jessie's eyes grew to the size of lightbulbs. "No—no, really?"

"Yeah."

"And you didn't tell Paige?"

"I couldn't. I'm still not sure about it. Maybe I misheard him. He's never brought it up since. I know Paige could deal with it. We've even wondered whether it was possible and talked about it before we decided to have kids. I just don't want to worry her about something more. She's already got her plate full at the hospital. Those people can be pretty hard on RNs."

"So, is he like you?"

I let out the breath I'd been holding. "I'm not sure. From what he said, I just don't know."

"What'd he say?" Jessie asked, his words coming quick and excited.

"His exact words were, 'Grandpa said to tell you that you've made him proud'."

"Oh," Jessie replied, the tone of his single word rising and falling as if he'd had an epiphany. "Yeah, maybe you're right then." Opening the car door, he flipped up the shirt collar of his polo shirt like a mobster and mimicked the stereotypical voice, saying, "Now look here, see. We've got a lot to do and little time to do it in. Now march on up there before I have to bring down the hammer of this here gun."

I shook my head at the bad impression as he dropped his thumb down on his finger-gun.

He dropped the impression and shouted as we took the stairs two at a time, "And don't forget to put on cologne. You stink, and you've gotta make a good impression if you're gonna be my best man."

My jaw dropped, and I stopped in front of his door on the third floor. "What? Is it that serious?"

"Like I said, things are gonna change. That's somethin' else we talked about. Liz is one in a million. Why wait?"

I clapped him on the shoulder and gave him a broad grin. "I'd be happy to. Damn, that's great. I hope she says yes."

"Oh, she will. Who can resist the Jess-meister when he puts on his charm?" he said with a laugh and opened the door.

While changing, shaving, and taking care of the other necessities to look my best for Jessie's soon-to-be fiancée, my thoughts turned to Paige. I could still see the glitter in her eyes reflecting the small diamond ring. I presented it to her in an unusual way.

* * *

June 8, 1996

Graduation was more of a relief than anything. It meant I didn't have to worry about classes, Stone Face Easely, or the looks of condemnation and fear I still got from the rumor mill of Madessa High School. I tried explaining what I could do to get them off my back, but that didn't work. Eventually I was ostracized again. It wasn't much different from the beginning of the school year. That day marked the beginning of my freedom. Throwing that covered, cardboard hat into the air was like lifting a weight from my shoulders, but only one of many. My larger concern for that day was still to come, but for the time being I was frigid. Whoever's idea it was to make us wear "professional attire" should've been strung up by the field-goal poles naked to see how they liked it.

The cool night air slipped right through the maroon gown and my shirt and slacks. I was shivering before we'd even crossed the field and taken our seats.

Paige found me with her hat in hand and a wide grin, brimming with excitement. Her amber eyes, auburn hair, and even her pale skin glowed like a firefly. I couldn't help but be attracted. She shone like a beacon amongst the maroon and white robes littering the football field. The women wore white, and hers gave me the impression that I was standing before a beaming angel. She flung herself into my arms before I could get a word out, and I squeezed her close, whispering into her ear, "You're beautiful."

She gave me another squeeze in reply and pulled away. "Isn't this great?"

I nodded. "It's a huge relief. Can't believe I made it through."

"We did," she said, giving my hand a squeeze this time. I felt like I could drown in her eyes. They were like sweet honey.

"How'd I get so lucky?" I asked.

"With lots of hard work," she replied and giggled. "You ready for the party tonight?"

"Yep, should be fun. Can you pick me up?"

"Yeah, Mom and Dad surprised me with a car this morning."

"Congratulations!" I said as we made our way to the bleachers where my mother and Abigail were waiting with Paige's family.

"A Subaru: with airbags and four-wheel drive," Mr. Kurtley added with a wink. "Got to make sure our baby stays safe."

"Dad," she whined.

Her mother backhanded Mr. Kurtley's tall shoulder. "Quit embarrassing her. It's her graduation: her day to celebrate."

* * *

At home, I tore off the robe and black slacks I'd been forced to wear. Slipping into a pair of warm jeans, t-shirt, and a loose flannel, I felt more like myself once more. I slipped Dad's dog tags over my neck and under the heavy-metal t-shirt just as the doorbell rang.

The blue-eyed, orange and white kitten I'd acquired earlier that day peered over the edge of my top bunk, staring down at me as though I might have a treat. "Meow?" A second later my graduation hat evidently became too much of a distraction, and she pounced on the tassel after stalking it, her tail weaving back and forth through the air.

"Be quiet," I told her and deposited the small, purring animal into a cardboard box. She mewed through the gaps of the top flaps as I began tying a length of ribbon and bow around it. "Coming!" I yelled.

I shut the bedroom door behind me and sat the box on the kitchen table before opening the front door for Paige. Again, she looked breathtaking, now wearing a deep-blue top under a thin, open sweater, and black slacks. "Hey, gorgeous."

"How's it going, handsome? I see you found your way back into those comfortable flannels I love."

"Always. I about froze this evening..." I paused, then couldn't help the evil grin that perched on my lips. "You know, I think these pants are lined with flannel."

"God, don't I know it. Whoever's idea it was—" She stopped as soon as my second sentence registered. Then she slapped my arm. "Alex Drummond, you should be ashamed of yourself," she chided, but a subtle smile played behind her words.

I winked. "Maybe later?" We both laughed as I escorted her into the new trailer.

"Wow! I like what your mom did with the place. Looks like y'all got the boxes unpacked quickly."

"Yeah, it's pretty nice, but doesn't take much to surpass the last hellhole." Even the memory of the Drunk's cigarettes and beer-can-strewn living room made me gag. "Have a seat. I've got something for you." Showing her the way to the couch, I picked the box up off the table and held my breath when a soft mew came from inside. Turning around, I sighed with relief when Paige looked at me with bright eyes, but gave no indication she'd heard.

With soft steps, I carried the box over and sat it on her lap. "Congratulations," I whispered.

She looked down with confusion. "You didn't wrap it? That's not like you, Alex. You sure you're okay?"

I couldn't help but laugh. "Just open it," I said with a smile. "I promise I'll wrap the next one."

She began untying the folds of red ribbon until the box shifted on its own and another questioning mew echoed from inside. Her eyes widened as she lifted it out. "Oh, Alex. You didn't? It's adorable," Paige crooned, "but what's...?" Her mouth fell open, speechless, and her eyes danced from my smiling face back to the tiny diamond ring hanging from the collar.

She caught her breath and stared at me, kitten still in hand. "Yes! Yes! Yes!" she shouted, pulling me and the little feline into a tight hug. I breathed in her hair and perfume, relishing the scent of the woman I'd be lucky enough to call my fiancée while the kitten squeezed out another mew. Paige pulled back and kissed me, her sweet lips closing on mine. The ecstasy of the moment filled me until she tilted her forehead against mine. Nose to nose, she gave me a peck on the lips and whispered, "Now I have a surprise for you."

"What's that?"

She nibbled on her lower lip for a moment and then said, "I'm pregnant."

At that moment the world spun into night, taking my consciousness with it.

Chapter 12

Last to Know

June 8, 1996

"SWEETIE, ARE YOU OKAY?" asked my mother, her graying ponytail hanging over her shoulder.

I propped myself up on an elbow. "I think so," I replied, my voice wavering a tad. As I did, I spotted Paige's face amongst Mother's and Abby's and remembered my fiancée's last words: *I'm pregnant.* Then Mr. Kurtley's words echoed from earlier that day: *Got to make sure our baby's safe.* Looking up at Paige, I asked, "Does your father know?"

She glanced at Abigail and my mother, eyes wide. "I don't think so. Did you tell him?"

I caught the double meaning, but changed the path of our conversation. "Of course," I said as I rose to my feet. "I had to get permission to ask for your hand."

I wrapped an arm around Paige's waist and smiled.

Mom's hands slapped her knees. "And you said yes?" she asked Paige, more excited than I'd ever seen her.

Paige nodded. "Yes, ma'am."

"Enough of that, missy," Mom said, taking Paige into her arms. "You can call me Vivian—no, better yet, call me Mom."

Paige looked at me, wide-eyed, then back at my mother. "This is so new. Why don't we go with Vivian and take it from there."

"Okay," my mom said, rubbing Paige's shoulders, "we can do that."

"By the way, where's the poopster?" I asked.

"Poopster?" both women said in chorus.

"He means the kitten," Abby answered, holding the purr machine in her arms.

I looked at Paige and smiled, then gave her a subtle, sensual kiss.

"That's not Poopster. Her name's Diamond," Paige said after taking a breath.

As Abby was rubbing the little feline's chin, she caught her breath and held the cat up like it was the world cup. "Look, look, Momma." Paige and I both smiled as they passed the cat around, neither wanting to give it up long enough to remove the diamond from its collar.

"Let me," I interjected. Abby held Diamond still as I removed the ring and took Paige's hand in mine. Abigail—who was blossoming into a woman herself—and my mother watched with tears in their eyes as I slipped it onto Paige's finger. When I looked back into her eyes, I found that they were tear-filled, too. "I hope those are tears of joy," I whispered. She nodded and wrapped her arms around my shoulders. I clutched her tight and whispered into her ear, "Do we tell them the rest or wait for later?"

"Later," she answered, pulling back to give me a smile. A few joyful sobs came from behind us, and we turned to make our exit.

While Mom gave me a hug, Paige took Diamond from Abigail and crooned into the kitten's wide, blue eyes.

"We'll be back later," I said, taking Paige's free hand in mine. "Don't wait up."

"Be safe," was my mother's only response. Then mother and daughter grinned at one another, as though conspiring about our future.

On the way out to the car, I mumbled, "I think your dad might know more than he's letting on."

Paige gave me a quizzical look. Then her eyes widened. "I'm gonna kill my mother!" she hissed, but even then her mood was too good for the smile to fully disappear.

"So how do you think he found out?" I asked. "It's not like you're far along."

She turned a skewed look on me. "Alex, you may not be able to see it yet, but the mornings have been rough for a while. Mom caught on, but she swore she'd wait to tell Dad until after we saw what you were going to do. After how serious we've discussed things, I hoped you would propose, but wasn't sure."

"Well, I guess she told him... Hey, at least your dad hasn't killed me yet. That's a plus," I added, trying to make it sound like a joke.

She squeezed my hand. "And now he won't. Dad likes you, Alex. You know that."

I spun her around just as we reached the car. "Yeah, but I *love* you," I whispered to her lips and tasted them before running around the car and jumping into the passenger seat.

She shook her head and whispered, "What am I going to do with you?"

"Marry me," I answered once she'd gotten in.

"You bet your butt. There's no getting away from me now," she answered with a grin.

"Well, technically I'm the one that collared you."

She slapped my chest and gave me a playful, "Keep it up, bub." Starting the car, we headed back to her place and the waiting graduation-party guests.

* * *

September 16, 2011

After running a comb through my wet, black hair in preparation for meeting Jessie's girl, I shoved it into my back pocket and pulled out my phone. A few quick numbers and the phone rang.

"Hello?" asked a feminine voice I'd grown to love.

"Hey, darlin'. How are you?"

"Alex? Hey baby. I'm doing fine. The hospital's running me ragged though. How're things going?"

I let out the sigh of frustration. "Well, progress, but I feel like I'm back to square one." I told her about what had happened with Irene and the meeting with the professors, even the visions of Egypt, but I left out how long each vision took. She didn't need to worry about that. The likelihood of me encountering a vision from something old enough to put me in a coma was almost nil.

"So how's Jamie?"

"He's good," she answered. "Misses his dad though."

"I know. I miss him, too. Is he still up?"

"Honey, it's not even nine. You do realize he's a teenager now, don't you?"

"Yeah, I know. So you're telling me he isn't in bed."

"He's not even home yet," she said. "I think they went to see a movie, and you won't believe this…"

"Yeah?"

"It's a double-date."

"Well ain't that somethin'," I mumbled, almost in disbelief.

"Yep. You weren't much older than him when you proposed."

"Yeah, but three years makes a hell of a lot of difference at that age," I muttered, remembering my own horrifying high-school years.

"Yeah it does," she whispered, her own voice sounding nostalgic, too.

"We're getting old."

"No we aren't. Get your head out of the Washington clouds and get home. I've got a surprise or two waiting."

"Wh-what?" I stuttered, but her end of the line clicked off. The words she used so many years ago when I proposed echoed through my mind once more: *I'm pregnant.* I shook it off, dismissing the possibility. *No way. Not after this many years,* I told myself.

Dialing my partner Hector Martinez, I brought him up-to-date with what was going on and what we were looking for. "Oh, and by the way, can you look into a guy for me? He grew up in our neck of the woods."

"Any connection to the case?" asked Hector, his Latino accent evident in his words.

"Nah, I don't think so, but there might be another murder up here, and I need to find out all I can. His name's Rayson, Greg Rayson. They've found all they can up here: some DUIs, a domestic-violence call and subsequent divorce and such, but nothing serious. I need to know more about his past."

"Sure, Al. No problem."

"Also, take a look at the victims from last year. If Victor Harris wasn't victim fifteen, there's probably someone that hasn't been accounted for."

"We checked out the people reported missing in the area during that time, but I'll check again."

"Yeah, and search the surrounding counties. Might have been someone from out of town, or maybe they were reported later."

"On it. Any idea when you'll be back?"

"Tomorrow night's the plan. That's when I scheduled the return flight for, at least. Got a few loose ends to tie up here. Finishing up with the Egyptian professors, and then I'll be heading back."

"Alright. Well, make it quick. I think Lieutenant Tullings said he was taking this time out of all that vacation you've got built up."

I knew when he was pulling my leg. "Miss you too, buddy. I'll be back to help you pull the rest of those cats out of the trees soon enough."

"You won't believe it, but I had to rescue a dog the other day," Hector added. "A freakin' doberman pinscher somehow got up a tree. Damn thing nearly took my hand off. Wound up tranqin' it."

We both chuckled. "You serious?" I asked.

"Yeah, it was the damndest thing I ever saw."

At that moment the doorbell rang. "Hey, I gotta go. Take care of yourself, and get me what you can on Rayson."

"Yep," he answered and ended the call just as a brunette in her late twenties sauntered through the front door to give Jessie a kiss.

"Hey, Jess," she said, tossing her black purse on the couch. Her high heels, short skirt, and frilled, shoulderless blouse gave her a Latin flare that any man would find arousing.

"Hey, doll. I'd like you to meet my best bud." Touching a hand to her lower back, he led her into the living room where I was pocketing my phone. He gave me a wink. "Alex, this is Liz."

"Oh, so this is the man Jessie's always talking about. Nice. Not looking too shabby either," she said, walking around me as though deciding what outfit she should show me next in a clothing store. She slapped my butt as she strode past and slipped an arm around Jessie's waist. "Good to meet you, Alex." Her dark-brown eyes danced with an energy not unlike Jessie's. Both of them smiled.

"W-well, it's nice to meet you too, Liz," I said, clearing my throat at the awkward introduction and telling myself, *This is going to be an interesting night.*

* * *

The evening began with a late dinner at a local French restaurant on the top story of a high-rise. It was called Jardin de Nuit. I thought the thirty-story elevator ride was bad enough, but when the maître d' checked Jessie's name off the registry, I was shocked.

"How'd you get us a reservation?" I hissed as the balding, gray-haired man took our coats and hung them in a massive closet in the front foyer. A dark-haired waitress in a black apron and white polo motioned for us to follow her.

Liz interrupted by saying, "Jessie's got connections."

Jessie nodded. "Pretty much."

I just shook my head, wondering how large the bill would be for a DC establishment where each table had pristine, white tablecloths and a pale hanging light centered over the table with a seamed, alabaster-glass shade. The room was almost pitch black except for the tables, each illuminated like solitary islands in a sea of darkness. A string quartet was even playing softly in one corner of the room, the musicians' shapes silhouetted by the faint light of their music-stand lights. I followed behind Jessie and Liz, barely glimpsing the chair backs and heads of people around me. A soft chatter emanated from each table.

I took a seat at the vacant, lit table that the waitress indicated, and Jessie explained, "I've worked for lots of people with money over the years. Believe it or not, when you're good at something, people notice and keep coming back." He winked at Liz, and she took his hand in hers. "I'm good," he whispered in a tone that seemed half sarcastic and half serious. "The foreman says I'll probably replace him some day."

"Evidently," was all I could come up with.

"So, Alex, I hear that you're a cop?" Liz said, breaking her gaze with Jessie.

"Detective," I said with a nod.

"And you followed someone up here?"

"Yep, he did. Turns out it was a bit of a downer though," Jessie added. Evidently he hadn't spoken with her about me in the last twenty-four hours, but she certainly was up-to-date with my arrival.

"Oh, how so?"

"Well, it's an ongoing investigation, so I'd rather not talk about it much."

Jessie's brows furrowed. "Alex, really? I've been a part of it every step of the way."

"Yeah, but it's different—"

"No, it's not," he interrupted.

"It's okay," Liz began, "if he—"

"No, it's not," Jessie repeated. "It's fine to tell you. It isn't like we have any new suspects or anything." Turning his attention back to me, he added, "Right, Alex?"

I shrugged. He wasn't wrong. I shouldn't have involved Jessie, but he knew the lay of the land. "We're in DC, hours from Tranquil Heights. It's not like this will get back to Tullings. Go ahead."

Jessie nodded. "True. So, basically we found out that Irene

Harris, that lady that burnt down her house with her husband in it, like I told you before…"

"Yeah, you mentioned that."

"She's innocent," Jessie finished. "While she got away with murder with practically a slap on the wrist, she couldn't be our serial killer. She wasn't even in town at that point."

A quizzical look appeared on Liz's face. "Then who did it?" she asked. My gaze found its way down to the bare cleavage revealed by her shoulderless shirt, but then I became distracted by a gold ring on a slim, woven chain around her neck. She fondled it in her fingers while listening, and it glimmered under the table light.

"We don't know," Jessie answered. "Not even sure if there was a murder last year or not."

"Well, that's good isn't it? Maybe there wasn't."

"Maybe," I answered, unable to take my eyes from the ring. It looked warped and a little twisted. She seemed to caress each curve and facet with the ends of her fingers.

Unable to help myself, I asked, "Where'd you get the ring?"

The question halted the conversation and her massaging fingers. She shook her head. "It's nothing, just some bad memories," she answered, letting it slide back between her generous mounds of supple flesh.

I've gotta get home. Paige would kill me if she knew what was going through my mind. Hell, Jessie would, too. Paige started it though, threatening me with such enticing promises.

Jessie looked at Liz and gave me a sideways nod as if to say,

"You can trust him." The motion pulled me from my thoughts.

She let out a deep sigh and whispered, "It belonged to my previous lover. We traded rings, but before we could exchange vows and make it official with a wedding, he was killed in a car wreck."

"Sorry to hear that," I mumbled, feeling guilty at having brought up such a touchy subject.

Thankfully, the awkward topic was interrupted by the waitress taking our drink orders. After Jessie ordered a bottle of wine that I couldn't pronounce and was astounded to hear come from his lips, the waitress said, "I'll bring that right out. If you'd like to take a walk through our high-rise garden while you wait, feel free. The stars are beautiful tonight, and the flowers are in bloom." Then she vanished into the dark room.

"High-rise garden!" Liz squealed. "I've heard it's beautiful."

"You've never been here before?"

"No, never," she whispered with a childish grin. Pulling Jessie to his feet, she said, "Let's go walk under the stars. Jennet told me that when she came to Jardin de Nuit, the gladiolus and moonflowers were beautiful in the moonlight."

Jessie rose with an adoring smile, his eyes taking in every inch of her. "We'll be back in a few," he said, turning his attention to me long enough to wink.

"Take your time, Jess. I'm not going anywhere."

They passed through two windowed doors. Staring between the curtained glass, I watched their shapes walk hand in hand along the paved walkway. The white, pink, and purple petals of various night flowers opened wide amongst the foliage around them, soaking in the night's rays.

Paige would love this. I sat admiring the enclosed garden from my limited vantage until the two lovebirds disappeared around a river-rock fountain. Then my thoughts returned to Paige, the morning of our wedding: her glowing skin, grinning face beneath the white veil, and bright eyes that could have lit up the church on their own. Jamie, my growing son, lay in her protruding belly under folds of decorated lace. She couldn't have been more beautiful. The kiss was electric, and the room filled with the families' applause.

My thoughts wandered to other boys around Jamie's current age: fifteen. Junior Lee had been about the same age when he died. Anger at this serial killer's insanity bubbled inside me at the thought of someone stealing the remainder of Jamie's life, ripping it away. I bit my lip, trying to restrain the raging emotion. In an effort to control myself, I unfolded my cloth napkin from the elegant, folded silverware napkin. Laying it on my lap, I maneuvered my silverware in order on the tablecloth, nudging them apart a little at a time to perfect the spacing between each one. I focused on their polished shine and the mirror image reflecting back at me from my fork handle.

What am I doing here? My hand tightened around it, framing my narrow, oblong reflection. *I should be out looking for that murderer, not sitting in this elegant restaurant. This is Jessie's time, his moment with Liz, and I'm in the middle of it while the seconds are counting down to the next murder.*

At that moment, Liz appeared leading Jessie by the hand. "Alex," she said through a grin a mile wide, "we're getting married." She held up her hand, and the ring glittered under the table's focused light.

Only then did I notice that the prongs of my fork were digging through the tablecloth and into the table. I quickly set it down.

"Seems she had one for me, too," Jessie added. The ring that was previously on a chain around her neck now encircled his finger. He put his hand out to me, and the light seemed to bend around the twisted metal. What I thought before was design, upon closer inspection, seemed to be the result of fire. The metal itself looked as though it had hardened outside of a mold while still fluid. Before I could see more, Jessie pulled out Liz's seat like a gentleman and then took his own.

"You won't believe how beautiful it is out there," Liz whispered, leaning over the table in her excitement. "I could never have imagined a more beautiful proposal." She turned to gaze at Jessie. "I do. I do. I do," she whispered." Jessie laughed and smiled more broadly than I'd ever seen.

"My, my. I'm so happy for you two."

"Who would've thought?" she murmured, taking Jessie's hand in hers. The light from overhead glinted off his ring, illuminating the liquid folds on its surface.

"I have to ask. I'm sorry for the question after such wonderful news, but the band you gave Jessie is just so unique. What happened to it?"

Liz paused and sucked in a quick breath. "I-it was my fiancé's, like I said."

"Right, I understand. I'm sorry to even ask, but did it burn in the wreck?"

She shook her head and Jessie quirked his eyebrow. "No, no nothing like that," she said. "He was a firefighter, and over the years he ran into too many fires to count. The heat took its toll on the metal, flexing and molding it around his finger."

"I see," I said, nodding. "Sorry to ask. It just looks so distinct."

"I understand. Not a problem."

"But on a happier note, congratulations again! I look forward to seeing you two walk down the aisle. However, I think this night should be left to the lovebirds." Standing, I took Liz's fingers in mine and kissed the back of her hand. "Take care of him. He's a great guy," I whispered.

"I will," she mumbled with a shy smile.

"But how will you get back to the apartment?" Jessie asked, rising from his seat.

I shook his newly adorned hand and wrapped an arm around his shoulders. The subtle streams of light from our table and others flashed into darkness, preceded by a whiff of worn leather.

Chapter 13

Memories in Need of Justice

September 16, 2011

THE DIM LIGHT of a campfire flared to life before my eyes. Leaves littered the ground under my knees and feet as I knelt before Anubis, staring at his dark work boots from barely a foot away. The flames leaped as though dancing, their shadows playing across the murderer's jeans as though coming to life.

"I see you went so far as to decorate my mark... with roses no less," the beast muttered. "That just won't do. It needs to be fresh and visible for Anubis."

The voice was the same lifeless female's. The victim's thoughts echoed through my mind. Sweet Jesus! Marla, help me. Anyone? *I tried to speak, but all that came out was a garbled collection of indecipherable sounds. I even felt drool course down my lip and coat my chin's whiskers.* Drugged, heavily drugged, *I concluded through the mental fog.*

A long, glowing stick emerged from the fire, and the Anubis clone carried it past me. Suddenly a burning sensation flared in my calf. I jolted to the side, but my bound legs and wrists allowed me only to tumble onto my side. The smell of seared flesh wafted to my nose, enhanced by the drug. My nose scrunched at the smell and the lingering pain.

"*Don't give me that. You are my golden bull, not some weakling. You chose the mark and the location, Greg.*"

I chose this? What? *I tried to mumble an explanation, but incoherent sounds dribbled from my lips.*

Her heavy boots and legs squatted before my tilted eyes as I stared past her at the trees. The glowing length of metal appeared inches away from my face, and then the searing pain blessed my forehead. I screamed and tried to rock away, contorting my body across the ground, but the damage had been done.

"*There, that's better,*" she continued. "*She'll be so happy to see your sacrifice.*"

My tongue felt thick and dry, and now the smell of burnt flesh permeated throughout my nostrils. I couldn't get away from it, but soon the dancing shadows of the forest returned. I squinted at them, trying to make out the beast who had stepped away, but she was nowhere to be seen.

"*Are you ready, my prized flesh?*" she rasped with a hint of joy in her otherwise-distant tone. "*It's almost time.*"

Cool liquid streamed onto my cheek and shoulders, then down my body, soaking my white undershirt and jean shorts. A scent stronger than my burning flesh wafted to me—lighter fluid. "Oh, not again!" I screamed, but a moan so low it was almost a grumble was all that escaped as I succumbed to the inevitable, mentally broken.

Holy Mary, Mother of God, pray for us sinners now and at the hour of our death... *I began chanting unbidden in opposition to those the beast began speaking.*

I tried to distinguish the woman's words, but they were in a language I couldn't understand.

The tall, shadowy figure paced around me, disappearing from view. She circled time and again until the words finally stopped. The monster threw a bucket of fluid into the flames, and the bonfire roared. I was on my fifth repetition of prayer when the stranger's hand jerked me upright.

"Anubis, accept my offering and see that my mother continues into the Duat," she commanded.

Suddenly something slammed into my back, and I flew forward... into the flames. Orange, red, and searing-white colors flared as every inch of my body screamed in pain and horror.

* * *

I was left panting in the dark a moment later, relieved by the instant absence of pain. *Oh man! So that's what happened to the mayor's son.* Greg Dihler had been a suspect in the early investigation because of his involvement with the team, although his father hadn't known. At least the police thought Greg might be involved, until his name made the list of victims. Since then, Mayor Dihler goes on a rampage every September. Another thought crossed my mind, answering a question I'd been trying to resolve for years. *Her mother. That's the* she. *How—who?* Before I come to any further conclusions, a fourth whiff of aged leather came to me. "Oh no. No more, please," I pleaded, but nothing stopped the assaulting vision.

* * *

"Oh my-my-my," hissed a melodious, yet intrigued woman's voice—the same one as before. "I must say that I love what you did. It screams 'Child of Osiris'," she muttered, her voice carrying to me from afar. "Celtic knotwork. Anubis will approve of your sacrifice."

Her boot heels clopped on the asphalt and a red neon sign bloomed to life out of the darkness. My eyesight was fuzzy, and the world seemed to shift under another round of drugs, but I finally deciphered the scrawled, glowing words. Ernie's Autobody, it read above the door. The faint glow of the words reflected off the blue, metal roof of the building. I stared up at it until the jackal head floated into view, its dark gaze staring down at my kneeling body and piercing my heart. Something was gripped in its hand, the end glowing bright orange.

"Help me, please," I tried to scream, but I felt even more drugged than before and barely heard my own gurgle echo across the rows of abused and beaten cars parked in the lot.

"What was that?" hissed the mutant creature, a hint of curiosity in its feminine voice.

I tried to scream again, but only drooled down my chin. Even that sensation was numb. I was barely aware, but knew full well the outcome of this night. Frustration at my inability to help simmered within me, melding with muted panic. I can't do a damn thing.

"Let's decorate it a bit more, shall we?" she said and stepped out of sight, the branding iron finally visible in her gloved fist.

Although numbed by the drugs, the pain still registered when the scalding metal was pressed against my spine. I screamed, and this time words were unnecessary. When she pulled it away, momentary relief washed over me. Then the bar of burning metal touched my side, searing skin to ribs. I let out another howl of pain that only ended when she took the brand away.

She giggled. It was crazed, happy, and... young. "One more," she whispered with another short giggle. "Sound good?" She didn't wait for my answer, instead ramming the rod into my other side. "It has to be even!" she roared. I tried to jump up, but I was bound and unable to stand.

The chanting began again a moment later, the sounds filtering through the air as though distant. I shuffled around on my knees, turning to find the source of Anubis's chanting, and found the monster standing next to a burning, metal barrel. My eyes widened at the sight. Sweet Lord, guard and protect Isabelle. I love her with all my heart. Make this quick, and don't let her see me like this.

The beast prodded me toward the barrel once she finished her chant. "Stop!" I tried to shout. Tears streamed down my face and onto my flannel shirt as waves of flame billowed closer, singeing my hair and eyes. The pain grew as Anubis shoved my head into the raging barrel from behind. I tried to fight, to pull back as the roaring fire blistered my face and shoulders, sending the gruesome smell of burning flesh and smoke up my nostrils and clogging my mouth, but bound and drugged, a moment later I was tipped headfirst into the inferno. The last sound I heard beyond the roaring echo was my own reverberating cry.

* * *

I stumbled in the dark, but was unable to see anything beyond an absence of existence. Yet somehow I panted, free from the confined barrel, searing flames, and choking smoke. Taking a haggard breath, I closed my eyes. It was no different from the pure darkness that surrounded me. "Oh Lord, help me," I muttered. Robin Gemanc had endured all of that, and now so had I. Taking one final breath, another vision assaulted my consciousness.

* * *

"No one can help you, Kevin," the murderer answered, startling me.

Yellow porch lights flickered to life like fireflies attached to a ranch home.

"I've been watching you."

"Wait, wh-who are you?" I stuttered, another strange male voice coming out slurred.

"A friend. Your best friend," the feminine voice answered as though almost trying to seduce me. "You're going to save my mother. Don't you want that?"

I shook my head, but stammered, "Y-y-yes." The world wobbled around me, but seemed clearer than the visions before.

"Good," she answered, drawing out the word and cinching the leather strap tight around my wrists.

I tried to pull away from the latticework wall I was backed up against. The wooden lattice crunched and flexed, but the leather straps around my chest and waist held me to something stronger. The four-by-four beams, *I thought with diluted frustration.* I built the thing too damn sturdy! *I glanced up to see the cheap, wooden paneling I'd attached years before when I built the large playhouse for my young daughter.* She wanted a sandbox or a playhouse for Christmas; she couldn't decide which, *I remembered.* So, I gave her both: a playhouse on stilts, with a ladder entrance, above a lattice-enclosed sandbox. *The yellow light from my porch across the yard illuminated the white, painted wall. It was almost gray now, but rainbows spanned the playhouse's outer wall with leprechauns prancing at each end, their black, curved smiles brightening their chubby faces with half-moon dimples. Even in the dim light, the vibrant colors Jacqueline helped me paint still brought a smile to my face. I wasn't sure if it was real, or a mind-altering effect of the drugs that lunatic stuck in me, but the thought of her, my Jacqueline, now four years old with brunette hair and dimples to match both her mother and the leprechauns, made me grin even wider.*

Scratching sounds, thumps, and the murderer's voice echoing through the darkness around the playhouse interrupted my nostalgic memory. "I know you want me to be happy, Kevin, and this is how it can happen. You are a prize, a golden bull, my annual sacrifice of flesh. What's more is, in addition to your personal sacrifice, you will give up exactly what brings you happiness."

My thoughts went to Jacqueline—her dimpled, innocent smile and cherubic cheeks. My grin vanished. "Stay away from my daughter, you bitch!" *I yelled. Anger flared inside me.* "You'll never get Jacqueline!" *I shouted.*

A laugh tinged with insanity echoed back. "Oh don't worry. If I wanted her, I would've taken her. I branded you years ago, you and the others. I know you've got fancy tattoos, but the one on your forearm is mine. You are mine. Remember?"

I glanced down. A tattoo with roses wound around the bottom of an ankh, but the ankh was newly seared into my flesh and throbbed.

"You're one of my golden bulls," *she continued,* "head of the football team, celebrated by everyone, the upcoming leaders of our small hamlet. I want you and your happiness. This... thing you are so proud of is perfect. It will make a wonderful funeral pyre. Now it's time to pay the piper."

I shut my eyes as my thoughts swam, slowly pulling the pieces of the night together, but it was like building a house of memories in quicksand—four supports in, and three would vanish. Jacqueline and Cindy are at the movies, *I finally remembered.* Girl's night, Jacqueline calls it; got it from Cindy. *Remembering Jacqueline's name for the weekly event brought her childish voice and face to mind. The memory brought tears to my eyes.* I'll never see her again, my sweet Jacqueline and lovely Cindy. At least they aren't here. They're safe. *I breathed a sigh of relief and sniffled, but it wasn't just the tears or the drugs tickling my nose... smoke.*

Smoke wafted through the lattice wall, and the back of my jean-clad legs felt warm. After a few seconds, or eons, I felt a noticeable difference. *The warmth had filtered through my clothes and was growing hotter. The pop and curl of singed, overheated branches and tinder filtered to my ears. The heat moved up my leg and began warming my hands until the skin began to blister. Every sensation was distorted by the drugs, but the pain seemed immense, especially from my ring fingers. I roared, bellowing in pain, screaming at the realization of my more vividly illuminated surroundings. I glanced up at the painted wall and watched the rainbows and leprechauns' faces blacken and change, distorting their cheery smiles into maniacal, demonic grins filled with malice. It seemed as though their eyes glared at me until the paneling and paint became charred and flaked away, drifting on the rising waves of heat from the growing bonfire. The flames surrounded me, lighting up the latticework everywhere I looked. I struggled to free my blistering legs, arms, and neck to no avail. I pressed my back against the latticework, hoping to massage the flames out of existence.*

It was then I saw the great dog-headed beast—half human, half jackal—dance around the burning playhouse into view, a book in her hands, chanting. "This can't be happening!" I screamed, but all that came out was another guttural roar. My throat felt raw as the sound dwindled, but whether from the smoke, flames, or my own inner anger, I didn't know.

As the bonfire grew, engulfing the playhouse, my clothes, and even my sizzling skin, the creak and groan of collapsing wood echoed through the growling fire inches behind my head. Once more I pulled at my bonds, wincing as they dug into my burned flesh. Instead of pulling free, I felt the small building shift and then topple on top of me. Scalding-hot boards, splinters, and nails embedded themselves throughout my back like a collection of enraged demons, poking and prodding. The pressure of hitting the ground under such weight expelled whatever breath I had left. I tried to take another, but felt the creak of my ribs. Smoke and ash rushed into my nose and mouth. A coughing fit took me, sending sharp pains throughout my gut and chest. I struggled for a breath, a tiny ounce of air that wouldn't come, until my head swam in the flames. Be safe, my darling. Take care of Jacqueline.

* * *

I opened my eyes to the dwindling smell of burnt leather, but every other sense found nothing in the darkness. No wind howled or trees scraped, and even the chanting had stopped. *Kevin, victim four. He left his daughter Jacqueline behind and his wife.* I took a labored breath, sucking in what moments before was impossible. *God, I hate this,* I silently swore. Instead of finding Jessie or Liz standing in front of me, the world blurred yet again, accompanied by the familiar smell I'd grown to hate. *Victim five, Chow Winn,* I told myself.

Another hail of fire and drugged, ritual sacrifice came upon me, this time in an overgrown field. *Mina, my wife, take care. I love you,* were Chow's final thoughts before succumbing to the blazing fire beneath his bound body.

Then victim six, Ernie Cobb, flared into my thoughts. *Wh-where am I?* he wondered. Looking back into his memories of the night revealed that the drugged effects I was feeling were a mix of the beast's concoction and intoxication. My own hatred of the Drunk and what had happened to Frank came to mind, and I struggled not to hate the man I was inhabiting. He, like the others, was fed to hungry flames, but this time behind a long-forgotten train depot. *Dad, I'm sorry,* came his unbidden thoughts before I was thrust into yet another victim.

As Davon King, I died in an abandoned factory on a rolling conveyor belt, one of many machines and pieces of furniture left in the building. My bared chest throbbed at the newly branded ankh, and the rollers singed my back in strips as the killer built a bonfire beneath them, leaving me bound to the metal contraption.

Fiona... I'll miss you, doll. Take care of Momma, was Davon's final thought.

The monstrous beast's parting words echoed through the three-story tall building before she pulled the great, metal doors closed behind her. "Anubis, that is seven. Grant my mother grace and entrance into the Duat."

Cesar Chavez, victim eight, was left in a fifties diner after they'd closed down for the night. The flames reflected off the aluminum plating on the countertop and chair legs. A round, plastic clock with a faded hula dancer in the background clicked the seconds, marking time as the flames engulfed the counter where Cesar was lying, bound, drugged, and helpless.

The only change in the pattern was the serial killer's

acknowledgement. "Save him," she cried, her voice quaking. "Allow him into your fold, past the test of purity, and into Osiris's realm."

Victims nine through fourteen continued the same way: in an abandoned trailer, a building, graveyard, coal mine, and even on a decrepit coalminer's railroad on the outskirts of town. The fourteenth, Timothy Sterling, I relived yet again in the vacant parking lot. I was certain of two things by the end: Liz was somehow involved with our killer, and two, that each victim wore the ring. By the end, having it absent from my hand made me feel like something was missing. While it seemed as though I were standing in limbo yet again, I trembled as I took another breath, wondering, *Is it over?*

"It's never over," answered a man from the darkness. "Not for people with your skills."

Although we'd never met, I recognized the sound. "Kevin, is that you?"

The disembodied voice didn't respond to the question, but said, "You're close. Thank you."

"Yes, thank you," came Cesar's distinct voice from somewhere distant. Then others repeated the phrase and similar words of appreciation, many men's voices. However they grew distant quickly and the islands of lit tables replaced the ghostly words.

* * *

My legs felt weak, and my knees buckled, but Jessie took my weight and helped me back into my chair.

"Alex, you okay?" he asked.

"I... I..." Giving up trying to phrase my thoughts, I simply nodded. I grabbed the glass of water that had arrived in my mental absence and downed it in a few large gulps. Wiping my mouth on my sleeve, I lurched back to my feet.

"Ho-ho-hold on, buddy," Jessie said, gripping my shoulders. "You sure you should be standing?"

"Yeah, I should go."

"How will you get home?" Jessie repeated

"I-I'll take a taxi," I stammered. My gaze turned to Liz as Jessie and I parted. *How... Why?*

She stared back, but seeing my face, her excitement diminished. She still smiled, but it looked forced. "Good-bye, Alex. Take care of yourself," she said.

I purposefully grabbed Jessie's left hand this time and pulled him close, whispering, "You should come home with me."

What remained of his energetic façade vanished, replaced with a frown. "No, not a chance."

I bit my lip, unsure what to do. *If I leave, she could kill him tonight—wait, it's barely the sixteenth. I've got time. She doesn't know I know.* Looking into my old friend's pleading eyes, I was aware that I couldn't convince him. *Let him enjoy tonight. I'm sure his heart will be broken tomorrow.*

Chapter 14

PTSD—of the Paranormal Kind

September 17, 2011

THE NEXT MORNING I awoke to my cell phone vibrating off the kitchen counter and clattering across the linoleum floor. I open one eye a slit and peeked over the couch arm, still fully clothed. The sun was shining through the apartment windows on the far side of the dining room, and I evidently hadn't even made it to the guest room the previous night. My head felt as though it was in a vice, and one of Kevin's devilish leprechauns was chuckling while spinning it tighter. The drug-induced murders I'd relived left me with quite the hangover, unfortunately without first enjoying a party. "Fifteen visions at once," I muttered, astounded at the thought. "And what was that first one?" I tried to shake away the heavy weight that descended on me as I sat up. *My God! Is a leprechaun actually sitting up there?* I wondered, cocking my head to the side for good measure. No shamrock-toting, tuxedo-clad leprechauns fell off, but the feeling remained.

The phone buzzed again, making its way across the floor of its own accord. "Coming. I'm coming," I muttered to the gadget and moped over to it, hitting the *Brew* button on the coffeemaker before leaning down to pick the phone up. "Hello?" I said, flipping it open. Although I didn't intend it to, it came out as a question.

"Alex, you okay?" said Hector Martinez.

My mind shifted gears, perking up, at least as much as it could through the morning fog cluttering my brain. "Hector... yeah, how's it goin'?"

"Going fine, Al. You sound like you just woke up. You do realize it's after nine, right?"

I glanced at the ornate, wooden centerpiece on Jessie's table. On either side was a bowl filled with apples and pears, while a wooden clock tower rose from the center like a miniature cuckoo clock. It read 9:15. *Got forty-five minutes to get to the college,* I thought to myself groggily. *Holy shit! I'm not sure I can take doing that again so soon.* My head pounded. "I do now. What ya got for me?"

"Man, don't tell me you had a go at the bottle. You know that ain't good for you," Martinez complained. "And Paige'll kill you if she finds out."

"No, nothin' like that, Hector. It was a long night." Thoughts of Liz and the visions came to mind, along with wavering suspicions of Liz, or at least her minor involvement. *Where'd she get that damned ring?* "In more ways than one," I added.

"Well, I checked out all the runaways and MPs from the surrounding counties and got nothin', bubkes. There's no one that went missing within a month of September 20 last year."

"I see." My mind wandered to the previous night's visions again. Something about the missing victim from last year made sense, but my head was swimming and I couldn't decipher it all. After the ghostly visions I barely made it to the taxi, and the ride home was more like a distant trance than a recent memory.

"I also checked on that Rayson guy," Martinez said, interrupting my thoughts. "He had it rough for a while after the divorce, got in a bit of trouble, like you mentioned. He even lost custody of his kids, probably due to his drinking."

I nodded to myself. "Makes sense. How many kids did he have?"

"Two, but the younger one, a boy named Trevor, ran away a few years after the divorce."

"Damn, that's rough. I take it they never found him."

A few clicks from a computer mouse filtered through the line. "Doesn't look like it."

Wow! No wonder he didn't mention the boy. That could explain his move, though. "Any luck finding out about his potential connection to these murders?"

"I pulled everything I could. Even scanned the old files into the computer in case you wanted me to e-mail them." A few more clicks echoed to Alex's ear as Martinez's voice paused, probably to read the monitor. "Nah. He was here for a few years before the murders began, but according to his credit cards and bank statements, he moved after his wife died of cancer."

"His wife's dead?" I asked.

"Yep."

"Then who took care of the girl?"

"Says here the father wasn't around so her grandmother took custody, a woman by the name of Deborah Easely."

My jaw dropped. *Stone Face Easely—no, it can't be.*

"According to the report, she's a—"

"Teacher," I finished for him.

"Yeah, how'd you know?" he asked. Hector hadn't grown up in Tranquil Heights, so sometimes the nature of small towns was still a surprise to him.

I took a deep breath and then let it out. "I took classes from her. She was a real piece of work. If her daughter died of cancer, that explains why she was such a cigarette Nazi on bathroom patrol." Suddenly I remembered the comment I made to Greg Rayson and his moment of thoughtful silence afterward. As soon as the dots connected, the conclusion hit me like a slap across the face. *He knows her. She is—was his mother-in-law!* "We didn't part on good terms," I added, remembering my outburst in front of the school.

"You want me to talk to her?" Hector asked. "See what's what, how the girl's doing and all?"

"Please, if you wouldn't mind," I replied, breathing a sigh of relief. The last thing I wanted to do was to interview Stone Face Easely as part of this murder investigation.

"You want I should look into this Rayson fella more?"

"Nah. He hasn't even been in town since the murders began. He's got no connection with his own kids, let alone these murders." Although I was tempted, I didn't mention his connection to Evie's death. If anyone needed to hear about that, it was Sergeant Rollen. Plus, I still hadn't decided how to approach the issue. It was delicate, and the more I learned about Greg, the more I was sure he

206 | The Golden Bulls

was suffering through his past losses. Evie's death and a potential court case would drive him over the edge… maybe even literally. "Don't spend too much time on it, though, unless you get a feeling. Easely is a lot of things." Things I didn't want to mention. "But she doesn't fit the bill for this. Just be careful, and you probably don't want to tell her that you know me."

"Oh, so things *really* didn't end well then."

"No," I confirmed. "I have a meeting with some professors on ancient Egypt again today, and then I'll be heading home late tonight."

"Got it. See you tomorrow then, Al."

"Yup, you too," I replied and hung up.

I shook my head at the coincidence, but that nagging feeling had returned. *There's no such thing as coincidences,* I told myself. *Something's up here, but what?* Then my thoughts turned to Jessie, and my eyes flitted back to the wooden centerpiece. *Just thirty-five minutes to get there. I'd better check on Jessie.* Although I wasn't looking forward to the conversation I would have with him, I was still unsure what to say. Liz was somehow involved. The victims were wearing her ring. Although her voice wasn't the same as the killer's, there was still too much coincidence for my comfort.

I showered and changed. With fifteen minutes to spare, I shrugged into my overcoat and knocked on Jessie's door. There was no answer. I knocked again, but still heard nothing. Peeking in, I found his bed sheets disheveled like normal, but nothing seemed different. The khakis and shirt he wore the night before weren't atop the full hamper against the wall and his cell phone wasn't on the charger. *Of course,* I concluded. *He didn't come home.* For a split-second my heart skipped a beat, but then I reminded myself of the previous night's significant moment—for him at least. However, she had seemed overly excited, too. *If she is the killer, she couldn't have been that excited about someone she was going to kill, could she?*

I pulled out my phone again and speed dialed Jessie.

"Yo," he barked into the receiver after a few rings.

"Wow! Well it's good to hear you so energetic," I said with a smile and began heading to the car. "Glad you're still alive."

"Why wouldn't I be?" Jessie asked, his voice sounding perplexed.

My thoughts again went to the coincidences and last night's visions. *He's gotta be with her. If she's involved, something could happen,* I worried. Then I reminded myself that we were still three days away and Jessie was a big boy. I needed to warn him, but it could wait a few hours. I still had to get everything figured out first. *I can't just go accusing a man's new fiancée of being a serial killer without some proof.* "No reason," I answered. "We just gotta talk soon. I take it you didn't come home last night."

"Now, that's the detective I know. You're spot on, Alex."

I laughed. "For once, right?"

He chuckled. "Something like that."

"You do realize that aside from this one killer, I put away more murderers than any cop in the region," I reminded him while starting the car and pulling into traffic.

"Yeah, and I know you're good, Al. I just like yankin' your chain," he replied with another chuckle.

"Listen, Jess. I'm headin' over to see the professors for that meeting this morning. You coming home soon, or wanna meet me there?"

"Do I?" he asked rhetorically. "No, but Liz might. She's into that stuff, remember? Hold on."

"W-wait, Jess," I said, trying to stop him, but he'd already vanished from the line. *She can't be there, not if she's involved. She can't see how I work... what I do.*

Fortunately, when Jessie came back on the line, he said, "Nah, she's not interested today. Maybe another day. We've got a lot to do, errands to run and things to get rolling for the wedding."

I nodded to the empty car and hoped it wouldn't be in vain. *I hope I'm wrong. Maybe there's an explanation for her having the ring.* There were still too many unanswered questions. "Sounds good, Jess. I'm heading out tonight on a nine-o'clock flight, so if we could talk some time before then, I'd really appreciate it."

"Sure. I'll give you a ring when we finish up and see if you're done teaching the academics."

"Right," I replied with a halfhearted laugh, "like I'm teaching them."

"Believe it or not, you are. Who else better to explain *what you do* than you?" he said, emphasizing the generic reference to my specialty.

"True. I'll see you then. Maybe we can grab coffee. Stay safe."

"Will do," he replied, and the line clicked off.

* * *

I arrived at the university over half an hour late and found the two professors talking outside Dr. Kamal's office in the hallway. "Get lost in traffic?" Dr. Mayna asked, already cloaked in her lab coat. She was wearing heels again, but this time with a brown skirt and thin, black, turtleneck sweater.

"Yeah, it's a little daunting without Jessie to navigate."

She laughed. "Nothing beats having a good local to show you around."

"Don't I know it?"

"Are you doing okay?" she asked after looking him over. "You look a bit pale."

"Yeah, I'm fine. Just had a long night. It would be great to spend a day recovering, but there isn't time."

She nodded with excitement. "You're right, there's not. I couldn't help myself. I stayed up until early this morning typing my notes and everything you mentioned onto the computer, and that was after spending a late night here with Sacmis. I didn't want to chance forgetting something. The quicker we record and document everything, the closer we'll be to publishing our discoveries. Just have to make sure there's a legitimate way to explain it all." Dr. Mayna's eyes took on a distant look, and her brows knitted in thought.

Dr. Kamal asked in his thick accent, "Any luck with your investigation?"

I took a deep breath, unsure whether to reveal everything. However, they knew and seemed to believe me. "More than I had hoped, and unfortunately from an unlikely source."

The Egyptian professor's bushy brows rose in curiosity. "Oh yeah?"

"Yeah." I gave them a quick summary of the detailed rituals and the wording of the sacrifices before asking, "Was the number seven important in ancient Egypt?"

"Why, yes it is," he answered in his deep, knowing voice. "In essence, it is supposed to symbolize perfection. There are many examples of seven in ancient Egypt and Egyptian mythology. There are two references I think you'll find most appropriate to your investigation. The first is the symbol for gold in ancient Egyptian writing. It had seven spines on its underside. You did say that she called these murders golden bulls, right?"

I nodded, considering the new information.

"The second, and possibly most important, is that the god Set tore Osiris's body into fourteen pieces, one group of seven for each region of Upper and Lower Egypt."

Dr. Mayna nodded. "That's just what I was thinking."

My eyes widened. "This woman is pulling from all over Egyptian mythology. Any record of someone doing something like this, sacrificing groups of seven?"

Both professors shook their heads. "No," Dr. Mayna replied. "We know a lot about it, but human sacrifice was practically nonexistent in Egyptian history, unless you believe that theory we talked about before. We have evidence that some civilizations practiced it, especially in South America, but probably not the Egyptians."

Dr. Kamal held up his hand to stop her. "That isn't false, but it's not quite true either. We don't know much about the early dynasties of Egypt and the predynastic period, but there is a theory about Abydos and the early pharaohs of the first dynasty."

"What's Abydos?"

"A capital city, and one of the most important cities in all Upper Egypt. It was called Abdju back then, but it is said by some that during the first dynasty of Egypt, they *may* have sacrificed courtiers and high officials, or had them commit suicide. This was done so they could be buried in the royal tombs and serve the pharaoh in the Duat after death. There is little to no evidence of this beyond their buried bodies accompanying the pharaohs', but some think it is so."

"Then where did this woman get the idea to sacrifice these people, her *golden bulls*?" I asked, emphasizing the murderer's lunatic name for them.

The Egyptian professor shrugged. "It's almost like she's picking and choosing bits of history. The bull was symbolic of Osiris, and they valued gold. There may even be some odd translation of a text she read about. From the chanting you mentioned, it could even be a funerary spell. We will probably never know."

"She has to know a lot about ancient Egypt though, right? Especially if she's casting spells."

"Yes, but I don't think she has a firm grasp of the history," Dr. Mayna replied. "It's like Dr. Kamal said: she's picking and choosing. She knows quite a lot about it, but that could be from the internet for all we know. You yourself found it to be helpful, although not quite perfect."

"True," I said, looking down at the floor. How many people's lives could have been spared if I'd just made the trip to speak with people who know? Would this information have made a difference? I didn't know, but I still hadn't caught her yet, and other lives were at stake. *Less than three days left*, but I was close. The victims' ghosts knew it, and I felt it in my bones. "Look, my flight home is tonight, and I've got to talk to Jessie before then. If we're going to take a look at that last John Doe—"

"Curly," Dr. Mayna interrupted with a smile.

"Curly," I said with a nod and continued. "Then we need to get to it. Who knows how long this will take?" A panicked thought struck me. "This guy's not from the first dynasty is he? I've been burnt alive too many times to count in the last twenty-four hours."

The university professor's eyes widened as though just realizing the enormity of what I'd endured since she saw me last.

"I'd also rather not end up in a coma," I added.

"No," Dr. Mayna whispered. "He should be from around three thousand years ago, too. At least, that's what we think. Carbon dating puts it around there, give or take a hundred years."

"Thanks," I said and followed the two of them back through the gallery and labs into the room we'd visited yesterday. It was empty, either the result of it being a Saturday and or because Dr. Mayna made sure we had the room to ourselves. Either way, I was appreciative.

Curly still lay where I'd seen him before. The remains of the woman were nowhere to be found. "Where'd Sacmis go?"

"She's in another room now while we further excavate around her hand. It's a long process, and people will want to know about that artifact you found."

Dr. Kamal added, "It didn't take long to convince my superiors at Cairo University to allow further excavation. If I hadn't been here, though, I know they would have demanded Sacmis be sent home."

"Just based on Alex's vision?" Dr. Mayna asked.

"No, based on you damaging the artifact without permission."

"I didn't damage it!" she shouted.

Dr. Kamal held up both hands, motioning for her to stop. "I know that, but that's what they would have seen if I weren't here to vouch for you. I trust you, Lilly. I know what's happened. I believe Alex, but not everyone thinks as I do. They are very protective of our history. So much of it has been destroyed or stolen already. Just think how much knowledge was lost when the Library of Alexandria and Serapis were burnt."

Dr. Mayna's chin fell to her chest. "I know. Thank you, Mohammed."

Silence permeated the room as she avoided looking at him. Evidently there was a past between them that I wasn't aware of.

"Well," I said, breaking the silence as though it were an ice-covered lake, "let's get to Curly, shall we?"

The two professors huddled around his bones.

"What can you tell me about him?" I asked, pulling up the stool.

Dr. Mayna crossed her arms and stared at the skeleton in the large box between us. "His bones were broken," she said, waving her hand at the contents, "as you can see. We found most of them, at least we think we did. We pieced them together, but it's like they're fused with other bones or something. It's been a difficult process."

"But you were evidently able to make out that this was a guy?"

"Yes, a boy, around puberty."

Dr. Kamal stared at the hundreds of bones, most no bigger than an inch or less, all arranged into the form of a human skeleton. The Egyptian doctor's dark eyebrows were furrowed in thought.

I looked back at the remains and spotted a quarter-sized, green stone in the shape of a beetle off to the side. Time had taken its toll on the small item, and whatever was used originally to paint the stone had flaked off, but a shadow of the original image remained. There was even a hole drilled through each side of the beetle's head, as though it could have been worn on a chain or necklace. "What's that?" I asked, pointing.

"It was found with the body," Dr. Mayna replied.

"It's a scarab," Dr. Kamal mumbled, his accent so thick I could barely make out his low words. "They were believed to be good luck and help the dead transform into whatever they would become in the afterlife." He leaned forward and plucked the stone from the elongated box.

Dr. Mayna's mouth opened as though to say something, but no words came out.

Dr. Kamal nodded and asked, "Are you sure this scarab was found with the body?"

"Yes," she said.

Closing his eyes, he slowly ran his thumb along the bottom of the stone, his bearded mouth forming subtle words without saying a thing. I wanted to say something just to ensure some ghost hadn't discovered a way to mute the world around me to get my attention. I glanced around the room, but saw nothing.

Finally the Egyptian professor opened his eyes. "Nakhtiokpara," he said. The words resounded through the room. "That was his name. It means 'Strong firstborn'."

"You sure?" Dr. Mayna asked.

"Yes, the person's name was often inscribed on the bottom or the back of the stone. His is here." Dr. Kamal rotated the stone for both of us to see the minute markings. They'd faded so much I could barely see more than a couple scratches. "You can feel them," he said, "like braille." He rolled the stone in his hands and peered at the back for a couple minutes.

I examined the skeleton once more, leaning over to inspect each part. "Was there an impact wound?"

Dr. Mayna didn't acknowledge the question. Instead she asked in a curious tone, "What'd you find, Mo—I mean Dr. Kamal."

I caught sight of her glancing at me warily, which reaffirmed my suspicions. They were more than colleagues. However, their love life was none of my business. It might concern Dr. Kamal's many wives, but if he already had three, maybe he was looking for Mrs. Four.

Dr. Kamal nodded at the stone. "Spell thirty from the *Book of the Dead*, I think. It's chiseled into the stone like the name, but I can only make out a phrase here and there. See, here it says, 'O my heart which I had from my mother.' That is a normal phrase from the beginning. Here," he said, pointing at one small section with the tip of a finger, "is where it talks about the balance. It reads, 'Do not rise up against me as a witness in the presence of the Lord of Things.' It is the heart spell." The Egyptian professor stared into the distance and began reciting the entire spell from memory, as it would have been said in ancient Egypt.

His words made no sense, but kindled a memory from the previous night. As I stood strapped to the playhouse, the beast's chanting melded with Dr. Kamal's. The words were the same. I struggled to think of other visions where I'd heard the odd chanting and brought to mind a few, but my mind still wasn't what it should have been. However slowly, the memories surfaced, but the words were different. "That's what the murderer was chanting during Kevin Simmons' ritual sacrifice."

He stopped mid-phrase.

"She chanted other things for the other murders, but that was one of them. What did you call it?"

The Egyptian professor swallowed and his Adam's apple bobbed. "The heart spell. Then it's as I suspected. She's reading from the *Book of the Dead*, and in Ancient Egyptian no less."

I nodded, having already come to the language conclusion after the previous day's early visions. "I'll catch her. Right now we're running out of time."

The skeleton looked twisted and grotesque, as though the archeologists might have mismatched some of the parts. "What can you tell me about how Nakhtiokpara died?" I asked.

"Well, the biggest thing is that he was born with a disease that affected his bones," Dr. Mayna answered. "He had massive deformations throughout his body. We're really not even sure how he survived to adolescence with this many skeletal problems. They didn't have the healthcare we do today, and this looks to be something most people die from before they reach ten years old."

"So there was no other likely cause of death?" I asked.

"No, we suspect it was the disease. However, his bones were found in such disarray that nothing is certain."

"If the disease took him, I'm not sure I'll be able to do anything for you, but we'll see." My hand hovered over what looked to be parts of Curly's shin bone. I licked my lips and muttered, "Here goes nothin'." Touching the tips of my fingers to the bones, my body stiffened in anticipation, but no vision came. I glanced up at Dr. Mayna.

"Anything?" she asked.

I shook my head.

"Where did you touch the other skeletons?" asked Dr. Kamal.

"On the wound," I answered. "I guess this means it probably wasn't the disease that killed him. Otherwise, I'd think most of his bones would contain the memory... assuming there is one at all."

Dr. Mayna nodded.

"May I see that?" I asked, holding my hand out for the scarab gem.

I prepared myself for what might come, holding my breath as Dr. Kamal handed it to me. However, nothing happened. I breathed out a sigh of partial relief and handed it back. *Maybe one of the other bones?* Stepping up to the upper portion of the body, I gently grasped the edge of a shoulder between two fingers. Still nothing. Bracing myself once more, I touched the shattered remains of the skull, but got nothing: no scents of aged leather, antiques, or even a dimming of the lights.

Dr. Mayna frowned. "I guess you came out here for nothing this time."

"Maybe," I mumbled, but then spotted a solid, curved section of what looked to be ribs, but they seemed to have grown together into a four-inch wide triangle: what was left of his ribcage. It was one of the largest sections of skeleton remaining. "You said his bones were deformed, right?"

Dr. Mayna nodded. "Yes."

"That doesn't happen to leave sharp indentations, does it?"

"It can leave pockmarks, pitting, divots, and such. What's on your mind?"

I leaned over, pointing at the piece that was now mere inches away. "What happened to the bottom of his ribcage?" A chip large enough for me to spot from a few feet away was gouged from the bottom rib.

She stepped closer and bent to peer at it. With a delicate hand, she lifted the shard and admired the jagged edge I'd indicated.

"Is that natural?"

"No," she whispered. Then louder she said, "But it does appear to have happened before his death. The bone seems to have remodeled itself. He must have gone for ages with this for it to have healed that much. It shouldn't have killed him."

"Why don't you let me be the judge of that," I said, coming around the table. Holding my hand out palm up, I said, "Do you mind?"

She gently sat it in my palm, and an immediate wind blew through the room. Papers scattered from the office desk and notes stirred from under manila folders that researchers had left on the countertops. "Mohammed, check the windows. If I find out who left it open, I'm gonna have their hide."

Dr. Kamal went to the far window while Dr. Mayna grabbed at papers and checked the window latches on the nearest wall. I was immobilized as a voice echoed in my ears, chanting like Dr. Kamal had done earlier. This voice was different, a tenor, and distant, as though it were travelling on the wind and over the seas. The subtle beat of drums grew in the background like a voice or sound you might imagine accompanying the waves of the ocean when you hold a conch shell to your ear. *It's not the wind,* I tried to say, but the words only drifted through my mind. My eyelids grew heavy as the scent of antiqued leather drifted to my nose. Trying again, I managed to whisper, "Be right back," before my eyes shut and the world vanished from around me. The last sight I had was of Dr. Mayna in her lab coat pausing to gape at me.

Chapter 15

Saving Nakhti

September 17, 2011

"KHERED, YOU'RE SUCH a strapping young lad. Isn't he?" asked a grandmotherly voice that began as the Ancient Egyptian speech I recognized, although, the latter question seemed directed at someone else.

As the dim light of a room with mottled, red, mud-brick walls revealed itself, I felt a wide hand on my slim shoulder. I blinked, clearing dark spots from my vision, and stared into the warped, copper mirror her wrinkled hand held in front of me. Through the waves of polished metal, I could make out my straight, dark hair and a few specks of white decorating my tanned skin. The onyx eyes staring back at me through dark lashes were hardly more than a child's.

A man harrumphed from behind me, but I couldn't tell whether it was in agreement with the old woman. She had enough wrinkles and gray curls to be over a hundred.

I spun to face the voice and asked in a childlike voice, "Father, when did you get here?"

"Now what did I tell you about calling me that?" replied the bald man in a white, linen tunic. He cradled a carved, ivory wand in the shape of a crescent moon. His forehead was wrinkled, and years in

the sun had sunken his cheeks, however, his eyes flared with life.

I dropped my head to stare at the dirt floor. "Sorry, Fa—High Priest Senbi," I said, catching myself.

"So why did you call for me, child?" the man mumbled.

"High Priest Senbi," I said, raising my eyes to meet his narrow glare, "I wondered when I could come to the Temple of Ptah to worship with you."

"You want to be a priest?" Senbi said with a chuckle, as though the idea were absurd.

I nodded with enthusiasm. "Yes, Fa—I mean, High Priest Senbi."

"Aunt, leave us," the high priest commanded.

The elderly woman patted my shoulder and gave me a pitying look. I returned it with a halfhearted smile then looked back at my father. My stomach was doing somersaults, and I felt a bit woozy, having mustered the strength to finally summon my father for the request.

"You know, Khu wants to follow in my footsteps," he mumbled, his lips curling into a subtle smile at the admission.

Images of a dark-haired boy a few years younger than myself flashed before me, sporting with the other boys in the village, something I was never allowed to do. I could be a priest, though, be revered by the people, and help them. My magic could be the strongest in Upper Egypt. Senbi had named me for my strength. Raising my chin and attempting to straighten my crooked back, I said, "I know, High Priest Senbi, but I am your firstborn. I am Nakhtiokpara. Do I not have the right to choose first? I am almost fifteen."

Senbi spat on the hard-packed floor. "You are to never speak of our relation. You know this. How many times do I have to tell you? You're an abomination, a freak. You can't even walk straight. How would you kneel at the stone pool? You have to be clean to even enter the Temple of Ptah. How will the people trust you to heal them if you can't even heal yourself? You're a cripple and will die soon."

I bit my lip, clenched my jaw, and lifted my face to meet his. "I am strong. You and the others have said I will die by year's end ever since I can remember, but I live on. Let me help others. Teach me," I pleaded.

A glint flickered in his brown eyes and then softened. He took a quiet step toward me and wrapped my bared chest in his arms. He flinched, drawing his hand away from my back and side where bone had grown in place of skin after a particularly brutal scrape while wrestling with three older boys. That was when we learned the extent of my ailment; it was also the last time I played with others in the village. Senbi's hand settled on an undamaged portion of my back. I smiled and hugged him, feeling his aged ribs creak in my slender arms.

He hissed down to me, "You are unclean, cursed, and impure. You are a stain on my reputation... on my life."

The words hurt, but I'd grown used to hearing such things from the other boys. However, hearing it from my father was too much. I tried to stop the tears from welling in my eyes, but could more easily have straightened my contorted back. The only thing that hurt more was the sharp pain of something suddenly plunging into my side, just below my ribs.

Senbi angled his engraved, ivory tusk up and thrust it deeper, into my chest cavity. My breathing came in ragged gasps, and it felt as if I were drowning in the Iteru like I almost had years before, but this time there was no water to surface from. Warm liquid coursed down my side as he pulled his staff free.

"Why, Father?" I asked.

He let go of me and backed away as if I were a curse to be shooed away with one of his spells. "You have shamed me for too long, Nakhti. Why couldn't you just die? Now I will have to spend hours cleansing my wand of your cursed blood. It may never work right again."

I crumpled awkwardly to the floor, my stiff left leg jutting out while my eyes focused on the bloody wand with engravings of Ptah, Osiris, and other gods he often used for his spells. My blood dripped from its tip and coated half the wand. The engraved depictions stood out darker in the murky, red liquid, as though soaking in my essence. "But, Father—"

"Don't ever call me that, you cripple... you cursed fiend. You could never be a priest, and now you will no longer stand in Khu's way." Wiping the wand on a spare tunic that lay next to my sleeping mat, he muttered, "I need to at least make sure your spirit leaves. We can't have you hanging around causing trouble." Lifting his smeared wand in the air, he began chanting, waving, and leaping on one leg, calling to Anubis and Osiris."

While taking my final shallow breaths, I smiled as Senbi spoke the spell to reincarnate me in Ptah's image. Maybe I will be strong like the Apis bull.

* * *

My eyes fluttered open to find a muted conversation taking place between Dr. Kamal and Dr. Mayna. Their words slowly filtered to my ears, growing easier to comprehend, but before they noticed me once more, another gust of wind swept through the room with the words, "*Em hotep nefer*," floating on it as light as a candle flame.

Shaking off the fogginess that seemed to have renewed my alcohol-free hangover from the previous night, I said, "Dr. Kamal, what does '*Em hotep nefer*' mean?"

Their banter stopped as though an anvil had dropped, and they both stared at me. The Egyptian professor thought for a moment, his eyes drifting into the distance. Then he replied, "Be in great peace."

I smiled and muttered, "You too, Nakhti. You too."

"Don't tell me," Dr. Mayna quipped, "that was—"

"Nakhti," I supplied.

"A ghost, I was going to say."

I shrugged and nodded. "That too. Nakhti is the real name of the guy you call Curly. Dr. Kamal was right. Oh, and by the way, he didn't have curly hair. Didn't even make it past fifteen."

"What happened?" Dr. Kamal asked in his rich accent, his deep voice flushed with excitement. He and Dr. Mayna both leaned forward on stools that had appeared in my mental absence.

I readjusted myself on the stool and leaned over to glance out the window. The sun had moved a good distance farther into the sky and was now almost directly overhead. "Well," I said, turning back to the professors, "I get the feeling that Nakhti is happy someone took notice. Most of the time, the ghosts don't interact, but two of your three bodies have. They must've been waiting a long time."

We circled the stools and settled into a powwow between the recently vacated table and Nakhti's remains. "Okay, go on," he said, his dark his glittering under the phosphorescent lights in the stark room.

"Firstly, his bones weren't always like that."

Dr. Mayna gave me a quizzical look. "They had to be. I don't know of anything else it could be."

"Apparently he was born healthy, like anyone else—at least, that's the impression I got."

She frowned, having just gotten settled, and glanced back at the computer on her desk. "So, the bones grew over time?" she muttered, turning back to me, but I could tell she ached to search for the disease and discover what ailed young Nakhti.

"Yes. Any time Nakhti was injured, his body somehow grew bone there. That's what caused his back to twist and become partially covered in bone."

"All those extra pieces...?" she asked.

I nodded. "They were part of his back. His left leg was also basically fused together—at least, that's what it felt like."

"How did he die?" the Egyptian professor asked, greedy for answers.

I smiled, but it was a sorrowful memory. "While he didn't want to die, it was still a relief. The disease had been so hard on him that when Senbi—"

"Senbiwosret?" Dr. Kamal interrupted with a curious tilt to his bushy head.

I nodded.

"He was a high priest, wasn't he?" Dr. Mayna asked, her attention refocused on the story.

"Yes," Dr. Kamal and I said simultaneously. Then he glanced at me with a surprised, but knowing, smile. "He did much for his people. They lived on the outskirts of Giza, what they called Kher Neter, the Necropolis. He was also a trader and made a good living from what we can tell."

"At what cost?" I asked.

"What do you mean, Detective Drummond?" he inquired.

"I mean, his eldest son was Nakhtiokpara, and High Priest Senbi murdered him."

The Egyptian professor's eyes widened. "If that's true, then that would change a significant piece of Egyptian history, at least for the people of that region. I grew up near there, and his name is on the temple list of revered high priests."

"Well, if you really wanted to shock them, you could just

analyze his ceremonial wand. It was this large tusk with engravings running along its surface depicting the best forms of the gods."

"It is nice. I have seen it," Dr. Kamal said. "But what would that prove?"

"So it still exists? In my line of work, we call it the murder weapon."

His eyes widened further, this time threatening the boundaries of his thick eyebrows. "He wouldn't."

I nodded. "Stabbed Nakhti in the side with it, jabbed it up under his ribs and into his lung."

"But their wands were sacred."

"Yeah, but he called me—I mean, he called Nakhti cursed. He said having a son like that shamed him. When Nakhti expressed a desire to follow in his footsteps, to be a priest, Senbi took him in his arms and stabbed him from behind."

Both professors stared at me in shock.

"He did say he would have to clean his wand to try and cleanse it of Nakhti's cursed blood, but with any luck, it might still have traces in the grooves. I doubt it's still viable for DNA, but you might be able to at least prove it's human blood. That would be of some support to anyone interested in knowing the truth."

"They won't believe it, even if there is blood on the wand," Dr. Kamal mumbled.

"Well, you're probably right, but we can get started anyway," Dr. Mayna said, rising to her feet. "It's back in the gallery."

This time my eyes widened. "Seriously? Here?"

"Yep, everything uncovered by that archeological dig is here temporarily," she answered over her shoulder, heading back through the doors and toward the front. Dr. Kamal and I leapt up to follow.

In the dim light of the gallery, each artifact was illuminated by its own special set of lights inside the glass enclosures. Between a large Was staff and a carved depiction of a pharaoh's head sat the carved, ivory tusk I'd seen only minutes before. Dr. Mayna knelt before it, staring at the engravings. It looked just as it had in my vision, although I didn't get a good enough look to make out the details. Now I saw that a bull was pacing along one end, its rear replaced by another identical head. On the center and pointed half of the tusk were depictions of a stalking leopard, a spread-winged eagle, and what appeared to be a human-like lizard carrying a sword. The lizard creature even had a ruffled frill coursing down the center of its head and back, and its tongue flicked out from between its jagged teeth. The oddest part of the image, however, was that it seemed to be smiling. Looking at the thing sent a chill down my spine.

"I can't believe it's right here," I muttered, staring into the glass box. My side twinged, remembering the moment it entered my flesh, and I had to remind myself that was Nakhti, not me. I pointed a third of the way from the point. "The blood coated up to here."

"His name's on the back," Dr. Mayna said, watching the object with a look of wonder on her face, "along with engravings of other beasts."

"So will you test it?"

She nodded.

"But carefully," Dr. Kamal reminded her, "and under my supervision."

Her shoulders slumped an inch, but a moment later she smiled up at him.

We admired the staff a few minutes more and then returned to the sparsely decorated room. "So how will you convince them, Dr. Kamal?"

He shook his head. "I really don't know. First we'll see what we can find on the wand. Then we'll take it from there."

"I'm really not sure where to go from here either," Dr. Mayna mumbled, taking a seat in her computer chair and punching away at the keyboard. "I was curious as a child, but eventually gave it up, choosing scholarly science. However, I always wondered if there might be some truth to mysticism and ghosts. What you've told us is just incredible. It's really overwhelming," she continued, staring at the computer screen and multitasking, her voice a bit more distant. "I don't know how people react to your approach, Detective Drummond, but I'm sure they will be very skeptical."

"You can say that again," Dr. Kamal interjected in his thick, Egyptian accent while staring over her shoulder. "We will have to find proof to back up what you say."

I gave them a knowing smile. "That's the way I've had to work for years. Welcome to my world." After a brief pause, I asked,

"Have you ever read the ending of a book first?"

This caught their attention, and both of them turned from the monitor to look at me.

"It's like that. Given this ability, I know what happened and even who did it sometimes, but proving it is key. Knowing the ending can be a guide to let you know if you're going astray in the investigation, but you still have to find the evidence to connect the dots in between."

Dr. Mayna's eyebrows rose as she considered the analogy. "That's a pretty good way to look at it." Then she turned her attention back to the computer monitor and read through an article. Pointing at the screen, she said with excitement, "I think this is it. It's really rare, but it's like you said, the boy's body repaired itself by building more bone." She looked from me to the Egyptian professor expectantly.

Knowing she was waiting for one of us to ask, I bit. "So, what's it called?"

"Fibrodysplasia ossificans progressive."

Both of us stood stunned at the name. "Fibrodysplasia... right," I said. "I've heard of that."

"Yes, but this is a special type." She clicked the mouse a few times. "You wouldn't believe some of the pictures they've got up here."

Dr. Kamal leaned in, his chest hovering next to Dr. Mayna's ear. Morbid curiosity got the best of me, and I came around to join them. The pictures were gruesome: contorted backs, fused bones, and bone overlapping skin in various places. While accustomed to seeing dead bodies, these depictions of what people had to live with, and the knowledge of just how difficult it was to move from Nakhti's memory, left me unsettled. "Looks like you found Nakhti's curse," I mumbled.

Over the next few minutes, the two professors took notes on the remaining details of the vision. Dr. Kamal informed me that if I was ever in Egypt, to look him up. He was certain he had some things he'd like me to *examine*. I gave them both my card, and we parted ways soon after, because a feeling kept gripping my stomach around the middle, pressing me about something else I'd been putting off: Greg Rayson and Evie.

* * *

In the car on the way to Jessie's, I finally made a decision. Flipping open my cell at a stoplight, I pulled Rollen's card out of my coat pocket and dialed his number.

"Rollen," he answered after two rings.

"Hey, Keen. This is Alex Drummond. We spoke the other day."

"Yeah, good to hear from ya. How's the investigation going?"

The light turned green, and I went with the flow of traffic. "It's taken a few twists and a curve ball, but I'm getting closer. I have one more suspect up here. She's involved somehow, but I haven't quite figured out the details." I thought about having Keen look into her, but it occurred to me that I still didn't know her last name. "Looks like I'm probably gonna have to head home before the twentieth and begin the search again down there, depending on what I find out later today. But I've got some information for you on a separate case that I saw on the television."

"Oh yeah. What's that?" he asked.

"Evelyn Cervantes, the girl who went missing about a week ago, I know where she's at."

Rollen said, "I thought you might." His tone was enough for me to know he was smiling. "When you told me to look into that Greg Rayson character, I thought it had to do with your case, but then this afternoon, in walks Mr. Rayson to confess."

The words surprised me, and I had to slam on the breaks to keep from hitting the slowing car ahead. "He did what?"

"He walked right into the precinct, seemed happy to do it, too. I get the feeling that man's conscience has been weighing heavily. He's lost more poundage than any weight-loss program could hope for, especially in a week. I just took a look at his driver's license and could tell."

"Yeah," I agreed, "I only met him once, but I could tell he wasn't doing well, looked like he was on his last leg. You know he didn't do it on purpose though, right?"

"I'm sure you're right, but I don't got a say in that. I'll put in a word for him with the DA's office. They should show him some leniency, but he ain't gonna shrug the delinquency charge. He confessed to that. Considering he got her drunk, he could go away for a long while. If Mrs. Sanchez pushes it and goes for statutory rape, it could be even longer."

I doubted she'd go for that, knowing the legal status of her and her workers. She probably wouldn't want to make it out to be any bigger than it already was, but anger often makes people do irrational things. However, unsure of what Sergeant Keenan Rollen had on Mrs. Sanchez, I didn't want to give him ammunition to go looking. "She could. Rayson's been through a lot already. Hopefully he can deal with this."

"Well, like it or not, he's goin' to. Honestly, the way he came waltzin' in here, I think he made peace with his past and accepted whatever comes his way. He was still depressed, but knew he was doin' the right thing. How long you been sittin' on this information, anyhow?"

I didn't want to admit it, but he was right. I'd been sitting on it far too long. "Uh-h-h," I stuttered into the phone. "You caught me. About twenty-four hours."

"Figured as much," Rollen said. "It's those hard ones that make us really question whether what we're doin' is right. Glad you came around to your senses though. How'd you figure it out anyway?"

This was the question I'd been dreading. "Keen, you wouldn't believe me if I told you, so I'm not gonna try."

"Detective, you're one of those mysterious guys, aren't you?"

"You might say that, but I get the job done and don't break any laws doin' it." My thoughts went back to Irene's house and a jolt shot through my gut as once again I remembered turning around to see the smiling face and waving hand of a neighborhood girl. The lie settled on my shoulders, and I knew Jessie had been right.

Gotta watch those lines.

"Well, keep it up," Rollen replied. "Got any other juicy info?"

"Nah, nothing else. Gotta see what I can find out about this last suspect and talk to a friend, then I'm on a flight home." I pulled onto Jessie's street and into a spot.

"Sounds good, Drummond. If you're ever up this way again, let me know. We'll get a drink. Some day you gotta tell me how you're getting this information."

"Sure thing," I replied.

Folding my phone closed, I slipped it into my pocket and noticed Jessie's truck parked a few spots away. The passenger-side door was open and a suitcase was resting on the seat. *Ahhh, Jess, what are you doin'?* I bolted up the stairs and into the apartment. "Jessie!" I shouted.

"Alex," came his voice from the far bedroom. "I thought you were gonna call me."

"Yeah I was. Just got off the phone with Rollen," I said, throwing my overcoat onto the end of the couch.

Jessie came into the living room with two more bags, a small, bathroom travel case, and a laptop bag. "You're just in time. I'm meetin' Liz at the Metro. We're eloping."

I held up my hands. "No, Jess. Just stop."

"The hell I will," he shot back, "and if you try any of that bullshit about tattoos, I swear I'm gonna slap ya."

The promise gave me pause, not due to its violence, but the reference to tattoos. "What are you talking about?"

"Look, I know why you wanted me to come home the other night, but we're in love. This infatuation you've got with ankh tattoos is too much. Just 'cause she's got one too doesn't mean anything."

She's got one too? I wanted to ask, but that would give it away. Jessie still had some unexplained things to fess up to; that much was obvious. Playing along, I said, "But how much do you really know about this girl? You've known her for what, a couple months?"

Jessie shrugged, but set down the laptop case as he thought. "The better part of a year now." After saying as much, he paused and mumbled, "Has it really been that long?" His widening eyes confirmed the math.

"And are you sure you know her well enough?"

"Yes, I'm sure," Jessie said, glowering, his tone stern. He grabbed the bag handle again and strode toward the door.

"Jess, wait," I said, following behind. "It wasn't the tattoo that concerned me."

"So what was it, how she slapped your butt? Come on, man. I like 'em a little freaky. You know that," he confessed, stopping in front of the door.

He was right there. I wasn't concerned about the monogamy aspect, at least not too much. They were practically a perfect fit. "It's not that either. Look, when I touched her ring, I had a vision— well, not just one vision, fifteen visions."

"Bullshit!" Jessie shouted over his shoulder and swung the door wide.

"Why do you think I couldn't stand up straight afterward? Why else would I have had to struggle home and pass out on the couch? Damn, Jessie! I woke up this morning with a pounding headache worse than any hangover, and I didn't have a drop to drink."

This stopped Jessie. He turned to look at me, a considering look on his face. "No joke?"

I nodded. "No joke. Come back inside. We just gotta talk for a couple minutes."

Jess lifted a wrist and peered at his watch. "Alright, I've got a few minutes, but you're not stopping me from catching that train."

"Okay, but hear me out," I said, stepping out of his way so he could get past. I shut the door, locked the deadbolt, and we returned to the living room. If he was determined to get out, I wouldn't physically stop him unless my hand was forced, but I most certainly wasn't going to make it easy.

Chapter 16

Revelations

September 17, 2011

SETTING HIS BAGS DOWN, Jessie slumped onto the couch. "So, what were the visions about?"

I wiped my eyes with my thumb and forefinger and lowered myself into the recliner. After collecting my thoughts, I asked, "How many murders were there?"

Jessie gave me a curious look. I waved my hand in circles, motioning for him to answer. "Fourteen," he said, "not counting Irene's husband."

"Right, and how many visions did I say I had last night?"

"Fif—" he answered, pausing as he made the connection, "teen." His face brightened, and he looked at me with more concern. "Are you serious? That means the ring had to be present at all of the murders, right?"

I nodded.

"On all of those dead guys' fingers?"

His eyes pleaded for me to say no, but I couldn't lie. I nodded once more.

"Then how'd Liz get hold of somethin' like that?"

"I don't know," I said with a shrug. "Trust me, I don't want to think she had anything to do with it, but that can't be ruled out."

Jessie quirked an eyebrow at my mention of her potential involvement.

"However, let's put that on the back burner and not jump to conclusions."

The look vanished. "Yeah, 'cause there's gotta be a perfectly good explanation for this. She's not that kind of woman. She's crazy, but in a good way—my kind of crazy," he said with a smile, his eyes distant, remembering something specific.

I cleared my throat and got his attention. "Right, so when did she get the ring?" I asked.

"Liz and her ex got them from a pawn shop, because it was cheaper. Neither of them could afford much at the time."

"Jesus, then that leaves any number of people it could have belonged to. When did they get it and where?"

Jessie thought for a moment. "She said it was about a year before we met, so around December or January of '09," he said, sounding less than certain.

"You sure?"

"As good as I can be."

"Crap! That's after the last victim."

Jessie glared at me. "Whose side are you on?"

I winced. "Sorry. It's not that I want her to be guilty. I really hope she isn't involved. You're just shootin' holes in my theories, leavin' me with more questions than answers."

"Sorry to shoot down your theories, Alex, but I'm glad to hear Liz isn't the one."

"Wait—where did she get it?"

"Some shop back home, I guess."

"Colorado?"

"Yeah, I don't think she moved up here until after things went south with him."

"By going south, you mean, when he died?"

Jessie nodded quietly.

I pressed my head into my hands and massaged my temples with my thumbs. *It doesn't make sense. How'd the ring get to Colorado in less than a couple months and then happen to make its way here?*

"Why do you think there was a fifteenth vision?" he asked, doing the math.

I shook my head. "The ring must have been in contact with that boy."

"It was a boy?"

"Yep, some kid playing around like he was one of those monks in orange, the ones that set themselves on fire."

"Buddhist monks protesting Vietnam... yeah, I remember. That's damned weird, but evidently that ring came from somewhere far off. Look, Al, I gotta go. I get it—this ring." He shook his hand, fingers splayed. "It's been through some gruesome stuff, but that doesn't mean my fiancée is guilty of serial murder." He looked at the ring once more and gave a visible shiver. Then he got to his feet and picked up his bags. "I know it's freaky, but Liz gave it to me. I'm gonna be wearing it for the rest of my life, and now I really wish you hadn't told me."

The thought of what he must be feeling made me shrink inside. I hated having hurt one of my best friends, but it still didn't add up. "Something's not right, Jess. You know that. What is Liz's last name anyway?"

"I do, but I also know that Liz is innocent. What are you going to do with her last name, look her up and judge her based on her past?"

"Yes, I'm going to look her up," I stated in frustration, "but her past will speak for itself. It will either exonerate her or incriminate, depending only on the truth. That's all I'm looking for here, Jess, the truth."

"Alright, but if you ruin this for me, so help me..."

I held up a hand to forestall the statement. "The truth shall set you free."

Jessie rolled his eyes. "Only because it's you, and I know you're thorough. You and I both know cops that will twist the truth to make it fit into their pretty, little theories."

"Thanks, Jess. I appreciate your confidence."

"It's Reider... Elizabeth Reider, and I don't have time to sit around and help you figure this stuff out. This is my time for happiness, Alex. I've been waitin' for years, and now it's happened—to me. Dr. Kamal was right. Life's too short. You've gotta seize what's right in front of you."

"I realize," I said with a grin. "Carpe diem, my friend, carpe diem."

Jessie smiled. "Horace, right?"

"Yep." We exchanged knowing smiles, remembering Mr. Broaderick, the English teacher who preached that phrase, among others, throughout the year. "Take care, Jess. Where're y'all heading?"

Jessie shrugged. "Not sure. We're gonna pick a random flight when we get there. It's kind of exciting." As he strode out the door, he said, "Be sure and turn off the lights and lock the door. Don't know when I'll be back."

Then the door closed, and I jumped up from my seat. Grabbing my coat off the couch arm, I slipped out the door when Jessie's sun-dried, green and white truck began pulling out of his parking spot. I took the stairs two at a time, my car keys in hand. By the time I pulled out, I could still see Jessie's truck cab looming above the roofs of the four cars between us. "Don't look back," I mumbled to the silent car through clenched teeth. "Don't look back."

The nearest Metro station was a few miles away, and I followed him into long-term parking, maintaining my distance. Grabbing my fedora, I leapt from the car once he passed a few aisles of cars ahead. Having overcome my naïveté during my previous trip, I quickly followed him through the gates of the Vienna Metro Station and the turnstile, down the escalator, and over the brown tile. He made it to the appropriate stop just as a large group of travelers were entering the Metro car. Jessie peered through the windows until he spotted a casually dressed Liz waving in a burgundy sweater. A large, offset collar spilt over her right shoulder. He stepped inside, and I entered the far end with a small crowd of stragglers. Taking a seat in the back, I tilted my hat down over my face and kept the two lovebirds in sight.

They sat in a section of available seats facing the center aisle. Each of them smiled and held hands while Liz whispered in Jessie's ear, her right hand playing up under the sleeve of his jacket. At the next stop, I moved closer, but kept four rows of seats between us, keeping my head down and grabbing a newspaper off a free seat. They were so absorbed in each other that I probably could have sat across from them, but that would have just been asking for trouble. A multitude of voices and people surrounded us: a well-dressed man talking on his smartphone, others heading home from the office, a couple ladies in pizzeria outfits who must have been on the way home, and even couples enjoying a vacation to the capital. The cacophony of muttering voices made it impossible to hear Liz and Jessie's whispered conversation well, but when he grabbed her wrist and jerked her hand out of his sleeve, his sharp reply of "Stop!" was clear and even drew glances from the nearby passengers.

He closed his eyes for a moment, took a deep breath, and said, "Please don't."

"Why?" she asked, cocking her head slightly.

"It's a scar... from something I don't like to think...," he explained, but his voice calmed and became indiscernible.

"Can I see?" she asked. I was unable to hear it completely, but watched her mouth the words.

Jessie's shoulders slumped, but he shrugged out of the blue jacket and rolled up his sleeve. My eyes widened as a four-inch-tall, dark shape appeared there, covered in scar tissue. It was the same as I'd seen in each of the visions: the ankh.

What the hell? I'd never seen it before, but come to think of it, I hadn't seen him without a long-sleeve shirt since fall of our high-school senior year.

Liz ran two fingers over the scar, slowly, as though savoring the touch, and a visible shudder ran through Jessie. He brushed her hand away. "Now, how come I never saw that?" she asked. "I've seen every..." This time her face disappeared behind Jessie's, and I couldn't make out the rest of what was said.

So she is surprised.

I shook my head, disappointed. She continued to caress the scar and Jessie gave in. She even lightly grabbed his arm as they talked, and then held her hand over the brand, glancing down at his arm when Jessie wasn't watching.

Something's off here. This doesn't feel right.

They whispered a bit more, the conversation going back to various things I could barely make out, but when she said, "Back at Madessa High, Grandma wouldn't let..." I couldn't help myself and leapt into the aisle, rushing toward them.

Jessie stood up and stared down at her. "Madessa High School?" he demanded.

Her eyes widened when he repeated the name, but she tried to play it off with a wave of her hand until she spotted me come to a stop next to Jessie. "You were spying on me?" she screamed at me.

Jessie looked and did a double take. "What the hell are you doin' here?" He glanced from me to her. "And I thought you were from Colorado."

She slumped in her chair and stared at the floor, her hands folding across her belly in an attempt to hug herself. Then she began sobbing. "I th-thought you loved me, Jessie. Wh-why does it m-matter where I'm from?"

"It doesn't, doll, but if you're lyin' to me, then that's different. I love you and want to spend the rest of my life together, but we can't have secrets from one another." Turning a condescending gaze on me, he said, "And you. What the hell gives you the right to follow me?"

"I had your best interest in mind, Jess. You know that," I replied, feeling the awkward silence of the other passengers watching this performance worthy of Jerry Springer.

"Maybe, but you sure as hell don't trust me, either." Waving a hand at his fiancée, he said, "This is what I want. Liz is what I want."

When she heard this, she looked up at him with a tearful smile and reddened eyes. "I love you too, and I wanna spend the rest of my life with you. Let's go. We'll leave Alex here. We can get off at the next stop," she said, quickly grabbing her leather purse and standing. She began rooting around in it.

Shifting my jacket so I had access to my holstered pistol, I said, "Please put the purse d—"

But Jessie interrupted, saying, "Alex, I can't believe you!" Disappointment tinged his voice. He shook his head. "I just don't think this is going to work," he mumbled. I tried to keep an eye on Liz, but his words pulled my mind back. "If you can't let me be happy, then I can't deal with you anymore..."

"But what about Madessa High?" I asked, and he stopped rambling. Both of us turned to look at Liz.

She peered up from her purse. Her wide eyes glared at me. "You think you can ruin my life, everything I've worked for? All I've ever done has been for other people, and I finally find the right man, and you just have to come along and ruin it."

"You said, 'Madessa High'," I repeated in a calm, regulated voice. "You obviously aren't from Colorado."

"I am too! There's more than one school named Madessa." Her eyes moved to Jessie's face, and her determination faltered. Her gaze fell and she mumbled, "It is Madessa High School, and you're right, I'm not from Colorado. I'm from Tranquil Heights, just like you."

"And you murdered fourteen people," I said, staring holes through her.

Her head flew up, and with brown, red-rimmed eyes blazing with hatred, she pulled a nine-millimeter pistol from her purse and leveled it at my chest from barely two feet away. It looked much like my own. My free hand subtly felt my side. The holster was occupied, and I breathed a silent sigh of relief.

Jessie's eyes went wide as saucers, as did most people in the train, but the shock of the moment left them stunned. "Jessie, honey, you coming?" she asked, turning loving eyes on him that glanced back at me a moment later, again filled with hatred. The quick emotional change at a split-second's notice and her steady aim caught me off guard, but told me she was capable with the weapon.

"B-baby," Jessie stuttered. "Why'd you go and do that?"

"What else could I do? He was going to put me in jail."

Jessie shook his head and looked at me. "Alex wouldn't do that, not unless you really kill—" Stopping himself, I watched the denial slide away from his eyes. He turned back to Liz, who was backing toward the door, but maintaining a solid grasp on the handholds with her free hand. A pained look infused Jessie's face. "You didn't really do it, did you?"

It seemed as though a pin drop could be heard throughout the Metro car. The slight muttering that had begun stopped to await her answer.

She nodded. "I did, but that doesn't change who I am. I'm still the woman you fell in love with, Jessie." At the acknowledgement of her murders, people began to scatter, jumping over seats, panicking and screaming.

"You can't do this, baby," Jessie said, pleading, both hands rising to frame her face as if in slow motion. Tears streamed from his eyes, and a pain-filled grin of denial plastered itself across his face. "I love you. You can't have done this."

"I did, but if you love me, we can be together. Come with me."

"I... I c-can't," Jessie stammered, shaking his head. "Not like this."

The heartbreaking moment was instantly contagious, and Liz's face contorted in grief and then rage. "But you love me!"

Jessie nodded. "With all my heart, but you can't do this. Killing those people wasn't right. Some were even my friends."

For a moment Liz seemed to feel his pain, her face pitying him, but then rage took over once more. Turning her hate-filled eyes on me, she said, "You're to blame for this. If not for you, I could have been happy—we could have been happy!" She was at the edge of the doorway now, waiting for the doors to open so she could make her escape as the other passengers ran past, trying to get as far from her as possible. Then, someone hit the emergency brake. The train wheels screeched and flung passengers forward just as the shot rang out. I ducked, but felt nothing. When I looked up a second later, Jessie had collapsed to the floor clutching his chest. Liz stared at him dumbstruck, then turned her dark orbs back to me, all evidence of humanity and rational thought seemingly gone from her. With a crazed look, she lifted the gun.

I dove at her, knocking it away and shoving her into the doorway alcove. Seeing the blood blossoming on Jessie's shirt and blue coat, my training disassembled like the tumbling of a Jenga tower. I began punching, kneeing, and kicking her folded form as the train shuddered. Lifting myself in the unsteady Metro car, I silently wished I had a sledgehammer to make each hit that much more painful. She curled up as I rained blow after blow into her slender form. Adrenaline coursed through my veins, pulsing like lava and feeding my rage. Pulling my nine-millimeter Smith and Wesson, I aimed it at her prone form, my finger caressing the cold trigger with desire.

"Alex," rasped a weak voice from behind me.

It took a few seconds for the owner of the voice's identity to sink in, and I turned to find Jessie reaching out to me, his bloody hand wavering as he lay in the aisle. Shock blossomed in my mind at the sight of his weak, wounded state. The blood sent what felt like a host of spiders running down my spine and clutched at the pit of my stomach. The wound was bad, worse than I thought. Fury raged inside me as I peered down at Liz's unmoving form. I forced my gun back into its holster and pulled a pair of handcuffs, attaching her wrist to the handle railing. Grabbing her gun off the floor, I rushed to Jessie's side, collapsing to my knees as the train came to a noisy halt. The folding doors opened, but she wasn't going anywhere, especially handcuffed.

Jessie's slick fingers trembled against my cheek and gained my full attention. His usually tanned complexion was taking on a paler hue, and I bundled up the loose folds of his shirt and jacket, applying pressure over the wound. Fortunately, it was the right side of his chest, not the left, so it wasn't near his heart. However, I could tell the bullet had pierced his lung. Blood coated his lips, and his breathing was ragged.

"Does it take long?" he asked, gripping my hand over the bundled folds.

Knowing what he was referring to and being all too familiar with it, I couldn't stop my own tears. I clenched my lips and jaw, struggling to stay strong while I pulled out my phone with my free hand and dialed 9-1-1. "No, it doesn't." I shook my head. "But you're not leaving us, not yet," I swore. The other passengers picked themselves up and ran for the doors, or huddled by the walls, chairs, and the far end of the car.

Jessie gave a haggard chuckle that turned into a bloody cough. "Not s-so sure about that," he stammered in a faint voice and squeezed my hand.

"I am. You aren't going anywhere, Jess, except the hospital."

Lifting the phone to my ear, the woman's voice asked, "What's your emergency?"

"I have a man down on the orange Metro line, around station..." I looked to the huddled passengers remaining.

A man with a skeletal-print shirt and shaved head supplied, "East Fall's Church."

"Near East Fall's Church Station," I told her. "Hispanic male with a GSW to the chest. It looks to have pierced his lung. Send medics. The shooter is in custo-dy..." My final words died off as I glanced at the Metro car door. The hollow tube of railing I'd attached the cuffs to was bent and had dislodged from the wall. Liz was nowhere to be seen. *How the hell?* I wondered. *She must not have been as unconscious as I thought, and with all the noise... Dammit!* The voice on the phone refocused my attention.

"Emergency services are on their way. Did you say the shooter was in custody?"

I licked my dry lips. "No, not anymore. She escaped. The shooter's a brunette in her late twenties, five-foot seven, wearing jeans and a burgundy sweater. She goes by Liz Reider. She's armed and dangerous."

"Thank you, sir. Please stay on the line..."

I sat the phone down on the floor and turned my attention back to Jessie. His eyes wavered, trying to focus on me, and they were getting glassy. "Stay with me, bud. Help's on the way." I would have to find Liz later.

"I l-loved her, Alex," he mumbled.

"I know," I whispered. "I know."

"But I—I never knew."

"Knew what?"

"That's Shelley."

"Shelley who?" Confused, I watched as he tried to explain.

"Sh-she was a freshman wh-when I was a senior. We all took turns, and g-got these." His glazed eyes looked down at the revealed scar of the ankh on his forearm. We got together at Greg's lake house. I j-joined in, havin' some fun, but only once. We all t-took turns with h-her. We even w-went out once before I gradu-uated."

"You and Shelley?"

He gave a shaky nod.

"And Shelley is Liz?"

Another shaky nod. He hiccoughed and gave a partial cough,

wincing.

"Stay with me, Jess. The fat lady ain't singin' yet."

He chuckled, or tried to. Just then, bobbing lights and footsteps echoed through the tunnel on gravel; a pair of uniformed Metro officers and three medics tramped up the stairs and into the car.

"The cavalry's here, Jess. Stay with us. You're gonna make it." I slid my hand out of his and shuffled to the side so the emergency team could get to him. However, I hovered nearby, watching every move they made. One grabbed Jessie, muttering about C-spine and getting a pulse, while the other checked my friend's airway and ripped open his shirt. The third medic mopped away the blood and slapped a large bandage over the wound in his chest and the exit wound in his back. But he kept Jessie's attention. "Are you in pain?"

Jessie nodded.

"Got any allergies?"

Jessie shook his head, but remained focused on the third medic, their eyes never parting.

The questions continued, things I could have answered like, "Are there any drugs in your system?" However, I'd heard it all before at many crime scenes. They had to cover everything and keep his attention. The world seemed to have slowed, but they worked at a fast pace, like a well-oiled machine, operating in tandem. Before I knew it, they had an oxygen mask over Jessie's mouth and were hoisting him onto a body board.

I followed them out of the train, worried about my life-long friend, but his confession plagued me. *They all took turns.* I shook my head at the grotesque images that came to mind. She was barely in high school. Then the rest of the confession came to mind. *Shelly is Liz.* My thoughts wondered to Shelley, the young ninth grader we'd interviewed so many years before.

Chapter 17

Choices

September 17, 2011

SHE HAD TO have had help, I concluded. No girl her age could have done those things, especially one as puny as she was. The repetitive beep of the heart monitor echoed from inside the curtained room. A host of doctors and nurses bustled around Jessie's medical bed, the swinging curtain offering only a fleeting view here and there. I'd followed him this far, but even a badge didn't get me past the E.R. bay curtains. *Come on Jess. You can't leave me, bud. I'll get that murderer. You know I will.* He could be as stubborn as a mule from time to time. I just hoped this was one of those times.

My mind going yet again to Liz, or Shelley, I flipped open my phone and dialed Hector's number.

"Martinez here."

"Martinez, it's me," I said, trying to get his attention as quickly as possible.

"Alex, aren't you supposed to be on the way here?"

"No, not yet. Nine o'clock, remember? That's not why I'm calling, though."

"What's up? Somethin' wrong?"

"Yeah." I sighed. "She shot Jessie."

"What? Who?" Martinez exclaimed.

I paused, panting as I tried to collect my thoughts. After almost sixteen years of looking, we almost had her. While frightened at the prospect of losing one of my best friends, the detective in me was on the edge of his seat. "Liz Reider. She probably went by Shelley years ago. I think she might have had help though."

"Alright, I'll see what I can dig up. I just wish we'd caught her before it became such a horrible spree."

My shoulders slumped. "Me too. I can't help but wonder if someone would have caught on before, how many lives could we have saved?" *I also wish Jessie had told me before. If only his shame about being involved hadn't clouded his judgment.*

Hector's tone became concerned. "You'll drive yourself nuts thinking like that. It wasn't your fault. You broke the case. Who knows how many lives you've saved?"

I wasn't so sure about that. "Hec, no one was killed last year."

"You don't know for sure. This could have gone on forever. Even if someone wasn't, serial killers don't just say, 'Eh, murdering's gotten kind of old now. Why don't I take up wind surfing?' It just doesn't happen. You know that it always gets worse."

I nodded to no one in particular. "I get the feeling this was more religious than anything. Fourteen seems to be her lucky number, or seven to be precise."

"Seven?"

"Yeah, don't worry about it. I'll fill you in later."

"Okay, but what concerns me is this: is Jessie gonna be number fifteen?"

"I hope not. They're working on him right now."

"You see, it's never over, Alex."

He was right and I knew it, but I still couldn't rid myself of that nagging question. "So will you look into Liz? She got away tonight and knows I'm onto her. I don't know what she'll do or where she'll go."

"I'll check the airports and her financial records. I'm sure Tullings will okay a rush on it, too. Give me a few minutes, and I'll get back to you."

"Sounds good. You can coordinate with Sergeant Rollen," I said, giving him Keenan's number and listening to the medical chatter echoing from the room. A distinct sound caught my attention and Martinez's voice became a dull buzz.

"Clear!" said a female behind the curtain, followed by a silence disturbed only by a *phwoosh* sound.

My phone dropped to the floor, clattering on the tile. *Come on, Jess. Stay with me, buddy.* I swear I heard the paddles' humming as they charged.

"Clear!" she said again. *Phwoosh.*

There was a brief commotion behind the curtain. Then she shouted, "Again!"

Tears drizzled from my eyes, and my jaw clenched. "I'll get you, you little bitch! You're mine now," I spat, hoping she heard me, wherever she was. Snatching my phone off the ground, I slapped it closed and stormed out of the hospital, intent on finding her if it was the last thing I did.

* * *

For the next hour, I sped down streets near the Metro station and even found myself doing laps at Reagan National, but the effort seemed futile and infuriated me more than anything. However, I had to do something. Fortunately, on my fifth lap around the airport, my cell phone rang. The digital screen read 'Martinez.'

"What ya got for me, Hec?" I demanded, spinning the wheel around another corner, avoiding the passengers crossing the road.

"Well, you're not gonna believe this."

My patience had been shredded. "Try me," was all I said.

"Shelley Reider was previously known as Shelley Rayson."

I slammed on my brakes, skidding to a halt behind a parked taxi. Piecing together the parts and connecting the dots, the inordinate coincidences took shape. "Jesus!"

"Yep, I know what you mean, and I checked out Easely this morning. She seems like an abrupt old woman and a little rude, but I can't find anything wrong with her besides the fact that she raised a serial killer."

I wished she did have something to do with it. It would have answered a lot of questions, but Hector had a good head for people. Shelley, or Liz as she was now called, must have been the product of such a harsh woman's upbringing, combined with the loss of her entire family. "Any word on Liz?"

"Yeah, something, but I don't think you're going to like it,"

Martinez added. "Liz boarded a seven-o'clock flight coming here..." He paused, then said, "She landed fifteen minutes ago, Alex. Is she running home to hide?"

"Go back and see if she went to Easely's house. She might have done just that." I didn't believe it, but that would be the best place to check. My heart began pounding in my ears like war drums prefacing inevitability as the true reason for fleeing to Tranquil Heights came to mind. "But...," I began, hesitating, "I don't think that's why she went home, Hec. She knows we're onto her. She's too smart to do something so stupid. Remember, she hid from us for over fifteen years. She blames me for losing Jessie. That's the real reason."

"Oh man," he muttered. "You know what that means?"

There was no question in my mind. "Paige and Jamie. Get a cruiser to the house, quick!"

"On it."

"And put out an APB out on Liz. I'll be there a little after ten."

"Already did," Hector replied. "Just get here. Lieutenant Tullings will submit the NLET, so you won't have to worry about that happy-ass procedure of waiting for them to get your pistol out of the lockbox when you get in. I'll go check on your family myself."

"Thanks, Hector," I said, meaning it with all of my heart. Ending the call, I speed dialed Paige. It rang and rang, but no one answered. Leaping out of the car, I tried again while rushing to the teller. Still no answer.

Striding past the line of customers, I flashed my badge at the pudgy, middle-age agent and asked, "You have a sooner flight than nine to Tranquil Heights?"

"What state is that?" she asked in a pleasant, patient tone.

Any tolerance I had left vanished with the unanswered phone calls. "Virginia!"

She blanched.

"Sorry, but it's life or death. Do you have anything sooner?"

"No, sir," she said promptly. "They'll begin loading for the nine-o'clock flight in about twenty minutes though."

Pulling my ticket from my pocket, I jogged to customs, checking in at the side entrance for special personnel and making it to my gate before they began loading. Struggling to keep my cool while my thoughts ran laps that would have put a roadrunner to shame, I paced in front of the boarding counter, hoping and praying.

* * *

When I stepped out of the glass doors of the Tranquil Heights Airport, I found a frantic Hector Martinez standing just out of the driver's seat of his brown and white police cruiser. He banged on the roof with one hand and waved for me to come with the other. "Alex, get over here!" he shouted. "Forget your car, we'll get it later."

I ran to the curb and threw my bag into the backseat, removing my hat as I folded myself into the passenger seat. I'd never seen him this anxious. Something was very wrong. Before I slammed the door closed, the cruiser shot into traffic. "Did you find Paige and

Jamie?" I demanded.

He spared a glance before returning his gaze to the traffic whizzing by. His eyes held pity and concern, having watched Jamie grow up and often joined us for holidays. His silent answer was more worrying than anything he could have said.

"Tell me you haven't found their..." I couldn't quite put the horrid thought into words, but another look from Hector told me he understood. "At least then I'll know there's hope."

He shook his head. "No worries there. We haven't come across them, but that's also the problem. They're missing."

I slammed a fist against the car door. "They've gotta be close. Did you check the Easely place?"

"Yeah, we even got a search warrant. Tore the house apart, but no dice."

I thought for a minute, remembering Jessie's last confession: *We got together at Greg's lake house.* "Remember Greg Dihler, Mayor Dihler's son?"

Hector quirked an eyebrow. "Of course. What of him?"

"Mayor Dihler has a lake house where she met the other victims."

"Up at Mountain View Lake?"

"Yeah, probably."

"Put a call in and see. A lake house would be someplace no one would think to look normally." He handed me the walkie-talkie.

I reported in and asked. Taylor, our dispatcher, came back a few minutes later. "281 Trout Road. It's good to have you back,

Drummond." Her voice was cheery, but held a wary tremble and pitying tone.

Hearing the address, Martinez shoved down the gas pedal, and the car revved forward. "We'll be there in less than ten," he mumbled, eyes peeled as the car shot over the slight hills. Flicking a button, the siren wailed, and red and blue lights shimmered off the buildings and windowpanes flowing past.

"Thanks, Taylor. I just hope it's in time."

"We're doin' everything we can on our end, sugar. Every officer is out searchin' the streets and followin' any potential leads. You need backup? I can pull a car if you want."

I glanced at Hector, who grimaced at the question. There are only a dozen officers in the entire department. Pulling one car could be the difference between finding them dead or alive. "No, not yet," I answered above the siren. "We're pretty sure, but best not put all our eggs in one basket yet. We'll get back to you if we need it."

"Sounds good, honey," Taylor replied, her local drawl always present. "You watch yourself."

"We will. Take care."

I sat the handset in its cradle in the middle compartment. Within a couple minutes, the town's streetlights and lines of small shops along main were dwindling in the rearview mirror. Slowing to forty-five, tires squealed as Hector spun the wheel. Then the car roared up a 60 degree incline of asphalt curves. Tall and slender pines and oaks flitted by along the edges of the road, the headlights barely grazing their trunks and lower branches. Piles of dead leaves fluttered behind as the large, modified engine gave it all she had.

"Now that's my baby," Martinez said with pride, sparing a second on a short straightaway to pet the gray dash. "She'll give any muscle car a run for its money."

I nodded, but my thoughts were elsewhere. Memories of Paige flew through my mind: the times we spent together in college working various cases and suspicious deaths, the few times I saw her illuminated by the autumn sun in front of the bowling alley, her glowing face saying, "Yes! Yes! Yes!" after I proposed, and the first time I held Jamie. I stared into the fleeting darkness until the asphalt turned to packed dirt rumbling beneath the tires. The smell of burning timber filtered through the vents and windows. Hector took a few back-road turns. Then my eyes widened and heart began to race as we slid to a stop in front of a large, three-story log cabin. Motion lights flared to life, illuminating the three-car garage and front of the house.

"Government office pays well," Hector said with a tinge of contempt, craning his neck forward to look at the roof through the windshield.

I jumped out of the car to stare, but not at the height, at the flames leaping from the windows upstairs. "Call it in, Hec. This place ain't burning by chance."

Hec yelled, "What are ya going to do, kick down the door?"

The thought had occurred to me. Tullings had said, *by any*

means necessary, although like the trip to DC, this might not qualify under his definition. "Damn straight," I replied, pulling my nine-millimeter.

I took the front porch steps two at a time. The stained wood groaned beneath me from a bit of weathering, but remained steady. Small rows of glass windows bordered both sides of the front door. I glanced in, but was surprised to see little inside but a carpeted, smoke-filled room. Slipping my hand inside a coat sleeve, I tried the handle. The door was unlocked and opened with a slow creak, swinging inward. *Either the mayor is very trusting, or someone's expecting me.* Gusts of smoke drifted out the top of the door, but didn't seem to have completely filled the house yet. However, they flared to life with the cool breeze drifting inside.

I took a deep breath, then dashed into the house, using my free hand to guide myself past the stairway and along the wall. I peeked around the corner into the living room. Smoke swirled higher in the large, three-story-high room, shrouding the beams above, but only obscuring the lower floor partially. Flames licked at the walls and the stairway steps, crackling and singeing the large, peaked house.

The television burst to life the moment I stepped in the room. "Alex," said a two-dimensional image of Liz standing in a dark forest, one solitary lantern suspended from a wooden crook like at most state campsites. A picnic table even sat to her right. Knowing she and Shelley were one and the same now, I thought I could make out the faint freckles that had littered her nose and cheeks in high school, but it was probably my imagination. She'd changed a lot. She wore the same blue jeans and work boots from the visions, but instead of an Anubis head, her wavy hair dangled over the same burgundy sweater she'd worn earlier.

"I'm glad to see you made it in time. I never doubted your abilities, but I must say that the last dozen years have made me wonder if you still had it in you."

There was a pause as shadows played across her face in the dim light of the lantern. It was as if she were waiting for me to say something. I opened my mouth, knowing she could be watching through a video camera or some such, but then she continued. "Jessie meant the world to me. I know you don't believe it since you're the almighty Alex Drummond, but you shot Jessie. What happened was your fault. You made him choose between our love and your friendship."

The accusation was expected. Years of training told me as much, but my emotions still flared. "The hell I did! I—"

However, the television's depiction of Liz interrupted me without acknowledgment. "Now, it's your turn." Rather than live communication, it occurred to me that this must be an activated recording.

The thought fled from my mind though as she snatched a large, white bottle of lighter fluid off the picnic table to her right and turned to reveal the shadowed entrance to a sizable shed built to match this house except for the shed's flat roof that stood about fifteen feet high in the front. The door hung wide. Logs were stacked neatly from the floor to a good two feet over her head. The top was barely visible under the ledge of the doorway. With a casualness that evoked curiosity, but also dread, I watched as the camera zoomed in on her dousing the logs and rough-hewn shed walls. She then moved around the side, spraying in wide arcs. A gnarled hand reached out from behind the camera and took the lantern down, then followed. The camera bounced and jolted with each step, all the way around to the back, but remained focused on Liz.

Once the squeeze bottle wheezed, she glanced back at the camera with a malicious smile. "Now you get to choose. Who will you save?" She threw the bottle onto the roof. It thumped and clattered along what must have been a tin roof slanted toward the back, but it was above the focused view.

"Choice... what choice?" I demanded, then covered my mouth again as the growing clouds of smoke clogged my lungs. The room's temperature was rising quickly, and beads of sweat flowed down my back and sides. The walls were engulfed in flames and their eager consumption of the building was growing to a roar. "Where the hell are you? You c-can't be far." I stifled another cough and wiped my watering eyes. I stepped closer to the television for a better look, struggling to see through the growing smoke.

Taking a matchbook from her jeans pocket, Liz struck all the match heads on a handheld sharpening stone. They flared to life, and she tossed the book of matches onto the glistening wall while she glared at the camera—at *me*. The camera zoomed out to reveal the back of the shed and lower edge of the silver roof. Atop it lay Paige: bound, gagged, and unmoving.

How long ago did she start this? I took a quick step toward the door before I could contemplate an answer, but her final words pulled at me, forcing me to stop: "Who will you save?" *Jamie, where's Jamie?*

As though answering my silent question, she said with a mischievous smile, "And while your beloved burns, will you take the time to save your only son? You may not be able to see him now. It really depends on how long it took you to get here. Try searching in the rafters above—that is, if it's not too late."

"Jamie!" I called, but only heard a short chain of coughs echo above in reply. I called again, louder.

Through the roaring flames, a soft voice croaked, "Dad?"

My jaw clenched. I wasn't sure if it was the smoke or the dilemma of my family, but hot tears coursed down my cheeks. The camera zoomed in further, intent on his face, and a four-inch tall mark appeared centered on Jamie's forehead. His olive skin was like my own, but now it had been marred. Freshly burnt skin appeared blistered and singed in the shape of an ankh, the base of it enflamed between his eyebrows. *She branded his forehead!* A solitary tear escaped Jamie's left eye, but my fifteen-year-old son held himself together and stood with eyes closed. As the camera zoomed out, I spotted his hands. While bound, his fingers were interlocked and clenched tight.

The television flicked back to Liz. The flames were quickly

consuming the stack of logs and storage shed. "So you see, now it's time for your choice. Who do you save, your beloved son or wife?" She quirked her head an inch to the side like a curious bird. "Choose quickly. However long it took you to find me means you have that much less time to save your loved one. If you truly have lost your edge, then you may lose them both. Wouldn't that be a shame?" The tone she used to ask the final question didn't seem to agree with her words. Then the picture went black.

"I'll get you, you bitch," I hissed. "Jamie?" I shouted to the rafters overhead.

"Dad, help Mom," came his trembling voice. "She's in trouble."

"Dammit! I know that, but are you still up there?"

"Y-yeah," he stuttered, "but I'll be okay. Dying isn't so bad."

"Jamie! You have no idea what you're talkin' about. Stay right where you are—" Pulling off my hat, I tried to fan the flames away to try and make out his location, but it only made things worse. With a frustrated growl, I threw the damnable hat at the television. Flames consumed it as they ate away at the melting plastic and glass.

"Alex," Martinez shouted from the entryway. "They're on their way."

I could barely make out his uniform jacket and tanned face. "Hec, you gotta help—"

"I know," he said. "I saw. Get Jamie. I'll take care of Paige. I promise" With that he jumped out the door, back the way he'd entered.

"I'm coming, son," I said over the sound of burning flames. I stared at the walls along the stairway. The passage was an inferno of flames rising to the next floor. My heart pounded in my chest, pushing me to find a way up to the highest beam spanning the room's peaked roof. Scanning the rustic wooden walls through the smoke, the gaps between rough-cut slats called to me like tree limbs begging to be climbed. "On my way, Jamie. Hang in there, buddy."

Sections hadn't caught fire yet, and I ran for the nearest, gauging the distance to the nearest support beam and the second floor balcony overlooking the large room. The rough planks tore at my fingers with each effort to pull myself up, but the sound of Jamie's coughs growing nearer bolstered my confidence. I cursed as my overcoat caught my feet, causing me to slip. Shoving it away with a leg, I pulled myself up by the tips of my fingers. I hoisted a leg over the first two-by-four spanning the living room. Stripping my coat, I stepped onto the indoor balcony railing and peered over the smoke-filled room. The slim wood flexed beneath me, wobbling and threatening to pull loose from either end. Regaining my balance, I flung one end of the coat over the next wooden beam, grabbed the other end, and pulled myself up. I was now close enough to make out his shape through the billowing smoke, but it grew denser the higher I got. "Jamie, I'm almost there. Stay with me."

He was only one level higher, less than fifteen feet away, but he was leaning forward precariously, a whip lashed around his throat.

It was stretched taut from his neck to the rafter above. His bound arms flopped forward and down as he forced himself upright and let out a litany of choked wheezes and coughs worthy of any fifty-year smoker.

"That's it, son. Keep your balance. I'll be there in a min..." Through the roiling, gray and black smoke, flames danced along the rafter he stood upon. I flung my coat up, beating as much of the flames back as were within reach. Keeping the wall to my back, I flung the coat up once more and hoisted myself onto the charred wood. It creaked and something snapped, jolting me. I stopped, holding myself in place and waiting for my nightmares to come true. A glance below displayed a mysterious hell. The floor of the room wasn't visible, only clouds of smoke with periodic flames lancing through them like forked tongues. Forcing myself to breath, I let out a ragged cough, but fortunately the wood was still intact. Rising, I made my way to Jamie, balancing in the boiling fog like a tightrope walker attempting to escape the clutches of hell. Breathing was difficult, so I held in as much as I could until I finally took hold of Jamie's zip-up hoodie.

At my touch, his face turned, eyes still held shut. Thankfully he'd managed to remain upright and there were a few inches of slack in the whip—at least for the moment. His wrists were bound in front of him with a zip tie. I patted his shoulder, trying not to throw either of us off balance, but seeing a blistered burn crisscrossing his forehead, I ground my teeth and my jaw clenched shut. More tears had found their way from under his eyelids, leaving streaks in the ash coating his cheeks. How much he'd grown over the last year surprised me. He was almost my height, but remained somewhat gangly, like I'd been at his age. He opened his eyes and met my gaze with dark-brown orbs; they were amber like his mother's, but much darker. They were heavy and stoic, but deep within he mourned for all he'd seen. There was no fear. *Yes, he's got the gift, but at what price?* His stare held me in place, grounding me on the wooden beam with the weight of experience, something his fifteen years shouldn't have granted. Again I silently cursed Liz Reider.

"Glad you made it," he said with a scratchy voice. Then he gave me a half smirk and sniffled.

I couldn't help but chuckle. "Anything for you, Jamie. You know that," I said, unwinding the whip from around my son's neck. The flexing leather pulled at his skin in places, leaving a collection of pinched marks circling his thin neck. He winced, but said nothing about it. "Are you okay?" I asked, knowing the question was stupid considering our predicament and his visible bruises, but I couldn't help myself.

Jamie nodded. Glancing to the side, he gave a slight nod to the smoky room. "Yeah, but we gotta get Mom."

"We will. Hector's gone after her. First we've gotta get down. Can you hold onto this?"

He took one end of the jacket in his hand and wrapped it around his wrist once. "Yeah, but can you?" he rasped. I hoped, and not for the first time, that whatever she'd done to him would heal.

"How do you think I got up here?"

"Good, stay strong." His voice was more firm this time, and I breathed a sigh of relief. *A small victory, but it's somethin'.* Jamie lowered himself down and hung from the beam like a monkey, moving a foot toward the far end of the room. Then he whispered up, "Oh, and Dad, you might want to make it quick. This beam's burnin'."

I glanced at the far end where his eyes were focused just as the beam splintered beneath our weight. A portion of the far wall where the beam was attached folded inward, and that side of the ceiling collapsed. Shocked, we tumbled free. I pulled at the coat, determined not to let him go, but when the wooden support one level below slammed into my side, it knocked the breath from my lungs. The coat stretched taut, sliding a few inches through my sweaty grip. Wrapping the end around my wrist and squeezing it in both hands, I grimaced at the pain of what were certainly broken ribs, or more.

A voice echoed up through the flames that were now roasting my side and back. "Hey, Dad," Jamie said with a strained grunt, "remind me to scratch this vacation off our (cough) bucket list."

My eyes bulged, and I forced myself upright, trying to shift him closer to the last two-by-four. "How can you j-joke at a time like this?" I wheezed, feeling the strain of his weight slacken as he gained purchase.

"When better?" he asked, staring up at me with a smile and red-rimmed eyes.

I shook my head and lowered myself down, wincing at each jolting pain.

The house fire had spread to the carpet below, leaving only patches singed, but not yet engulfed. "Jump over here, old man. Last one out the door's fixin' dinner." Before I could say a word, he leapt for a vacant spot, rolled like an acrobat, and turned to wait for me in the entryway. I followed, but with less majesty and flare—more like a hobbled retiree.

I took a deep, long breath of crisp mountain air as we finally stepped out of the burning house. After a few more breaths and an appraising look at my son, I added, "You know, how 'bout we eat out. I think your mother'll deserve it."

He smiled and nodded. "This way. You can see the smoke through the trees."

Sure enough, he was right. Orange flickers played through the limbs in the distance, and a sudden urgency grasped hold of my heart. I took off toward it, only seconds behind Jamie, and ignored the pain each step sent through me. *My blessed Paige. You'd better be alright. You have to be.*

Chapter 18

Madness

September 17, 2011

A GUNSHOT RANG out ahead, reverberating through the trees.

"Hector," I hissed.

Jamie and I pushed faster. Hoping we weren't too late, we barged into the trees, only slowing as the small clearing with the burning building came nearer. We ducked down to survey the scene for a moment. My eyes were drawn to the burning outbuilding, its walls and inner cargo growing into an inferno.

"How long has it been burning?" I whispered.

Jamie shook his head. "They only took Mom a few minutes before you arrived. Maybe fifteen minutes total." His lowered voice didn't sound certain.

Movement in the trees near the burning building some ten yards away caught my attention. In the foliage-covered darkness, even starlight was unable to penetrate, but I could discern the dark shape of a body lying on the ground, still and unmoving.

"Where the hell? I know I saw something."

Jamie pointed further beyond. A shape flitted through the trees, staying outside the firelight. A sudden crack of a branch from behind startled me, and I spun around, only to hear another gunshot sear the crisp night air. Before I could see who or what was behind us, something tore into my shoulder, bowling me over onto dead leaves and limbs.

"You're not taking my grandbaby," hissed an aged woman's voice from years back. Her words quaked, but whether from hatred or old age, I couldn't tell.

I rolled over, again forcing the pain into a far corner of my mind as I searched the night in the direction of the voice. Her figure stood beneath a tree, shadows crisscrossing her silhouette and hiding any distinct features beyond her bed of curls encircling her head.

"You and your cursed blood will die today," she promised. Her arms were extended toward me, embracing a gun. A strip of moonlight broke through the branches overhead, illuminating the crocheted, white sweater covering the arms and the butt of the gun. I recognized it as Hector's. He took pride in the forty-five caliber Heckler and Koch. He'd even replaced both sides of the grips with a customized etching of the Virgin Mary in prayer. Faint floral designs played off the arms of her sweater in a failed attempt to compete with the design. It was a sweater like any grandmother might wear when welcoming home her darlings, and never one you'd expect to find on someone while they aimed a gun at you. She stepped forward, and the light shone across her face and spectacles. She still had the stony face, but it had gained more wrinkles, even grown splotched and pale in places. Behind her glasses, her eyes pledged murder. She swiveled, and the forty-five caliber sought out Jamie, who stood frozen a few feet away.

"Including you, you little demon," she said. "I hear tell that you're just like your demonic father, speaking with ghosts and doing Satan's bidding."

I stared from her to Jamie, my world tumbling apart at the trembling pistol in the woman's hands. The flames engulfing the building beckoned to me, but I couldn't tear my eyes from this threatening woman or my son. A sudden bloodcurdling scream broke the silent night, stopping the distant sound of crickets better than the gunshots had. "Paige!" I shouted. My gaze swept over to the building, and again Paige's voice rang out in an unintelligible yell, paining my very soul.

"Don't you worry about that harlot," Mrs. Easely said. "My baby's takin' good care of her. She'll get the comeuppance she deserves, cavorting with demons like you and giving birth to more hell spawn."

Tears threatened, and my heart felt like it was ripping in two. *Time... not enough time. She might shoot Jamie if I make a move, but if I do nothing... Paige.*

"Mrs. Easely," Jamie said, holding a hand up, palm first, "you don't wanna do this. We're not what you think. Your granddaughter killed fourteen people. If you do this, you'll be no better than her. We won't be the one's goin' to hell, you will." He gave her a moment to think, but her jaw tightened. His other hand's fingers curled around something invisible, but remained lowered at his side. "Don't do this." He took a slow step forward, and panic entered my old teacher's eyes.

"Boy, you better watch your step," Mrs. Easely growled. "It's just like one of Satan's minions to try and turn me against my blood. Those boys raped my baby. Those horny sinners had it comin'."

Jamie took another step, closing the distance between them to under ten feet. "You're a good woman, Mrs. Easely. You taught children for years, helped them to grow up and be model citizens. I know you won't do this. Andrew wouldn't have allowed this. It's wrong."

Her arms stiffened, and the trembling stopped. "You are a wily one," she said, her voice quaking this time. "Bringing up my dead husband, I should shoot you right where you stand."

Jamie didn't take his eyes off her, and now only eight feet separated them. His voice was calm and soothing. "I know you miss your family, but you can't bring them back this way. Like you said, I can speak with them. You know I can."

"Uh, Jamie, admitting to that's probably not a good idea," I hissed, lifting myself on my good elbow and working my hand down to my waist.

"Quit movin'!" she shouted, glancing at me, then back at Jamie. "And you... you should be ashamed."

Jamie shook his head. "I'm not ashamed. I help people just like you. Andrew wants you to stop."

A tear ran from under Mrs. Easely's wire-rimmed glasses. "Don't you talk about him," she hissed, her arms shaking.

"He's holding my hand right now, Deborah, whispering in my ear," Jamie explained, taking another step, his hand still curled at his side. "Remember the good times. Even when things were hard and budgets were getting cut, y'all made it through by supporting each other. I know he wasn't a believer in the afterlife. He told me, but he's here for you now. You just have to accept him."

Mrs. Easely stepped to the side, placing space between her and us. "No, that's not right. He's in heaven." Another lance of light illuminated her more clearly as she shook her head, her gray curls quivering as though an uninvited spider had gotten into them.

"He's right here." Jamie held up his hand, maintaining the invisible hold. Smoke from the fire drifted through the trees, and I could have sworn it parted around a large, form standing next to Jamie. "He's with me. He's here for you," Jamie added.

"S-stop. P-please stop," Stone Face Easely pleaded, her façade finally breaking. The gun lowered to the ground, and I grasped mine, flicking open the leather fastener. However, they were now mere feet apart, with Jamie standing almost directly between us.

"Deborah, Andrew wants to show you something, but he has to use me to communicate. Please, take my hand." Jamie took another step forward, extending his free hand toward her.

"It c-can't be," she stammered. "He's in heaven."

"There are many places and states in the afterlife, Mrs. Easely. Andrew's here for you."

Freeing one shivering hand from the pistol's grip, Easely lifted her hand to his. She hesitated over his fingers, and Jamie grasped hers, wrapping his fingers around her small palm and wrist.

"It's okay, Deborah," he said, an older, much lower voice

underlying his words. "I'm here for you." The other voice was more pronounced in the final words, using Jamie's lips as though he were a ventriloquist's dummy.

Easely's eyes widened behind her silver spectacles. "Andrew?" Her tone was unsteady, but held an element of disbelief.

"Darlin', you can't do this. What would Elmore think? Your daddy would've strapped you good for even thinkin' about something like this," Jamie said, his voice now completely lost in the ghost's. "And I'm ashamed. I love you, doll, but this has got to stop."

More tears ran down her face, dripping onto her floral sweater. She dropped the gun to the leaf-covered ground and placed her other hand in Jamie's, staring into his eyes.

"Now, darlin', I've gotta show you somethin'," Jamie said. Deborah's deceased husband's baritone voice held a mountain drawl like many of the locals in the area. "This is for the best."

Mrs. Easely nodded her head and licked her lips, gripping Jamie's hand as though it were her lifeline. A burst of light flashed in their hands, growing until it coursed through both their bodies. Mrs. Easely's head flew back, her glasses spinning into the shadowy night. Her mouth and face contorted as though in silent anguish, highlighted by the bright light. Her mouth attempted to scream, but not even a croak emerged. Her hands began to vibrate then shake, growing more pronounced as it spread through her body like the light had. Soon her entire body seized as though suffering an epileptic fit. When it could not be controlled anymore, her hands slid out of Jamie's and she collapsed to the ground. The light dimmed and vanished, leaving her huddled form contorted and shivering. Jamie stared at her, panting and taking a teetering step to steady himself.

Another scream echoed through the forest. This time Paige wailed, "It *burns*. Help!"

Both our heads spun to see the building glowing like an enormous torch in the night. I couldn't see my wife's form since the front of the building stood in the distance, facing us. Jamie and I scrambled toward it, going as fast as our bodies would allow. *Paige... Paige... my beautiful, Paige,* was all I could think. Sirens and a woman's scream echoed in the distance, but barely registered in my conscious thoughts. Hurtling around the burning shed, I moved back until I could see Paige, still tied to the tin roof. Parts of it glowed reddish-orange.

She squirmed against the heat and held her head up, eyes wide and pleading as they met mine. "Alex, help," she croaked.

I didn't realize I was still holding my coat until I began beating at the burning wall with it, determined to make my way up. The heat was incredible, and sweat emerged from everywhere as I approached the scorched logs. Grasping the searing-hot wall, the pain in my fingers was but a distant thought compared to the need to save Paige, the love of my life. Throwing the coat across the roof of the shed, I pulled myself up and onto it. "I'm comin', baby. I'm comin'," I whispered.

Her hair hung in sweaty tendrils, but she'd been able to spit out the dirty cloth that was shoved in her mouth. "Alex, help," she whispered and coughed, pain-filled tears streaming from her red-rimmed eyes. Lengths of thick rope secured her to the roof like hospital-bed straps, and her wrists were zip-tied like the other victims.

I jerked on one rope and felt it give and snap, probably fraying at the end from the fire. It loosened, but didn't completely give way. I pulled harder, placing my shoulder underneath and standing, forcing it up and away from the roof. Paige's body shifted, lifting, but weighing me down since the cord was wound under her right arm and over her torso, then under the next arm. It finally gave way, and I almost lost my balance on the slanted roof. Paige sat up and rolled her upper body onto the coat at my feet while I steadied myself. I pulled at the one binding her legs. It held tight.

"Here," Jamie shouted from below and threw me a folding knife, the one with the faux-wooden handle I'd given him last Christmas.

I flipped the blade out and began sawing at the rope. *Should... have... sharpened... it,* I silently swore with each sawing stroke. Seconds passed like years. Clouds of smoke billowed from around the roof edges, and small tendrils emerged from nail holes and cracks. I blinked at my watering eyes, focusing on the taut rope wound around Paige's feet. After what seemed like an eternity, it snapped and I untangled her feet, lifting them onto the overcoat. I stood over her, my legs straddling her bruised and burnt body while I used the knife on the zip-tie. "Don't move, baby," I whispered.

She panted and closed her eyes, but her trembling hands and arms revealed the willpower it must have taken to remain still in that inferno. I stared down as she curled her hands out, away from the binding and Jamie's knife. Inside, each palm held a fresh brand to match Jamie's forehead. I cursed Liz in silence yet again, but worked at the plastic tie. Her hands came free a moment later, and pained, watering eyes opened to stare at me.

"We're goin' home, honey," I said, positioning myself on the metal roof so I could lift her in my arms. The soles of my shoes stuck at first, then squished with each step, but I lifted her, and she looked into my eyes with relief and love.

"Jamie, you down there?" I asked, unable to see him as I moved closer to the roof's edge.

"Yeah, right below you. Just drop her a few inches from the roof, and I'll catch her." Paige's eyes flew wide at his words.

I whispered, "It'll be okay, love. Trust in me… and your son."

She nodded. "I do."

Holding her out, I doubled-checked my distance from the edge and let go. She plummeted down, her mouth clamped shut, until Jamie caught her in his arms and carried her a few yards away into the trees. There he laid her on the ground while I grabbed my overcoat and leapt to the ground, wincing as the jolt enraged the gunshot wound and my broken ribs. The pain in my burnt fingers filtered to my mind. I gritted my teeth and shuffled the coat, draping it over my left forearm.

"You two okay?" I asked.

"Yeah, we're good," Jamie replied, helping Paige to her feet and placing her arm over his shoulders.

They followed me around the corner of the building just as an enraged woman's voice bellowed, "You!" Lifting Hector's gun from next to Mrs. Easely's shivering body, Liz stalked forward, aiming it at not me, but Jamie. "What did you do to her?"

"Now wait a second, Liz," I said, stepping between them and raising my hands. "Let's put the gun down. No one needs to get hurt here. Enough blood's already been shed."

"Alex, there's more than one bullet in this, and they've got both your names on them. Whoever wants to go first is fine with me."

"Shelley," came Jamie's calm voice from behind me, "this isn't how it's supposed to be. Your grandmother realized that. She'll be okay in time."

"You have *no* idea how this is supposed to be!" Liz screamed, her hand shaking as rage contorted her face. "Jessie should be alive. My mom should be alive. My brother shouldn't have burned." With her free hand, she gestured wildly, emphasizing each sentence.

Jamie let Paige slump onto me. Then he stepped closer to Liz.

"Jamie, *stop.*"

He didn't listen or even acknowledge my voice. "Look, your mother died of cancer. That couldn't be helped. The doctors did all they could."

Jamie's words surprised me. *How does he know?* A moment later it occurred to me. Andrew Easely wasn't the only one he was speaking to.

Jamie continued and closed the distance with another small stride. "But your father isn't dead. Your mom lied to you."

"Don't you dare," Liz demanded, motioning at him with the gun. "She would never do that. She was a professor in search of knowledge and the truth."

Jamie held up his hands as I had, showing he had nothing in them. "I'm telling you, he's not dead."

"He's not," I added, reaching an arm around Paige's waist and hoping to gain Liz's attention. Paige winced, and I loosened my grip. "Your father is Greg Rayson, right?" I waited for her to nod. "He lives in DC. He doesn't even know your mother's dead. I met him with Jessie. They work together."

"That can't be true," she said, almost talking to herself.

"Think about it," Jamie added. "Your mom didn't tell you because she and your father fought. She thought you'd be better off with her. All parents lie to their children if they think it's in their best interests. She didn't mean any harm by it."

"But how do you know?" Liz demanded, shaking the pistol at him.

I swallowed the large lump in my throat at seeing the unsteadiness of her hands. *She's goin' over the edge, Jamie. She might shoot you without even realizing it.* Paige's eyes met mine, pleading for me to do something. I held my coat in front of me and took a small step to the right, opening my view of Liz, and Paige followed my lead, sticking with me.

"I've talked to her," Jamie answered. "You know exactly what me and my dad can do. Your grandmother told you, right?"

Liz nodded. "Yes, she did. How do you think I knew to keep hidden?"

This time, Jamie nodded. "I realize. So you know I'm telling you the truth. I'm not crazy, but what you're doing is. You have to stop."

"But Mom is in the Duat," she explained, a tremor running through her words. "She and Trevor both are. I made sure of it. Osiris got his golden bulls. It says so in his prayers."

Trevor? Wait, Buddhist-wannabe Trevor? It dawned on me who the young boy was, and who the voice in the distance calling his name belonged to.

"That wasn't what Osiris meant," Jamie replied. "Shelley, your mother's work was precious to her. You know she loved every aspect of ancient Egypt, and you also know what you've done wouldn't have made her happy. You have a father who'd love to be with you. Don't throw it away."

The pieces in the puzzle finally began fitting together. The local Egyptologist that lost her job when the college closed its Archeology department must have been Liz's mother. This was all a morbid, twisted misunderstanding of her mother's life-long passion. It also occurred to me how pained and distorted Liz's view of the world must have been over the years.

Liz shook her head as though forcing out Jamie's attempt to reason with her. "Even if you're right, there's nothing if I let you take me in. Jessie's gone, and I have no future in a prison cell." The tremble in her voice vanished, and she steadied the gun on Jamie's head. "You know, that brand makes a perfect target." Her voice was ominous and decided.

Gripping my nine-millimeter, I jerked it free, leveled it on Liz, and pulled the trigger. Paige dove at Jamie, shoving him aside and to the ground. A split second after my shot rang out, Liz's gunshot permeated the air. Then she fell backward, blood streaming from her eye where my bullet hit. I slumped to my knees next to Paige and Jamie as they rose. Pushing back Jamie's hair, I inspected every inch of his face and head.

"I'm okay, Dad," he said, pushing aside my hands. "Mom, you okay?"

She knelt over Jamie on his other side and smiled. "Yeah, honey, I am."

I helped them to their feet, grimacing when Paige took hold of my injured shoulder. She pulled her hand away and stared at her bloody palm, then at me. "Oh, Alex?" she asked, worry etched across her face. "We've gotta get you to a hospital."

Sirens wailed in the distance, but much closer now. "They're comin'. Anyone seen Hector?"

"No," Jamie said while stooping over Liz's still form, "but you're a damn good shot, Dad."

"We've gotta find him. He might be hurt. I think I saw someone over here." I ran to where I'd first seen the prone form hidden under the trees and slumped to my knees as a glimmer of starlight played across a bloody wound on his head. I felt for a pulse and sighed with relief. It was strong.

Examining his forehead, Martinez winced at my touch. "Damn, woman!" he muttered. "Can't you leave me—" Opening his eyes, his words came to an abrupt halt as he stared up at me.

"Martinez, you call me woman again, and we're gonna have issues."

He smiled and chuckled. "Did you get the license plate of the freight train that hit me?"

"Can you get up?" I asked, shaking my head with a laugh.

"Yeah, if you'll give me a hand."

I offered him the lesser of my two injured ones, fortunately the hand not attached to my bleeding shoulder, and he took it.

Making our way as a group back to the large house that now looked like a bonfire of the gods, Paige commented, "You know, babe, I think we're gonna have to get you a new jacket."

I lifted the draped coat on my arm, staring at the bloodstains, burns, and torn sections, and that was just what was visible under starlight. "Yeah, you're probably right, but I don't think I'll ever get rid of this one. It saved too many lives today."

"Oh, is it a part of the family now?" Jamie asked. "Can I name it Fluffy?"

I couldn't help but laugh. "Sure, Jamie." Questions were flitting through my mind, and I couldn't help but ask one. "I think I know, but how did you really get all that information about Easely and Liz?"

He gave me a crooked smile that looked quite odd with the distant firelight playing across the blistered ankh on his forehead. "I'm sure you know. It wasn't a trick. Like you've always said, Dad, use what you've got." Paige watched us with interest, my free hand gently circling her waist, while Hector stared at Jamie in astonishment.

"Wait, you too?" my partner asked.

Jamie smiled wider. "Yeah, me too."

"How long have you been talking to them?" I interjected.

"A couple years. It started when I visited Grandpa's grave with you once."

Suddenly it hit me. About a year and a half prior, Jamie began visiting my father's grave on his own. I thought it a bit odd at first considering Jamie'd never met the man, but let it be.

"Grandpa spoke to me that time. It was out of nowhere, and I didn't know who was talkin', but eventually I figured it out. Now I can even see them. Their bodies glisten like they're covered in dewdrops. Is that how you see them?"

I shook my head. "I can't see them, Jamie. Never could. I can hear them, but normally only if it's part of a vision."

He gave me a considering look and stared at the approaching house fire. I followed his gaze. A collection of flashing lights in red, white, and blue were spinning in frantic circles, casting wide arcs of color across the tree line, gravel road, and grass. "That's how I knew about Mr. Easely and Sandy."

"Sandy?" Hector asked.

"Sandy Easely, Shelley's mother," Jamie supplied. "Andrew Easely wanted to talk to his wife, to explain and show her what Shelley had done, the pain she was causing. Mrs. Easely's probably having a hard time coping right now. I don't think she could see past Shelley to what she was doing. Mrs. Easely needed to know."

"She already knew, though," Paige complained. "She was protecting Liz. She may have even helped kill all those people."

"Yeah, but knowing in retrospect is different than experiencing it from a different perspective while it's happening," I added, thinking back on the hundreds of visions I'd had over the years. "Sometimes parents can excuse anything."

Jamie nodded and stared into the distance.

Chapter 19

Troubled Thoughts

September 21, 2011

I WALKED PAST the graveyard where my father was buried and up the stone steps of the church. Stepping out of the gray, cloudy day and inside the old building was a little strange considering it wasn't an Orthodox church. The atmosphere even seemed odd after missing the last few weeks of Sunday attendance. The mayor was riding us hard, like every year. Then, a comfortable hand settled onto the shoulder of my new black overcoat, gaining my attention. A glance to my left, injured shoulder told me that no one was there. *Ghost?* I wondered. Shaking my head, I took a seat a few pews inside in the left row and sat both bouquets down to the left with my bandaged hands. One of the bouquets was orchids, my father's favorite, and the other spring flowers. A casket sat in the front of the church, below the dais and elegantly carved podium. It was closed. The thought of who lay inside sent a chill down my spine.

The rest of the pews were filled with people scattered throughout. A few were people I knew from school and the community. They purposefully glanced away when they caught sight of me. *People just don't understand the unexplainable, nor do they want to.*

The minister walked out and began his homily/eulogy. I watched the people around me, keeping a spot open next to the aisle, more focused on the late arrivals than anything the preacher had to say. Thankfully, a pair of belted, black slacks stepped up to my right. I'd been afraid he wouldn't make it. The doctors had thrown a fit about his coming after flatlining and then only taking a few days of bed rest, but I knew what it would mean to Jessie.

He slid into the spot I'd left vacant without a word wearing a burgundy dress shirt, the same color as Liz's sweater. *Liz probably bought him that thing.* His brown hair was trimmed and combed, and he twirled a single rose in his hands, back and forth, mimicking the decision I was sure he'd been juggling until now.

I'm glad you could make it," I whispered.

He nodded with a frown. Shaking his head, he said, "I just—No matter what she did, I loved her, Alex."

I patted his shoulder. "I understand. It'll be alright. You doin' okay?"

He nodded and stared at the priest at the podium. I turned back to the front, and we both watched the remainder of the ceremony in silence. Partway through, Jessie clenched his jaw and tears began streaming down his cheeks.

At the end, we both filed through the line, each person paying their respects in their own way. Women stumbled out in tears, leaning on their husbands' arms, and various other members of the community said a few words, but some spat on her coffin. The priest stood watching, but did nothing.

Mr. Lee and his distraught wife were ahead of us. "Why'd you have to take our boy," Mrs. Lee pleaded, barely remaining upright with her husband's assistance. "What'd he ever do to you?" She waited for a response that would not come until Mr. Lee ushered her past and up the aisle, out the church doors.

I laid the spring bouquet in front of her coffin, but said nothing, leaving Jessie to lower himself onto his knees and prop his forehead against the dark-stained wood, the rose still clutched in his hands. "Why?" he whispered. "All of this, and why?" He sat silent for a few minutes, saying his goodbyes. He set the flower on her coffin as he stood and turned to leave.

When we made our way slowly through the pews, following the other attendees, Jessie asked, "How do you do it? How do you go to these funerals when the woman tried to kill Paige and Jamie?"

"How can I not?"

Jessie quirked an eyebrow and waited for a better response.

"She was a tortured soul. I could have come out just as twisted as she did."

"But you didn't," Jessie replied. "You didn't kill over a dozen people. You didn't do all those horrible things. You're stronger than her. You go out of your way to help people."

I shrugged. "I could have, though. Liz and I each had a very troubled past. We lost our families. If not for the friendship and support I got early on, I could have wound up just like her. Don't get me wrong, I'm not saying what she did was right. I hate her for it and had a real hard time stepping foot in here, but I can't ignore the similarities. It comes down to decisions. Any one decision I made in my past, or she made, could have changed who we became in the future. I could have turned out just as screwed up as she was."

Jessie shook his head. "I... I know why I came, but I'm not sure I could've done it if I were you."

"Well, I spoke with Mrs. Easely the other day. She explained a lot of things. I had my suspicions, but the extent of Liz's delusions is easier to understand now. She sacrificed seven people for her mother and seven for her brother to help them get into the Duat... the ancient Egyptian's afterlife."

"Yeah, but how did her brother die?"

"You might say he was victim zero. He started it all by accidentally setting himself on fire."

"The first vision you had," Jessie offered quickly.

"Yep, that drove Liz over the edge. She must've come across her mother's files or taken an interest in her mother's work, and all of a sudden the idea came to her as a way to save her family. From then on she sacrificed one person per year on the same date her mother died."

We passed through the church's double doors and down the stone steps. "Why not the day her brother died?"

"I don't know," I replied.

"So, the brands the football team got...?"

"That was her mark... marking you as a golden bull."

"You mean, marking us for death," Jessie mumbled. "Do you

think she really loved me, or was I gonna be another victim?"

"Jess, seven is a special number in ancient Egypt. She was done. I think you were her chance at a future. Unfortunately, you can't run away from your past."

We crossed the street and entered the graveyard. After passing the large cement fountain with the angel perched in the center near the front of the cemetery, we eventually came to my father's row. Jessie stopped and motioned for me to go ahead. "I'll wait in the car. Seems you have enough company."

I nodded and strode down the row of tombstones, approaching the old pine tree with wide, drooping limbs. Jamie sat beneath it in my reserved spot, his back against the smooth side of the trunk and a diamond-shaped Band-Aid covering the four-inch brand on his head. He wore a black t-shirt and blue jeans. Paige also stood at the foot of my father's grave staring down in silence. Her black dress and bowed head reminded me of a weeping widow, and a shiver ran down my spine. I'd asked them to come with me, but they both refused to come inside for the service. Instead, they waited here in the crisp morning air.

Shaking it off, I stepped between them. "Hey, you two. Everything alright?"

Paige nodded and gave me a slight smile. Her gaze then returned to my father's grave, and she was silent for a time. Her folded hands were bandaged like mine. Taking a deep breath, she looked up. "I'll leave you two to chat." Crossing her arms against the chill morning, she went to join Jessie in the black Lincoln where it was warm.

"So, is he here?" I mumbled, brief excitement bubbling inside me.

Jamie nodded, and then tilted his head back against the trunk once more as though exhausted. "He wants me to tell you something. He said it might answer a few questions."

I looked from the grave to my son and back again. Finally I returned my gaze to him. "Go on."

"I think I told you before, but he's proud of you, Dad."

I smiled. "Yeah, you did tell me that. It meant a lot."

"Well, he really is. You're doin' it right, a lot better than he ever could."

I was a bit confused. "What do you mean?"

"Grandpa had an ability like ours, too, but it wasn't the same. He was trying to reach a guy who'd sped off the road and was dying. That's why he went out that night."

"Wait, so he saw visions of people when they were dying?"

"Yeah," Jamie said with a nod. "Kind of cool, huh?"

"Then how—"

"Grandpa could function in both realities," answered Jamie before I could finish. "Unfortunately, that didn't make him invincible. He never made it to the guy to save him. They both wound up dying when that truck driver hit him."

I was floored and awkwardly fell to the ground at the foot of Dad's grave, settling onto the damp grass Indian-style.

"But he's proud of you. You're doing so many things and helping so many people. I want to help. I can do more than you—well, a little different I guess. I don't see visions like you and Grandpa. I can just talk to them and see them."

I tried to breathe normally and maintain control. "I'll have to think about it."

Jamie's dark eyes watched me for a minute longer. "Alright. Let me know." Rising from under the tree, he said, "I'll leave you to say a few things to Grandpa, like usual." He headed toward where Paige and Jessie stood waiting.

I moved over to take my old spot, which Jamie had vacated. It was a bit more cramped than it used to be. The limbs seemed closer now, and it was more confining. I looked at Dad's headstone, and the words 'In memory of a loving father taken too soon. We miss you, Terry, but will see you when we get home,' stuck out in my mind.

"Dad, I never knew. I wish I had, it would have made all these years easier to understand." He didn't reply, but I knew he was with me. "I hate what happened with Liz. She murdered so many people and almost took my family and a good friend with her, but I'm trying to keep things in mind. It can't always be personal, but it's difficult to do. She was crazy, and it could just as easily have been me."

I bit my lip, considering what else to say. "Maybe things are better where you're at, Dad. Can you look after her... try and make sure she finds her mother?"

I waited for an answer I knew wouldn't come, but I held out

hope. If Jamie could, maybe I could too. A cool breeze stirred the colorful leaves on the tree limbs at the edge of the graveyard and whispered through the pine boughs overhead.

I sighed and rose to my feet. Setting the bouquet of orchids at the base of his headstone, I said, "Thanks for listening, Pops. Although I can't hear you, I want you to know you mean the world to me." Kissing my fingertips, I touched the stone and walked over to join my family.

My cell phone vibrated, and I grabbed it. Glancing at the display, my shoulders slumped as I read 'Dispatch'. *Just another day in the neighborhood,* I thought with a sigh. The phone buzzed again, urging me to pick up. Flipping it open, I said, "What ya need?"

Taylor's youthful voice replied, "You won't believe this, but I think we may have a copycat. We need you down at the mortuary."

I stopped, my feet feeling as though they were sinking into the dew-covered grass. Sirens echoed in the distance, and clouds swirled with ominous procession overhead. I stared at my waiting family. *Guess crime never takes a break.*

"Alex, you there?" asked Taylor, her voice now tinged with concern.

"On my way," I mumbled and shoved the phone back into my pocket, deep down where it might be harder to find.

About the Author

WESTON KINCADE writes fantasy, paranormal, and horror novels that stretch the boundaries of imagination, and often genres. His current series include the A Life of Death trilogy and  the Priors. Weston's short stories have been published in Alucard Press' "50 Shades of Slay," Kevin J. Kennedy's bestselling "Christmas Horror" and "Easter Horror," and other anthologies. He is a member of the Horror Writer's Association (HWA) and helps invest in future writers while teaching English. In his spare time Weston enjoys spending time with his wife and Maine Coon cat, Hermes, who talks so much he must speak for the Gods.

For up-to-date promotions and information on new releases, sign up for the latest news here: https://kincadefiction.blogspot.com.

As a special bonus, the first three chapters of book 3 in the A Life of Death trilogy, *Sacrifices*, are included below so carry on. Happy reading!

A LIFE OF DEATH

SACRIFICES

Book Three

WESTON KINCADE
(Excerpt)

Chapter 1

Adolescence

March 8th, 2012

SIX MONTHS AGO, I almost lost my wife and son to a deranged woman. The delusional lunatic chose to interpret her mother's lifelong work as though it were the product of an Egyptian-Lovecraftian romance, brought on by a mushroom-induced haze. My family was lucky. Paige escaped with minor burns, but Jamie... every time I look at my son I'm reminded of him standing atop the crossbeams spanning that vaulted ceiling, seconds from being hanged within an inferno. *How does a man live with the visible reminders of such an event? How does a son?*

Jamie's footsteps came bounding down the hall, each one thundering in the double-wide trailer like the giant trundling after Jack at the top of the beanstalk.

"Slow down!" I shouted.

Jamie appeared out of the dark hallway into the living room, a smile spreading across his narrow face. It was a shadow look, a grin hiding something subtle but ominous beneath the surface. He had never been a troublesome child, but now that he was fifteen it seemed as though his mischievous nature was revealing itself, like the terrible twos had somehow grown into a five-foot-eight Clark Kent lookalike with an undeniable desire to borrow the car.

Was I ever like that?

"Dad, give it up. It's not like I'm gonna bring the house down."

I frowned and shifted in my generic La-Z-Boy. Its faux-leather surface squeaked beneath my light-brown slacks. "You're giving me a headache, boy. Are you ready for school?"

Jamie rolled his eyes, and I couldn't help but notice the ankh branded into the center of his forehead. The black bangs curling down around it failed to hide the scar—a visible reminder of my failure. I hated Shelley Rayson for branding him like cattle. And I hated myself for allowing it to happen. As a homicide detective, it's my job to ensure everyone's safety, but what seems like yesterday, I was practically helpless.

"Fine, Dad. Don't have a cow. I'm ready." He trudged into the kitchen, his long, blue t-shirt attempting to hide his sagging jeans.

"Are you taking the bus?" I pulled the lever on the chair, and my footrest descended, rocking me up to my feet. I stretched, then powered off the television and the murmuring news reporter with the remote.

"Nah," he replied. Leaning over the counter separating the kitchen from the dining room, Jamie asked, "Mind if I take the car?"

"Yes, I mind. You don't have your license yet. You can't drive without an adult present." I buttoned the top of my shirt and hiked up my tie.

"Awwww, why you gotta be that way?"

"What, like a dad?" I replied, unable to help a slight smile.

Jamie disappeared deeper into the kitchen, but his voice answered, "No, like a jerk."

"A jerk? I know you didn't just call me that." Striding into the kitchen, I gave Jamie a quizzical look.

My son's head was stuck inside the refrigerator as though searching for some place to plant a flag, claiming it for his own.

"Jamie, we have rules in this house, and you know it."

He shrugged out of the refrigerator with a bagel in hand and a rolled-up tortilla peeking halfway out of his mouth. He mumbled something around it I couldn't make out, but his dark eyes still held an element of mischief.

"Do I need to tell your mother?"

At this, the look on his face dropped. He removed the excess tortilla from his mouth and swallowed the rest. "Sorry. I've just gotta get to school early today."

"Why's that?"

"A bunch of us are getting together this morning to plan something for this afternoon."

"That sounds nice. Anything I should be aware of?"

Jamie scowled. "No. I can take care of things myself. You don't always need to come to the rescue. It's just some boys ganging up on my friends. We're organizing a defense. They'll lay off soon enough."

Our small town of Tranquil Heights seemed to be getting more violent every year, but if the events of six months before had taught me anything, it was that I needed to trust Jamie. I couldn't handle everything myself. "Well, let me know if you need my help."

Jamie rushed through the kitchen and dining room. "I could use the car."

"Not that. Like I said, you're not old enough."

"That's not fair. Grandpa said he let you take the car out when you were fourteen."

The mention of Grandpa was a bit irritating. My father had been killed by a drunk driver before I entered high school. Our family was a little different than others. I frowned at Jamie. "Those were different times. Get your bag. We'll head out now. That should get you there in enough time."

"Is Mom already gone?"

"Yes. The hospital called her in at five this morning." I knew he could hear the agitation in my voice. I was sorry to have directed it at him, but children could often be irritants, especially those who could speak with your dead relatives. How was I to argue with my father when I couldn't talk with him without being flung into a deadly vision? And controlling those was practically impossible.

"But, Dad, it's embarrassing—"

I held up a finger. It worked almost as well as a mute button. "Do you have a car?"

His mouth clamped shut, and he shook his head.

"Do you have a license y—"

"I've got my learners," he interrupted, pulling the identification card out of his pocket and waving it between us as though I wasn't the one who took him to get it one week prior.

"Let me finish. Do you have a legitimate license yet?"

His head drooped.

"Pay for insurance?"

It dropped more.

"And did you not just insult the one person you wanted to do you a favor?"

His shoulders sagged, and he disappeared back into the hallway, heading for his room.

"That's what I thought. I'm taking you, and pull your pants up before I get the governor to outlaw sagging for indecent exposure. I taught you better than that."

"Awww, Dad," whined Jamie from the other room, but when he came back into view, his jeans were on right, if not a little askew. "Why can't you just lend me the car?"

"I'll tell you what. Wait nine more months, pass your test, get your license, and we'll see."

Jamie huffed but said nothing more as I locked up. We jumped into the old, unmarked police cruiser. The half-orb, rotating light sat on the dash, idle and unmoving like a turtle hiding from predators.

Hiding from my son, I thought with a chuckle. *Teenage angst will scare anyone.*

The engine revved and we drove down the street, heading for Madessa High School, my old stomping grounds. The drive would take fifteen minutes. We passed the old cemetery lined with large pines and a black, cast-iron fence. I stopped at a red light. Many family members were resting there. I even had a great-great uncle who we believed was buried in the mass grave of Confederate soldiers. A small fence enclosed the long rectangle of space within the cemetery. It was a grassy mound topped off by a large, stone cross. From the road that split the cemetery, I spotted the stone raven sitting atop the cross's arm. The bird stared down at the massive grave as though attempting to decipher identities. A few of the mass grave's inhabitants had their names chiseled into the wide square of weathered stone beneath the cross, but far more remained unaccounted for. So many lives lost and so much mystery shrouding their battlefield deaths saddened me.

"Dad, the light's green. Why do you have to stare at the cemetery all the time?" Jamie asked.

I hit the gas and caught up with traffic as we passed through the small, picturesque town. Classic red-brick homes towered along the sides of the narrow streets, white columns framing the frontages. "There's a lot of history in that cemetery."

"I know, but that don't mean you have to get caught up in it every time it comes into view."

"Doesn't, not don't," I corrected. "Maybe not, but we owe them more than a passing glimpse."

Jamie glared, then waved a hand. "I know. I know. But life goes on. There's so much more to the here and now. You can't forget about that."

For someone with even more paranormal ability than me, he often said things that made me wonder where he had acquired years of wisdom. The next moment, he'd be back to his old, teenage self. It was hard not to be drawn into the past. The world of the dead beckoned around every corner. Jamie somehow walked the fence between the two worlds better than I ever did. "You know, you surprise me."

Jamie grinned. "You shouldn't set your expectations so low and that won't happen near as often."

From anyone else I would have been hurt, but this was Jamie's sense of humor showing through. We both laughed. "But if I set them any higher, I'm not sure you could meet them," I replied with a grin.

Jamie's eyes widened as he looked at me from the passenger seat. "You didn't just insult me?"

We both laughed again. "All's fair in love and war... and parenting, or so they say."

A woman's voice squawked over the radio, "Car thirteen!"

I reached down, picked up the receiver, and clicked the handset. "Car thirteen here. What do you need, Taylor?" Taylor Hicks was our resident dispatcher on days. The Tranquil Heights Police Department wasn't large, but it had grown with the swelling population in our small community.

Taylor's bubbly voice echoed through the speakers, "I know it's early, Alex, but we found something on Mark's Row by the train tracks. You really need to take a look before the weather turns."

I glanced out the window at the vacant lot of waist-high grass whizzing by, the ancient, gnarled oaks and pines separating housing divisions, and then the new mini-malls that just went up last summer. Above, gray clouds roiled across the skies, rolling over us and shrouding the sun's morning light as though Zeus himself had become irate. He was a father, so it was understandable. Thunder pealed in the distance. There was no need to ask what the situation was. The weather could destroy evidence. I was a homicide detective. It's what I did best. My abilities made me well-suited for such mysteries, no matter how much I hated enduring the visions. "How long?"

Dispatch replied, "Hector put up a tent, but the forecast is calling for high winds and sleet by lunch."

"On my way." Tossing the handheld microphone onto the center console, I asked Jamie, "You mind being a little late? I'll write you an excuse, but we need to get over to the scene ASAP."

Jamie gave a momentary frown but perked up. "Sure." He pulled out his cell phone and began punching a message in with his thumbs. "I'll have Donny get things organized this morning. So long as I'm there this afternoon, it shouldn't be a problem."

I shook my head. *Back to texting. Teenagers.*

Chapter 2

Lost Innocence

March 8th, 2012

I TURNED LEFT, exiting the main strip, and quickly entered farm and pasture land that could have been a scene from medieval England, just with more cows than sheep. The town's expansion hadn't reached here. We passed decrepit barns and houses that seemed willing to fall at the briefest touch; porch roofs slumped inward, and doors hung from the hinges. I turned right onto Mark's Row, an old road that had been paved some years back, but not kept up. Barbed-wire fence lined each side of the narrow street along with tall, green weeds and plant life erupting after the fierce winter. The fields hadn't been tended in years, and everything was overgrown. Breaking up the vacant scene was a pair of police cruisers parked at the rise in the road, just before the train tracks. Their lights weren't flashing this far out, but I recognized the marked number on the back quarter panel of Hector's car.

We'd been partners for years and normally rode in the same vehicle, but when more area needed to be covered, the department had given him one of the old cruisers—number eight. He liked calling himself "The *Ocho*" when responding to dispatch. Taylor always got a good laugh out of it.

I pulled to a stop and opened the door to another peal of thunder.

"Mind if I help?" Jamie asked.

Normally children wandering around crime scenes was a big no-no. I glanced over at the last cruiser present—Theresa's. "Sure. Just remember to stay out of the way. Let me know if there's something you need to touch before you do. Officer Fuller won't throw a fit about you being here, but she's a bit by the book. Remember that."

Jamie threw off his seatbelt with a large grin and exited the car. "Don't forget Fluffy," he shouted.

I pulled the long, black trench coat he'd nicknamed out of the back seat and slipped it on along with my matching fedora. The overcoat was tattered and singed along the edges after our previous ordeals, but it was difficult to replace, like a comfortable pair of shoes that have been worn in. Besides, Fluffy and I had been through a lot. I approached the large, blue-topped tent between the white-and-brown cruisers. There weren't sides to the tent. It was more of a pavilion covering for weekend campers you might pick up at the local sports store, but we made do with what was available in rural Virginia. Hector was leaning over something, peering down at the ground between rectangular containers and a drink cooler while Theresa watched over his shoulder. If I didn't know better, I'd have thought they were trying to start a camp fire, huddled as they were. Hector's beige sports jacket contrasted with Theresa's blue officer's uniform.

"So what do we have?" I asked. Just before stepping beneath the tent, a few raindrops spotted my shoulders and forehead.

Without glancing back, Hector replied, "Not much. The Meyers own this side of the road. Their son William reported it."

"Reported what?" Jamie asked.

I gave him a sidelong glance at the interruption, but Theresa smiled wide. "It's good to see you. Were you on your way to school?"

He nodded.

"Sorry to pull you away from your friends." She stepped over to Jamie and patted his cheek. "This is a little gruesome so you'll probably want to stay back."

"Okay," he mumbled without conviction.

He had no intention of following those instructions. He'd probably seen more death than Theresa in the last dozen years she'd spent on the force. *At least he's playing along.*

"Any footprints, tire tracks, some kind of DNA?" I asked.

"See for yourself," Hector said, rising to his full height of five feet eight inches. He waved at something on the ground. "This is all we found. It could have been here for a day or two. Thankfully it's in a gully. The sides sheltered the remains from the wind, but who knows how long ago it was dumped. We blocked it with everything we could until you got here. There isn't much." They had draped a clear sheet of plastic over the remains, but he pulled it back just enough for me to see a pile of chalky white dust.

I closed the distance between us, with Jamie inches away. The entire cone was no more than eight inches in diameter. However, a few larger chunks stood out amidst the rest. I squinted and knelt closer. Some particles had been blown into the surrounding grass, but who knew how much of the remains had been lost?

Hector used a specialized brush to knock some of the white sediment from one of the solid pieces. Silver glistened from the grooves of what now looked to be a filled tooth. Glancing at the others, they appeared to be more teeth and bone fragments from a cremation. It looked like dried clumps of white beach sand. "These have been here longer than a couple days, Hec."

My partner readjusted his knelt position to gaze closer at the remains. "What do you mean?"

I pointed at the sediment-like clumps. "These still contain some moisture. I think there was more here before, but when it rained last weekend some of the remains washed away. This is what's left. It absorbed the water. By now, the person responsible is probably long gone."

"We thought it might have been a fire," Officer Martinez explained. "Maybe a copycat killer like the one we found some months back."

I shook my head. "I don't think so. The location's not right. Fire can really damage bones and even destroy some, but these look to have been ground up and dumped here. There aren't any scorch marks from a fire or a pit. It's like someone just stopped their car, opened the door, and poured the cremated remains out like a soda that had gone flat. Plus, I doubt there's more than one copycat killer in Tranquil Heights. This is still a small town."

Hector gently lifted a fragile shred of bone from a small tray next to him. "This is the largest one we found. It's why the Meyers kid contacted us."

I held out my palm and readied myself for what was to come.

Hector set a bone from a human eye socket in my hand. It was smaller than normal, seemingly that of a child, and as soon as the pitted surface touched my skin, the long-familiar aroma of aged leather wafted to my nostrils. Darkness followed as though an inkwell had been poured into a swirling glass of water.

* * *

My vision lightened onto a blurred image that began to clear, revealing the decrepit front porch of an old house illuminated by moonlight. It looked huge. The wooden railing was at eye level, as if I had shrunk. The old, wooden boards beneath my black sneakers were painted gray but peeling, as though each step I might take could pull another layer off. I glanced up, inspecting the shattered glass in the front window, the splintered door frame, and the looming door cracked open six inches. A look over my shoulder revealed a dark night, forest, and overgrown plants around the house. I took a couple strides off the porch, down the fractured stone steps. Vines grew over the two-story house as though nature had returned to claim it, a vengeful but possessive mother I wouldn't want to tangle with. I turned my attention back to the drooping porch roof. It looked ominous. Crickets chirped, an owl hooted a three-syllable mantra, and something scurried through the dark underbrush a few feet away. I swallowed the lump of fear that had crept into my throat.

"Stay out here," Momma had said.

This place looked as though nothing human had lived here for ages, but hissing voices echoed through the open door. One was Momma's. I didn't recognize the other. It was masculine.

For a moment, memories separated and I recognized my own distinct mental self. I'm Alex, not some kid, *I thought.* Keep it together. *It was always hard to distinguish between the victim's memories and my own, always a losing struggle for identity.*

The child's thoughts returned, overwhelming my own and pushing my consciousness to the back, leaving me an observer. Stay out here, *I silently repeated to myself.* Stay out here. Momma doesn't know. It's scary, too scary.

"Who-whooo-whooooo," sounded the owl again. I jumped. Something else shook the nearby bushes, and I gazed into the golden eyes of a creature sitting in the dark. It stared back, sending a shiver down my spine.

"Who's there?" I whispered. My voice was light, youthful, and a tremor ran through it.

Nothing but night sounds replied. The gold eyes closed and then opened, glaring at me. My knees shook, and my heart thundered in my small chest. A small baseball cap and shorts were hardly enough to protect me from whatever wildlife was out there. Something swept past my shin, stirring the hair on my right leg. I jolted. Unable to remain still any longer, I ran back up the steps toward the comfort of Momma's voice, but stopped at the door. Stay out here. *"Momma?"*

The conversation inside continued, unwavering.

Something rattled from the depths of the overgrown front lawn. I looked back, my eyes widened, and I dove through the entryway. The house was dark with no lights, just dim moonlight shining through the windows. The walls were skeletal and bare. Sections had been ripped away, revealing boards and pipes beneath. Sheetrock littered the ground. Each step crunched. I passed through the remains of a doorway into a large room. The voices grew louder the closer I got, but they weren't in this room. The sound of footsteps echoed oddly as I crept into the kitchen. Metal pans hung from high cabinets.

Momma leaned against the kitchen island with one hand, her other massaging a thin man in a flannel shirt. "Please, just give me some more. They always pay. I can sell more."

In the dark room the man stood shorter than Momma, but his curly hair added a few inches of height.

Momma leaned closer to him. "I can make it worth your while. Trust me."

"Momma?" I asked, stepping up and tugging at her jeans.

She jumped and turned her narrow features to stare down in astonishment. "Tommy, what are you doin' here?"

"What the hell?" shouted her friend. He jumped back and ran a frantic hand through his hair. It stood up around his head like coiled

vibrating springs, as though his appendages had just been attached to jumper cables. "You brought a freakin' kid?"

"I was scared," I whispered. "Something outside was watching me."

Momma gripped my shoulder in a shaking hand but turned her attention back to her friend. "I'm sorry. I didn't have a choice. There was nowhere to leave him. He doesn't know anything."

"Of course he doesn't know anything," the man shouted. "He's a kid."

"He won't tell anyone. I promise."

"He doesn't know to keep his mouth shut," her friend said.

Momma reached for his shirt, pulled him closer, and ran a hand down the front of his pants. "You know I can make it worth your while."

"Worth getting locked up for? I think not." He grabbed something off the counter next to him. It scraped across the countertop before vanishing into the shadows at his side. He leaned down closer to me, and his hair gave him the look of a demented clown. "You and I are gonna have a little talk."

I couldn't see his eyes, but something in his tone made the soles of my sneakers itch. I took a step back and then another.

"N-no, please don't," Momma pleaded.

"Come on back here, Tommy. You and I are gonna be friends."

Momma stepped in front of him, running her hands up and down his shirt. "Please don't. I'll sell it all. I won't take any. You won't have to worry."

"Was I talking to you, you damn junky?" He shoved her backward. "Do you think I care how much you sell… you who brought her child to a drug deal?" He shoved Momma harder. She tripped and fell on the dirt-strewn floor. Then he slashed her across the face with something clenched in his fist. The far window illuminated the long, rusty knife.

"Tommy run—"

He slammed it into her chest.

She gurgled.

My heart pounded like a humming bird's. Momma said to stay outside. My fault. *The soles of my sneakers itched more. I ran.*

My fault. My fault.

Momma's angry friend pounded after me. I skidded over the boards and trash, almost falling. I turned into the hallway and up the stairs, leaping the steps that were missing or broken. Run, run, run. Almost at the top. *Over the lip of the second-floor's final step, a gust of wind fluttered a curtain in a far room where moonlight shone through the window. It beckoned to me like an otherworldly escape—until a hand clamped onto my ankle, jerking me backwards.*

"Get over here, you damn cockroach," the man shouted.

My chin slammed into the steps. As I tumbled downward, my forehead smacked into the railing. A blinding light broke my consciousness. My vision became vague, as though I had been thrust into a fog.

The man huffed and puffed. A strong arm gripped me around the waist and tucked me under one arm like a football.

Momma? Where are you?

"You've been a bad boy," said Momma's friend. "You're gonna have to suffer the consequences."

Momma? I'm sorry. *"Mom-ma?"*

"She can't help you anymore."

A shiver ran through my small body, but I couldn't understand why. My thoughts came slowly and were as hard to grasp as sludge. My... fault. My... fault.

Momma's friend clomped back into the first room I had entered. He set me on my feet and held me steady with a solid grip. "Tommy, I need you to stand still for a sec, okay?" the man requested in a forced pleasant voice. "Be quiet."

The world wouldn't stay still. The skittering I'd heard before sounded from the corner once more. I was having a difficult time standing. If not for Mommy's friend anchoring me in place, it would've been impossible. A wadded newspaper in the corner shuffled into the light amongst fast-food bags and other trash. I closed my eyes. My fault. My fault... but gotta accept the consequences, like Momma's friend said. *I forced my eyes open and stared at the dark corner. The same pair of golden eyes I'd seen outside peered from beneath the crumpled newspaper, looking at me. My knees trembled until a black nose and whiskers peeked out. A bedraggled, gray-streaked cat emerged. "Meow?"*

"Kitty," I said, raising a wavering hand toward it.

It hissed.

At that moment, the man reached around my head and slid
something sharp along my neck. It hurt. I couldn't breathe. Warm
fluid ran over my skin, down my neck and shirt. Kitty, why?
It hissed again.
No air... No words... My fault. My fault.
My legs gave way as Momma's friend whispered, "Good boy."

* * *

Another peal of thunder and the sound of sheets of rain
splattering against the cloth pavilion were the first things I heard.
As my vision cleared, I focused on the eye socket. Tommy's absent
eye seemed to be looking at me—calling to me. The words, *My*
fault, ran through my mind, repeating in his childish voice. A
shudder coursed down my spine. Now the vision was something I
possessed, a memory. It was difficult to discern between my
thoughts and those of the victim's whose death I was reliving. I
would now remember the events of Tommy's death until the day I
died. It was a blessing and a curse that haunted me daily. Every
victim was another memory almost indistinguishable from my
own.

"Yeah, it's getting pretty cold. That thunder gives me the willies,
too," Officer Fuller added, rubbing my shoulder. "It's going to be
one of those days."

"Don't I know it," I whispered, stretching my head to the left
and then the right. My tensed neck cracked audibly, like a

collection of snapping twigs. Paige hated the habit, but it relaxed my muscles and nerves.

Hector stared at me with knowing eyes from a foot away, where he still knelt. He'd grown accustomed to how I worked. After six years as my partner, we developed a relationship and got to know each other well—in some ways better than our wives. He was aware of my ability to relive people's murders; although, in the beginning he was skeptical, even after seeing the results. An ounce of that skepticism would probably never go away, but we trusted each other with our lives. He would take my secret to his grave rather than chance our supervisor, Lieutenant Tullings, finding out. They'd have me seeing a psychiatrist and probably drummed off the force. Science doesn't support my abilities, and neither does the justice system. I gave Hector a brief nod.

"Can I hold it?" Jamie whispered once Theresa had stepped to the edge of the pavilion tent.

Martinez's brows knitted. I ignored the look. He didn't know what Jamie was capable of, at least not yet. However, I was hesitant to agree knowing how brutally the boy and his mother were murdered. *Seeing such horrible things can't be good for a kid. Would I be a bad parent if I allowed it?* The ankh branded into the center of Jamie's forehead peeked out from under his curling bangs—a reminder of what he suffered and how he saved us all. *I have to give him a chance. He's capable of so much more than I give him credit, but Paige will kill me if she finds out.* "I'll take the heat if fingerprints turn up," I assured Hector. Turning my attention back to Jamie, I said, "Careful. Just hold it in your palm. It's a difficult one."

He nodded and held his hand out between us.

"Oh, and don't tell your mother."

He rolled his eyes. "Duh."

I sat the skull fragment in his palm, and a faraway look came into Jamie's eyes, much as I probably looked during my visions.

Hector watched my son, and his eyes widened, flitting back to me. "He can, too?"

I agreed silently. "Keep Theresa distracted, would you?"

My partner rose, and his knees popped. "I'm getting too old for all these *secretos*." His Mexican dialect slipped out. Hector strode toward Officer Fuller. I was barely into my mid-thirties, and he had just turned forty. Since then, every ache and pain was a result of The *Ocho* being "over the hill."

Chapter 3

The Search Begins

March 8th, 2012

JAMIE WAS SILENT after the vision, walking around looking at things. I began to question whether I'd done the right thing. Even in the car, he strapped himself in without being reminded and stared out the passenger window. The overgrown grass and barbed-wire fence whizzed past under his scrutiny.

Clearing my throat, I asked, "So, what did you think?"

Jamie turned to stare ahead at the glove compartment. "It's never easy seeing through their eyes."

Those were words I had said myself from time to time. "I know."

"I can't believe how cruel some people are… just because the guy was worried what a kid would say. Hell, most people wouldn't have listened to Tommy if he had tried to tell the world."

I was reminded of my own adolescence—a time when few people believed me, not even my mother. *Who would believe their own stepfather, or husband in her case, would have killed his first wife? Not many people. The drunk was a murderer, though. He'd admitted it.* I swallowed the lump in my throat. "I know," was all I could say again.

"And his mother… Why didn't she do more? She just kept trying to seduce the guy—I mean, come on!"

"That's something I've come to understand over the years, Jamie. It sounded like she was dealing for him and wanted to up the stakes."

Jamie quirked an eye at me as we passed from pasture and farm land back into residential Tranquil Heights. "It seems to me, she had her hand in the cookie jar a bit too much."

I could not help but chuckle at his comparison. The stark innocence of a childlike action being equated to drug use was an unexpected contrast. Jamie was quite observant for a fifteen-year-old. "It would make sense. Sometimes people develop a dependency on drugs. She was trying to get what she wanted and make more money at the same time. Honestly, most dealers I've encountered would have jumped at the deal... if not for this guy's paranoia."

Jamie nodded. "Probably. I just hate that Tommy had to go through that."

"You and me both. We still don't know how the boy wound up cremated."

Silence permeated the vehicle as I contemplated what might have happened. I turned up the street to Madessa High School. The new sign sat atop a low, red-brick foundation. It was digital and had a blue devil marching along, trying to stab the tail of a dancing goat that kept flipping and turning at the last second. "Skewer the Libsom Valley Goats!" scrolled by beneath the animation. Jamie groaned.

"What's wrong?"

He shook his head. "Nothing. I just hate basketball, and it's that time of year—March Madness."

I frowned. I'd never been much of a sporting type, but I wouldn't say I hated any. "Hate?"

Jamie rolled his eyes. "Fine, not hate. It's just annoying. Every time I get to school it's like, 'Hey, did you catch the game last night? That three-pointer at the buzzer was awesome.'" His imitation sounded like a modern version of Fred Flintstone.

I laughed as we came to a stop in traffic. "Okay, I get it, but you might want to keep your opinion to yourself. Who knows what some rabid fan might do if they overhear you at the wrong moment." With a grin, I grabbed my fedora from the back seat and plopped it onto his head. It slid over his forehead, reminding me of when he used to wear it before he could even walk.

Jamie raised his eyebrows, and they hid beneath the brim. "Good point." He paused for a moment as I turned into the circular drive at the front of the school. A tall, modern clock stood dark and sleek in the courtyard ahead, a waist-high, sandstone-enclosed flowerbed at its base. "You know, one thing I don't understand is why Tommy wouldn't talk to me."

I narrowed my eyes in thought and put the cruiser in park after pulling alongside the curb. "What do you mean?"

"Couldn't talk with Officer Fuller around, or she might think I had a few screws loose. I know Tommy was there with us because after the vision, I heard whimpering."

This was a part of Jamie's ability that differed from my own, the ability to hear and sometimes even see the ghosts of his victims. I could hear them on rare occasions, but to Jamie they were almost as real as flesh-and-blood people. "Could he have been scared or in pain?"

"I'm sure he was scared, and maybe something more than that." Jamie sat for a moment, then opened the car door and shouldered his half-full backpack, tossing the hat into the back seat. "I think he still feels like this is the consequence he deserves for disobeying his momma. See ya later." Jamie slammed the car door, bounced over the curb, and strode toward the school, the note I'd given him when we first got in the car gripped in his hand.

My fault... My fault, repeated in my mind. "Maybe you're right," I whispered. The sadness I felt for Tommy slipped deeper into my gut.

The ride back to the station was quiet and uneventful with only my thoughts to keep me company. *Who was this curly-haired murderer? What was Tommy's mother's name? Where was she? And the dealer?*

The brief look at the front of the house in the vision told me two things: one, that the place was run down and no longer occupied, and two, that it was out in the wilderness. The only sounds I'd heard were that of nature, so it could be a mile or a hundred. Since I had nothing to go on beyond where the remains were dropped and a vague impression of what the killer looked like, I played with the idea of calling the department's sketch artist.

I passed through the old, brick station house's side door, patted a few uniformed officers on the back, and strolled through the sea of 1970s wooden desks we called Homicide HQ. By the time I reached mine, I'd changed my mind. I sat down in my leather chair. It was old and worn in places, with the stuffing showing through, but it was comfortable. It squeaked a greeting.

I couldn't help but frown. If I called in Jim Lint, our sketch artist, we could search the criminal database comparing the sketch to photos of past arrests. We could even work up a sketch of Tommy's mother for the NamUS database to see if anyone alerted the authorities about missing or unidentified people. Neither Jamie or I saw Tommy, but with his name and association, that would be added information to make the job so much easier. Unfortunately, I couldn't explain how I got the information. People didn't just buy into the paranormal; most would be skeptical. The likelihood that they would believe me, even if they went along with it and I solved the case, was minimal. The more likely result would be me getting kicked off the force, and that wouldn't help Tommy or my family. Not to mention, anyone else I might have been able to help in the future would lose their chance. Lieutenant Tullings sent me the hard ones even though he didn't know about my talents. He asked few questions unless it related to what could be proven in court. His leniency and confidence were hard to come by in a supervisor. If I were to tell him, he'd be obligated to assign me a therapist and relieve me of duty. It was just the way the world worked, and I had to operate within its strictures.

Dismissing the idea of calling the sketch artist, I scooted stacks of case files and reports aside, revealing my computer keyboard and flat-paneled monitor. They'd updated our computers recently, but as a state institution, the update replaced fifteen-year-old computers with five-year-old ones. They were fast enough for me, though. *I'll just have to do it the hard way.* I booted the computer and accessed the NamUS database. I punched in Tommy and some general details about age and US region. DNA analysis would give us the personal details I used if anyone asked. For the first search, I narrowed it to Tranquil Heights and guessed the missing date to be within the last month. Two boys around the age of eight appeared on the screen with school photos. I had no idea what Tommy looked like, but a brief search into each revealed their mothers' photos. One had died over a year ago. The other was still living, but neither looked like Tommy's mother.

This could take a while. I revised the search parameters and reduced the name to Tom. He could have been called Tommy as a nickname. Fifteen results appeared, but none were likely matches.

I revised the search again, extending the region to twenty-five miles and the surrounding counties. Over a hundred fifty results appeared on the screen. *This could take a very long while.* I rinsed out my coffee cup in the lounge and refilled it from the newly brewed pot.

Two hours passed, the seconds measured by clicks of my computer mouse and sips of coffee. Steam drifted from the mug, and the dark liquid cooled. It was astonishing how many people had gone missing and for so many different reasons. Each picture and missing-person report required that I scan it for unique details that might align with the little I knew, but nothing seemed to fit. It was like a jigsaw puzzle with missing pieces. Worse, this one had a timer. If this curly haired, paranoid drug dealer could destroy a body, there were more to come.

The next revision of the search parameters quadrupled my previous result totals, and my face sagged. Lunchtime had come and gone. This task might take days. My stomach grumbled, and my eyes itched as though some ungodly maid had taken a feather duster to them in her haste to clean the place. I rubbed them and refilled my cup for what had to be the tenth time. *How many pots of coffee have I made now? Three? Four?*

Returning to my desk, I found Hector sitting in my chair, swiveling back and forth with impatience. "Oh, there you are," he said when he looked up from my monitor. "From the bags under your eyes, it looks like you ain't had much luck."

I took another sip of coffee, hoping the caffeine would give me a little boost, at least enough to socialize through the mental haze. "Nope, no luck. You'd think knowing what I know would make this easy, but without pulling Jim in, we're at a standstill."

"We've had this conversation before," he replied, his Hispanic accent flavoring his words. "Tullings likes you, Alex, but his hands are tied. There'd be no way to explain things. It's like connecting dots, and we have to be able to document every step or else the bastard'll win. Remember, there's no double jeopardy."

"I know. I know. It just irks me sometimes."

"Anything I can do to help?" Hector rose from my chair and seated himself at the next desk—a much cleaner one. A faux-wood placard on his desk announced to visitors, Det. Hector Martinez.

Glancing back at my cluttered office desk, I wasn't sure where my nameplate had disappeared. Shaking my head, I took a seat and ran a hand through my dark, wavy hair. A minor headache seemed to be coming on. I loosened my tie. After so many hours of futile searching, it felt more like a noose after a witch trial. I contemplated wearing a tie more ornate than just striped blue. *At least I'd look pretty the day I really am hanged by it.* "I just don't know," I replied.

"Why don't I go old school. I can call the local county stations and see what they know. Maybe they've got some missing persons they haven't added to the database. You know how some of these small, backwoods towns can be. They try to solve it for the first six months before throwing things online."

I nodded. "Good idea. Add a tidbit about Tommy and his mother potentially being another victim—no certainties, though. Just say it was an anonymous tip when we started asking around."

"Will do."

Swiveling back to my computer screen, I resumed my search.

Hector paused for a second. "Couldn't we say the same thing to Jim?"

I paused, mouse icon hovering over another search result. "No, it won't work."

"Yeah, it would."

"For the first time, but how many anonymous tips before people start getting suspicious. Word gets around. Once we do it, that will make it easier to do again. Best not to start. In another department and another city, it's not likely to come back and bite us in the butt, but Jim is a regular here."

Hector shrugged. "You're probably right."

I returned my attention to the screen. The lack of results was so distressing that I considered starting a new search, this time for the murderer. While I couldn't do much for the victim, or victims if there was more than just Tommy's cremated remains there, I could prevent future people from enduring the same fate—assuming the man did it again. I thought about going back to the remains, sifting through more bone shards. It might give me a different vision, one of Tommy's mother if she had been dumped with him. *But will knowing get me any closer to the killer? Probably not.* Besides, there weren't many bone shards left, and in my experience, fires destroyed both evidence and visions. It was lucky that the fragment of Tommy's orbital socket had contained a memory. Nothing else likely would.

Time is money. Without a clear look at the killer's face, it would be difficult. I had hoped to find a location to help narrow the search since there would be too many arrest records and photographs to go through manually.

Then my desk phone rang. I dug it out from under a pile of paper. "Detective Drummond, Homicide."

"Mr. Drummond," a male voice on the other end replied, "this is Mr. Cantril, the principal at Madessa High School."

The mention of the high school brought a flashback of Mr. Larkin, the young administrator who tried to help me as a teen. Adolescence hadn't been good to me, but during that final year, I'd learned to look at the world differently. Besides, from what I'd heard while attending college, Mr. Larkin moved on some years later. "Yes, Mr. Cantril, How can I help you?"

"I'm sorry to bug you at work, but we've had a couple problems with Jamie and his friends. Can you stop by? He's missed his bus and will need a ride. First I'd like to go over some things with you."

I let out a sigh. *What happened?* I would find out soon enough, but my gut told me it had to do with the group of boys he'd mentioned. *Things must've gotten out of hand.* "Sure, Mr. Cantril. I'll be there soon."

"Thanks, Mr. Drummond."

I hung up and glanced at my desk clock. It had been a gift from Jamie last Christmas. An old Civil War Confederate Soldier sat atop an upright pocket watch with an expression somewhere between consternation and constipation. In comparison to the gray-clad soldier, the watch was the size of a boulder. *Come on, Jack, get it the rest of the way out, ol' buddy. You can do it!* Between the soldier's legs, the hands of the clock ticked away. *Five till four.* I gathered my jacket from the back of my chair.

"Problems at school again?" asked Hector.

"Yeah."

"Did he say what about?"

I shook my head. "I'll find out in a few minutes. I'm guessing it's to do with something Jamie told me this morning."

"Well, have fun. I'll get on those calls."

"Sounds good." I headed for the car. Jamie had never been a troublemaker, but he was mischievous. At times that streak got him into trouble—nothing serious, but it got aggravating. However, I had a feeling this time was different. *What've you gotten yourself into this time, Jamie?*

Thank you for reading. I hope you enjoyed the excerpt. You can get your copy of book 3 in the A Life of Death trilogy, *Sacrifices*, on Amazon.

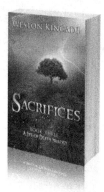

Made in the USA
Monee, IL
11 December 2019